ANNIE HAUXWELL

IN HER BLOOD

WILLIAM HEINEMANN: LONDON

Published by William Heinemann 2012

2 4 6 8 10 9 7 5 3 1

Copyright © Annie Hauxwell 2012

Annie Hauxwell has asserted her right under the Copyright, Designs and
Patents Act, 1988, to be identified as the author of this work.

First published in Great Britain in 2012 by
William Heinemann
Random House, 20 Vauxhall Bridge Road,
London SW1V 2SA

www.randomhouse.co.uk

Addresses for companies within The Random House Group Limited can be found at:
www.randomhouse.co.uk/offices.htm

The Random House Group Limited Reg. No. 954009

A CIP catalogue record for this book
is available from the British Library

ISBN 9780434021802

The Random House Group Limited supports The Forest Stewardship Council (FSC®), the
leading international forest certification organisation. Our books carrying the FSC label are
printed on FSC® certified paper. FSC is the only forest certification scheme endorsed by
the leading environmental organisations, including Greenpeace. Our paper procurement
policy can be found at: www.randomhouse.co.uk/environment

Text design by Laura Thomas © Penguin Group (Australia)
Typeset in Adobe Garamond

Printed and bound by CPI Group (UK) Ltd, Croydon, CR0 4YY

IN HER BLOOD

Annie Hauxwell was born in London and emigrated with her family to Australia when she was a teenager. She abandoned the law to work as an investigator for a private firm, and after working as a screenwriter she turned her hand to novels. She now lives in Castlemaine, Victoria, and travels to London frequently. *In Her Blood* is her first book.

For my sister

The great white shark never sleeps. It must keep moving or sink to the bottom and drown. It has a number of adaptations that make it an efficient killer and the first bite is frequently a death blow.

Wikipedia

What hath night to do with sleep?

'Paradise Lost', John Milton

The First Day

1

Catherine Berlin gazed down at the blue flesh swaying in the grey water, the outline of the woman's remains softened by a bone-chilling February mist. The backwash from a water taxi on the river rippled into the lock. Berlin felt her own body rock gently with the swell that roiled the corpse, exposing a deep, serrated gash at the throat, as if someone had taken a bite. With faint bewilderment, she recognised a quickening of her heart. So this is what it took to move her. Someone would pay.

The case conference with the Murder and Serious Crime Squad was perfunctory. The men at the table regarded Berlin with indifference. She was just a civilian investigator with a regulatory agency. At fifty-five her lean frame was tending to look wasted. Her hair, once blonde, was now a dirty melange of grey, streaked with tarnished gold.

The squad boss, Detective Chief Inspector Thompson, was about her age and seemed long past throwing his not inconsiderable weight around. He put down his bacon roll, slipped on his glasses and read from a notebook: '"A bite or a tear. A wound from some kind of serrated edge or teeth, anyway, which perforated the neck, almost severing the head." We're waiting on forensics. In the meantime, Ms Berlin, are you able to provide us with any more intelligence about this source of yours?'

He didn't look at her as he spoke, but his tone was mild and she sensed his apparent indifference towards her arose from professional disinterest rather than arrogance.

Berlin went through it again as the others shuffled their papers. 'She called the hotline and identified Archie Doyle as an illegal moneylender. Our first meeting was at Starbucks about four months ago. The date's in the file. She was well spoken, plausible, but nervous. I needed to win her confidence. We arranged another meeting. In the meantime further inquiries were made, approval was obtained for surveillance, and observation commenced.'

A cocky young officer spoke up. Berlin had seen him before, but couldn't recall where. She knew he recognised her too, but simply as a soft target. He wasn't going to waste the opportunity.

'So was she a concerned citizen, a disgruntled girlfriend or a victim? I mean, as I understand it, if the moneylender hasn't got a licence and is arrested, the debt is wiped, yeah? Big incentive.'

'That's correct,' said Berlin. She held his gaze, barely able to summon the energy to play this game. She remembered his name was Flint. The little weasel was a detective constable.

'So which was she? Citizen, squeeze or vic?' asked Flint.

'She didn't say.'

'No name, no address,' said Flint.

'She wanted to use an alias. Juliet Bravo.'

Flint looked blank. Clearly it didn't ring a bell.

'On the telly. Before your time,' murmured Thompson.

Flint's nod was curt. He was on a roll now. 'You had a mobile number for her, and that was it? I take it she was registered as a CHIS. You know what that is, don't you? A Covert Human Intelligence Source.' He said it very slowly.

'No,' said Berlin.

'No, you don't know, or no, she wasn't registered?' asked Flint. Berlin caught Flint's quick scan of his colleagues, to make sure they were picking up on his clever sarcasm.

'She wasn't registered,' she said.

Flint shook his head and threw down his pen, a pantomime of incredulity. Berlin cleared her throat.

'If I may explain, Detective Constable —'

'Acting Detective Sergeant,' snapped Flint.

Berlin decided not to bother. 'Look, I was waiting for her at the lock at the Limehouse Basin this morning. It was very cold, so I kept moving.'

'It was a bloody early meeting,' remarked one of the officers.

'A late night,' said Berlin.

'Party girl,' sneered Flint. Was he referring to her or the dead woman?

'Insomniac,' said Berlin, similarly ambiguous. In fact insomnia was a trait she had shared with Juliet Bravo.

She waited until Thompson nodded that she should continue.

'I walked around to the other side of the lock and something caught my eye. When I took a closer look I could see it was a body. At first I didn't even realise it was her,' she said.

Thompson sat back in his chair and Flint appeared to take this as a signal he could have free rein.

'Which of you wanted to meet at the lock?'

'She did. I —'

'Preferred Starbucks. Yes, we know. Who else knew about this meeting?'

Berlin let his question hang out there. Like she would be, soon enough. Taken in an open cart from Newgate to Tyburn, hung for public amusement, cut down while still alive, then torn limb from limb. Quartered. Her daydreams echoed her nocturnal wanderings. Sometimes she couldn't distinguish.

'Why did you go alone?' demanded Flint.

She didn't answer.

'Surely you people have standard operating procedures which you ignored by meeting her alone. Am I correct?' he tried again.

It was purely rhetorical. She remained silent.

He delivered the final blow. 'Where is this shark Doyle now?'

He knew, but he was going to make her say it. Now she remembered where she'd seen him before. And who he'd been with.

'The surveillance was withdrawn,' she said.

The collective groan wasn't even muted.

Someone would pay.

Making people pay was Doyle's business. He had never believed in light-touch regulation. An undisciplined system gave weak characters the opportunity to get weaker. He'd learnt that from Frank.

Doyle was a short, solid man with squirrel cheeks and a pale complexion. His eyes held a permanently hurt expression, as if he couldn't believe you were doing this to him, again. He stared into the lock and fiddled with his heavy gold rings. Rings on her fingers, bells on her toes. Concrete boots. On the other side the police were still working under floodlights. He stayed well back in the shadows. Word had reached him that the grass had been fished out. He thought it a pity they hadn't taken the opportunity to remove the rest of the rubbish. The canal was a disgrace.

The tidal stain on the massive timbers of the lock bore testimony to the effort required to tame the sullen river and render it fit for trade. Doyle gazed into the dark eddies and saw the silent plea in the eyes of so many victims as they were consumed in the rush of water. It was a hard city and an unforgiving current that ran through it. He should know.

When Doyle was a kid, Frank would announce that he was going to see a man about a dog. Sometimes he would take Doyle with him. His mum didn't like it, but she daren't make a fuss once Frank had his mind made up. At the age of eight Doyle had stood here and watched Frank dangle a bloke between the huge lock gates, limbs inches from the crushing pressure. He would never forget the screams.

Doyle thought about the dead girl and sighed. No doubt she'd been badly brought up. Spoilt. No values. Learning the hard way hadn't done him any harm. He spat into the filthy water. The sky was lightening and the police were switching off their floodlights and packing up their stuff. He should make himself scarce. He checked his watch. Time to go and see a man about a dog.

2

When Berlin had finished making her formal statement, Acting Detective Sergeant Flint directed a constable to see her off the premises. He stood behind the front counter with his mobile in his hand and watched her go, then made a call.

From the steps of Limehouse Police Station Berlin turned left towards Canary Wharf, where another inquisitor awaited her. Crossing East India Dock Road, she took Westferry and kept walking under the bridge into West India Quay.

Her route through Canary Wharf was monitored by 1750 CCTV cameras. So why didn't she feel safe? She couldn't shake the feeling that the footsteps of her dead informant were dogging her and any moment a cold, wet hand would grip her shoulder. Christ, it must be shock, she thought. I'm in shock. I need a drink.

The wind shrieked as it swept the deserted squares and empty walkways, a mercantile labyrinth encircling the soaring glass towers of credit that had made it possible. Upmarket shops. Few customers now broke the silence in the gleaming malls. The seductive hum of muzak had been replaced by the sound of shutters coming down on boutique businesses as the bankers fled to Geneva and a more forgiving tax regime. Britain was bust.

Berlin swiped her ID through three layers of security and finally reached the lair of the toothless tiger – the Consumer Affairs Branch of the Financial Services Agency, a non-departmental public body that sat, mostly on its hands, at the heart of the beast.

Her so-called colleagues surreptitiously monitored her progress from the lift to Nestor's office. Delroy, the only one she could rely on, didn't seem to be around. Nobody acknowledged her except Senior Investigator in Charge of Operations Johnny Coulthard, who peered over the top of his workstation and gave her a smug, knowing grin. She responded with one undignified finger.

She didn't knock on Nestor's door, just walked straight in. He didn't seem surprised to see her. Through the immense window behind him Berlin could see the pale sun fracturing the surface of the river. Tower Bridge engraved against the slate sky. What kind of a man would choose to turn his back on that view? Only the slight, tight-lipped, desiccated creature before her. Watery hazel eyes absent of passion, mired in irony.

In her mind's eye she watched the portcullis of Traitor's Gate rise. She knew what was coming.

'We enforce licence provisions. We enlist the assistance of the police to execute warrants. We don't run one-man, or one-woman, operations. We work as a team and follow process.' Nestor's voice never rose above a murmur, which required his listener to lean in and focus on him.

'We protect the market for corporate lenders. At the same interest rates as the sharks. Or worse,' she said.

'Corporate lenders rarely break people's legs,' observed Nestor.

There was a pause and Berlin waited for the axe to fall. But to her surprise Nestor softened his tone.

'You are assiduous, Berlin, I know that. But why persist in the face of a direct order?'

She stuck to name, rank and serial number. 'I logged her intelligence, then arranged surveillance on the target, which, as you are aware, was aborted due to procedural difficulties. I later tried to reschedule, but the resources weren't forthcoming. If you take my meaning.'

For the first time she saw colour suffuse Nestor's cheeks.

'The resources weren't forthcoming because the file was closed,' he hissed.

That wasn't the reason, but there was no point in arguing the finer points.

'There's no basis for the assumption that her death is associated with our inquiries,' she said without conviction.

'*Your* inquiries,' retorted Nestor. He raised his hand as if to slap it down on the desk. But didn't. 'For Christ's sake, Berlin, this loan shark, Doyle, could have had enforcers watching her.'

'She hadn't borrowed from him. She wasn't a victim.'

Nestor picked up on it immediately and she realised she hadn't entered this observation in the log. 'Why are you so sure?'

'She told me she owed him nothing.'

Berlin remembered the way Juliet Bravo had made the remark. She hadn't been talking about money.

'What else did you fail to log?' Nestor persisted.

'My report covers everything,' she said.

His knuckles whitened. 'You're stood down with pay, pending an inquiry. It will be intrusive. If you take my meaning. And Berlin, let's hope all this doesn't come back to bite you.' A small smacking sound escaped Nestor's thin lips. 'Now get out.'

Not a mile from Canary Wharf there was a street where there weren't any cameras because there wasn't anything to protect – except the people who lived there, who weren't worth much.

A couple of lads were having a laugh. One of them posted a dog's tail through the letterbox of number fifty-one, then together they sauntered back to the black Merc that Doyle preferred for conspicuous work. Sometimes the sight of the Merc cruising down the street was enough. But on this occasion Doyle had directed the lads to resort to sterner measures. He fancied himself quite creative in these matters; the dog had been his idea. He sat in the back seat now and waited for the inevitable scream. When it came, he grunted with satisfaction. The lads high-fived each other as they drove off. Job well done.

Inside number fifty-one, Sheila Harrington staggered back against the wall and slid to the floor, sobbing, unable to touch the bloody stump on the doormat. The kids had had that dog since they were little. What was she going to tell them? Terrified cries from the garden told her she wouldn't have to explain. Doyle and the lads had driven around the back and thrown the rest of the dog over the fence.

3

When Berlin left Nestor's office she strode to the lifts, pressed the call button, took the lift to the next floor down, got out and walked back up the stairs.

She ducked into the ladies and waited until she was confident that Coulthard would have made his customary announcement – 'Scoff!' – and like a flock of sheep the lads would be following him down to the canteen. Nestor always ate his mid-morning croissant in his office.

The request to revoke her computer access would have gone to the harried IT people, but the queue at the so-called Help Desk was always long. It was a fair bet that it would take them at least a few hours to get around to it. She never thought she'd be grateful for that delay.

Keeping low behind the workstation partitions, Berlin made her way across the office to her desk, logged on to her computer and slotted a memory stick into the USB port. Protocol strictly prohibited their use and she knew it would leave a trace on the system. But no one would be looking.

Nestor had closed the Doyle file but he hadn't deleted it. He was fanatical about logging every scrap of work they did, even when it came to nothing. The figures mounted up for the all-important Annual Report.

Keeping an ear out for the sound of the lift approaching, Berlin quickly downloaded all the work she'd done on the man who was now the obvious suspect for Juliet Bravo's murder: Doyle. She watched the documents sprout wings and fly to her memory stick. It was all there: scanned handwritten notes, data dumps, requests for information. The most remarkable thing about Doyle was that he didn't exist.

When she'd caught the call to the Stop Sharks hotline the informant who would become Juliet Bravo reported that Archie Doyle, aka 'Oily Doyley', DOB 21 August 1954, was a loan shark who lived at number fourteen in a block of flats overlooking Weaver's Fields, off Bethnal Green Road. Which made him and Berlin practically neighbours. The informant also said he drank at The Silent Woman in Poplar. As with most first-time callers she had refused to identify herself, but had given a mobile number.

Impatient, Berlin watched the audit trail of her work flash past: the log of that first call, the date-stamped file she had opened in the Agency system and the initiation of routine online inquiries.

The Agency's database had no record of a moneylending licence being issued to an Archibald Doyle. If he was lending money in that name, he was doing it illegally. She had checked the General Register Office for Births, Marriages and Deaths, but came up empty-handed. She had interrogated Experian for a credit history and run a search on the electoral roll, in the unlikely event that Doyle was committed to participatory democracy. She'd scrutinised Companies House records and all the other public domain databases. In accordance with the National Intelligence Model protocol, she had filled in the forms to flag other law enforcement databases. Then she had requested checks from the DVLC, CRIMINT, the local authority, and the Inland Revenue. No driver's licence, no criminal history, no council tax.

The Inland Revenue held the most accurate records, of course, but the tax man was always the slowest to respond. She would have had to wait three months or more for a result as hers was a low profile, quasi law enforcement agency. Loan sharks took a back seat to terrorists, although these days the distinction between them was often lost once you moved further up the food chain. Drug money had to be 'washed' before it could be used to finance arms deals. Channelling it into loans to small businesses meant the cash that came back appeared legitimate.

But the file had been closed and the request to the Revenue had been withdrawn. It made very little difference to the outcome. All her other searches had drawn a blank. By normal standards Doyle was the invisible man, at least under that name.

Just as the last document was winging its way to her memory stick, she heard the door of the stairwell close and footsteps approaching. She snatched the stick out of the port and slipped it in her pocket.

Coulthard strode across the office towards her.

'What are you up to, madam?' he said.

He always wore the same sickly smirk. She quickly stood up, hoping he wouldn't walk around and see the message on the computer screen accusing her of interrupting its copying operation.

'Just clearing my desk of personal items,' she said. Both of them knew her workstation was an impersonal wasteland.

She grabbed the single postcard stuck on the partition: a picture of Alcatraz inscribed 'Wish You Were Here'. She brandished it at Coulthard as she stalked past.

4

Sheila Harrington opened her front door only after checking through the spy-hole. It was that nice Daryl, bringing the kids back. Her ten-year-old, Terry, pushed past her and bolted down the hall in the direction of the PlayStation.

Daryl Bonnington gave her a soft smile and raised an eyebrow. 'Kids!'

He was only a kid himself, thought Sheila. Simon, her eldest, who kept reminding her he was nearly fourteen, hovered nearby. He looked up to Daryl. Which was not a bad thing, she thought. He needed a role model.

'Thanks ever so much for taking the boys while I cleaned up. I couldn't think of anyone else.'

'Glad to help out,' he said.

The sounds of Grand Theft Auto drifted to them. She sighed and it all came out in a rush. She couldn't help herself. 'It was that bloody thing, the PlayStation, that caused all this aggravation,' she said. 'You know what they're like, they keep on, all the other kids have got one and I thought it was only a couple of hundred quid, I'd be able to clear it quickly. But it never seemed to end, ten quid a week and that was the Christmas before last and they say I still owe them. But that can't be right, can it?'

Bonnington looked genuinely sympathetic.

'They... the dog...' She couldn't bring herself to say it.

'Yeah, I know. Simon told me,' said Bonnington and touched her shoulder lightly, a gesture of solidarity. 'Kids get over things faster if they talk them through.'

'Yeah, I suppose,' said Sheila, thinking that around here talking was the cure that killed. 'I just don't know what to do. I'm at my wits' end,' she continued, close to tears.

Bonnington was trained to manage desperation. 'Let's go in. I'll make you a cup of tea.'

Bonnington called goodbye to Simon and Terry as he passed the living-room door. Sheila followed him down the hall.

'I'll be back for the boys later then,' he said.

She hesitated for a moment. You heard so much about perverts these days. But then she told herself, don't be ridiculous. She was losing her faith in people because of recent events, that was all.

Bonnington checked his watch.

'This meeting is very important. The war on drugs.'

Sheila could see he wasn't joking.

'So I'll see you at about five.' He touched her arm. 'Remember what I said. Take some time for yourself, okay, Sheila?'

'Yeah, okay,' she said. 'Thanks, Daryl. See you later.'

Sheila watched him go. Her husband was doing ten years. Daryl said the boys would benefit from early intervention. As if they could inherit drug dealing from their father. 'Everything's connected, Sheila,' he'd said. He was well meaning, but a bit peculiar sometimes, she decided.

She closed the door and put the chain on.

There was the sound of screeching brakes and a sickening thud. Sheila went cold, then realised it was just the game.

5

George Lazenby slammed the surgery door behind him and set off across Victoria Park for his daily constitutional, which took him straight to The Approach tavern. He had to prepare for his meeting with the local NHS Trust that afternoon. It was an appropriately grim winter's day; even the ducks were shivering. It was definitely port and lemon weather. A heart-starter. For medicinal purposes only.

An hour later Lazenby caught Bonnington's look as they collided in the doorway of the old town hall where the Trust met. No doubt it was a reaction to the whiff of alcohol he caught on his breath. Bonnington was unfailingly polite, but Lazenby couldn't stand being patronised. He picked up on Bonnington's small, rueful sigh. It made Lazenby cross and discomfited, acutely aware of the irony: he was to debate the nature of addiction when he was half pissed.

'Up for it, are we, 007?' inquired Bonnington mildly.

Lazenby grunted in response. He did nothing to disguise his distaste for the earnest outreach worker, a bloody God-botherer. Bonnington's smooth skin, floppy blond fringe and bright blue eyes might beguile some, but Lazenby found his smile cold and unnatural.

He didn't like Bonnington's over-familiar use of his nickname, 007, either. He was aware the allusion was supposed to be witty. His belly hung over his belt, his drooping moustache was tinged brown with nicotine and his shirt frequently bore evidence of his breakfast. He lacked charisma. Anyway, the other bloody George Lazenby had only played the part once, in 1969. The nickname had come from his patients, which told you something about their vintage, and his. He didn't have a family practice.

The chairperson of the Trust, an academic with a PhD in the

semiotics of accident and emergency signs, indicated that Lazenby and Bonnington should take their seats on either side of her. She droned through the minutes from the last meeting and made her introductory remarks. Lazenby's gaze drifted up to the public gallery. There was the usual smattering of the homeless in search of warmth, but his eye was caught by a tall woman in a battered Burberry mac, staring into the middle distance. She struck him as very sad.

Lazenby reviewed his notes. The long, inglorious history of opiates in Britain was one of the good doctor's interests. His specialist subject, if he ever got to appear on *Mastermind*. Opium had been the means of forcing the Chinese to trade, back in the days when they were still smart enough to tell the West to fuck off. The Raj grew opium in India and exported it to China in exchange for another great drug, preferred by the British: tea. When the Chinese had objected to half their population succumbing to the pipe's dreamy charms, the Brits went to war, gave them a good thrashing, then went home and had a nice cup of fully imported oolong.

The Chair invited Bonnington to open the discussion. Game on.

'Madam Chair, ladies and gentlemen, members of the community. Dr George Lazenby, FRCGP, is a dinosaur. In a nice way.'

A couple of members of the Trust smothered their titters. Bonnington smiled at Lazenby, who tried to take the jibe in good part.

'He is one of no more than seventy medical practitioners in the whole country licensed to prescribe diacetylmorphine for addiction. And the Home Office informs me that there are only about forty left who actually do so – stalwarts who refuse to prescribe the universally favoured substitute, methadone. Dr Lazenby needs a special licence to give heroin to registered addicts, and the agreement of his local NHS Trust. That is the reason we are here today.'

Lazenby pretended to listen. He'd held his licence for a bloody long time and it wasn't easy for them to take it away. None were being issued these days. He half-heard Bonnington droning on about narco-terrorism. This was the mantra of the drug lobby these days, that massive industry of law enforcement, clinics, rehab facilities, academics and public sector policy wallahs whose livelihoods depended on illegal drugs. The marriage of convenience between the war on terror and the war on drugs.

Lazenby blew his nose loudly. The Chair glared at him. Lazenby knew the Trust was in sympathy with Bonnington's views because heroin cost more than methadone. It was always about money. But 007 regarded methadone as nasty stuff, and so did his patients, who were well-adjusted working people taking maintenance doses of pharmaceutical heroin. Their general health was better than his bloody own, thought Lazenby, reaching for his cigarettes before remembering where he was. He groped instead for an Extra Strong Mint. He became aware that Bonnington's tone had gone up a notch and tuned back in to what he was saying.

'Ladies and gentlemen, the continued sad decline of our community is hastened by heroin. The trade in this substance generates and supports crime locally and globally. Crime that threatens our way of life. Should we be using our taxes to buy a drug that is synonymous with immorality and dissipation? Or should we insist that those afflicted participate in a regime that will help them overcome their frailties and arrest the decline of our civilisation?' Bonnington's delivery was measured, but urgent. His message was clear.

Bonnington sat down to a smattering of applause from Trust members, which Lazenby thought was entirely inappropriate. The little bastard seemed so reasonable. The Chair nodded at him; it was his turn. He stood up. So did the woman in the Burberry mac.

Then she pointed a gun at him.

Lazenby felt as if his heart was going to burst out of his chest. Frozen to the spot, his gaze riveted on the small, snub barrel, he sensed the tide of fear that swept through the members of the Trust as, one by one, they turned their heads to the gallery.

'Murderer!' screamed the woman.

Lazenby lunged to one side as a sharp crack rang out. The sound of terrified pigeon wings beating against the thick glass atrium melded with the din of the Trust hitting the floor and the thundering feet of the fleeing homeless. One pair of feet ran in the opposite direction, taking the stairs of the gallery two at a time.

When Lazenby finally looked up he saw it was Bonnington, now sprinting towards the woman. She turned to face him, the confusion in her expression quickly replaced by fear. She held the gun loose in her hand, her arm extended into space over the ornate wooden balustrade. Bonnington launched himself at her.

Lazenby couldn't really see what happened next; it was so fast. They seemed to struggle, Bonnington reaching out to grasp the woman's extended arm and hold it rigid. They could have been about to waltz.

Then the woman toppled over the balcony as if performing a cartwheel. As she ploughed headfirst into the oak conference table her neck snapped.

The starting pistol slid from her hand.

6

It was early evening, but already black as midnight on the old tow path that ran beside the canal. It was the quickest route to the other side of Victoria Park, where Berlin had an appointment at six-thirty. She'd barely missed one in twenty years, come hell or high water. It would be hell if she did.

She kept her eyes on the cracked path in front of her and tried to ignore the sound of gentle lapping and the dark, floating shapes that loomed at the edge of her vision. Eventually she emerged onto a quiet street with a row of terraces. All had been smartly renovated. With one exception.

Every window of the decrepit Georgian house she approached was barred, but the faded green door was always on the latch. There were no cameras above the cracked portico.

Berlin pushed open the door and, without hesitation, she crossed the threshold of respectability and walked down a dim hall into an even dimmer room.

She plucked a magazine from the table and took a seat. *Time*'s Man of the Year in 1986 was Deng Xiaoping. Time stood still here. A well-dressed citizen of her own vintage usually had the appointment before hers. They had never spoken and had exchanged only the gravest of nods in recognition of their bond. Living up to the room's purpose. Waiting. But today he wasn't there.

His absence added to her unease. It was as if the wheel on which her universe turned had jumped a cog. Discovering a mutilated corpse before breakfast will do that to you, she thought, as she waited for the green light above the consulting-room lintel to come on, indicating that the current patient was leaving by another door. The last receptionist had fled years ago.

Fifteen minutes later the light still hadn't come on. Berlin was irritated. It didn't take that long. The surgery was silent apart from the dull rumble of the Central line emanating from deep beneath the foundations, a little plaster dust raining from the cracked cornice as each underground train sped through the darkness. Irritation turned to anxiety.

Berlin knocked on the consulting-room door. 'Hello?'

She knocked again, louder, then turned the handle. The door opened, but not far. Something was blocking it. Berlin put her shoulder against it and shoved, peering through the gap. A body was the obstacle. Lazenby. Her first thought was dead drunk. Then heart attack.

But as she lunged at the door and the body shifted enough for her to squeeze through the gap, the dark Axminster carpet rucked up, revealing the sheets of old newspaper beneath it. They were a sodden, wine-coloured mess. Vomit? Then she saw the small hole in his chest. Lazenby wasn't dead drunk, he was just dead.

Berlin took a quick step back and the newspaper slid underfoot. She put her hand out to steady herself and closed her eyes. The intense human emotion that had been absorbed by the wall for nearly forty years seemed to ooze into her palm. She snatched her hand away and tried to focus. She remembered to breathe and gulped for air. She had only one thought. *Shit.*

The door of the drug safe hung open. It was empty. She bent to touch Lazenby, but didn't dare. She had known him for more than twenty years, but he wasn't her friend. He was her salvation.

Panic enveloped her as she realised the implications of his death. Her phone was in her hand, although she couldn't remember how it got there. Instead of dialling 999 she put it back in her pocket and tore a bunch of prescriptions off the pad on the desk. Habit took her to the other door. She ran through the self-administration room, back down the hall and out into the world. Its edges suddenly seemed sharper.

Berlin and Mrs Ranasinghe, the local chemist, had grown world-weary together. Mrs Ranasinghe had stood her ground against many threats, from vandals and armed robbers to the machinations of corrupt councillors and their dodgy development schemes. She had met all comers with a placid taciturnity. The shop was a veritable fortress.

Sadly now she was to be brought to her knees by a bright, clean, shiny, soulless Asda supermarket, which was to incorporate a bright, clean, shiny, soulless pharmacy. Berlin couldn't see Asda providing addicts with a dispensing service. Buy one get one free?

'Plasters?' asked Mrs Ranasinghe.

Berlin frowned, confused, then followed Mrs Ranasinghe's gaze to her hand, which was smeared with blood from the surgery wall. She had a sudden vision of her perfect hand print inscribed in the spatter from Lazenby's aortic spurt. 'Oh no, thank you, it's fine,' she said, and wiped her hand on the sleeve of her black overcoat. It had seen worse.

Mrs Ranasinghe seemed unfazed until she glanced at the bunch of prescriptions that Berlin thrust at her. Lazenby's signature was on all of them. She managed Lazenby's diamorphine supply and also provided the surgery with bulk sterile syringes and other necessary paraphernalia. Mrs Ranasinghe knew the score.

'This is most unusual, Miss Berlin,' she said.

'Holidays, Mrs Ranasinghe,' came the quick reply.

Mrs Ranasinghe raised an eyebrow. A registered addict, travelling?

'Yours or his?' Mrs R would know both options were improbable. 'I should call him,' she said.

A buzzer indicated another customer at the security door. Cold sweat ran down Berlin's back. 'He's not there. The surgery's closed. Please, Mrs Ranasinghe. It's an emergency.'

Mrs Ranasinghe shrugged. 'What the hell. I'm retiring anyway.'

She disappeared for a moment and returned with a brown paper bag. Berlin reached for it, but before she handed it over Mrs Ranasinghe cautioned her.

'Seven days,' she said.

'Seven days?' echoed Berlin.

Mrs Ranasinghe was solemn. 'I've given you enough medication for one week, Miss Berlin.'

Berlin took the bag, nodded her thanks and went to the door. She waited for a click, the signal that Mrs Ranasinghe had released the security bolt.

'Miss Berlin?'

Berlin forced herself to remain calm and turn around.

'Yes?'

'Enjoy your trip.'

7

Doyle released the padlock, removed the chain and tugged at the rusty iron gates. They grated on the cracked concrete as he dragged them open, acting as an early warning system for the reclusive, paranoid old man who dwelt beyond. The family had been East End for generations and Doyle could never understand what drove Frank out to his 'premises' in Chigwell all those years ago.

Nineteen eighty-six. A year best forgotten. One thing after another. Nancy had buggered off without so much as a by-your-fucking-leave. She had taken her savings and left Doyle with their eleven-year-old, Georgina. He and Nancy had been childhood sweethearts and he'd worshipped the ground she walked on. Okay, they were de factos. But she'd never minded. None of them went in for certification.

It was the year of Thatcher's bleeding Big Bang, which had made it nigh on impossible to get a decent crew together. All the villains with brains had gone into the City. Only the muscle was left. Frank had said they had to diversify to make best use of it. Somehow he'd come up with a bit of capital and started lending to cash-strapped single mums. It built from there.

Nancy went and then Frank decamped to Chigwell. No support from that quarter. Doyle was left with Gina, a right little madam, who blamed him for her mum pissing off.

Eventually it all went pear-shaped. Gina walked out the day she was sixteen, and not so much as a Christmas card since. He was left on his tod in Bethnal Green to carry on the business. He loved it, mind, the business. But found the nights a bit long.

Frank's premises consisted of a crumbling, featureless postwar bungalow, a sprawling place of silent, square rooms and stained Danish furniture. It was on a couple of acres, dotted with ramshackle sheds, garages and outhouses. The land would be worth a fortune now. No mortgage – Frank paid cash for everything. He'd never borrowed money in his life.

Doyle had to close the gates behind him and secure the padlock after he'd driven through or Frank went ballistic. The grating noise irritated the shit out of Doyle. Just once he'd like to surprise the old man. Sometimes he didn't bother to fasten the padlock, a small act of defiance. Frank never went out; he would never know. The supermarket delivered his tins of spam, tea bags and what have you to the gates and Doyle paid the bill.

Towering weeds either side of the drive obscured the booby traps and broken glass that Doyle knew littered the grounds. Anyone would think Frank had the crown bloody jewels in there.

The old man opened the front door before Doyle got out of the car. He turned back down the hall as Doyle stuttered a greeting.

'Hello, Frank. How goes it?'

'Shut it. The premises are freezing.'

Doyle resisted the temptation to tell him to turn on the fucking central heating. It was pointless. Frank still lived in a fog of World War Two austerity.

'And a bit of fucking respect. I might be eighty-odd but I'm still your fucking father.'

'Yes, Pop.'

Frank drew the ledger out. He used to keep it in a kitchen drawer, but lately he'd taken to tucking it in behind his belt. He clutched it in his huge, trembling hand.

Doyle reflected that the old man was literally losing his grip. But the sinews in his skinny arms were still taut as wire, the knuckles great red ridges of bone, hard as iron. He was a foot taller than Doyle, his eyes sunk so deep into black sockets their colour was obscured. Grey hair curled from his ears and nostrils, adding to the gargoyle look.

Doyle shivered as Frank passed him the ledger. He sat down at the kitchen table and Frank stood over him and watched, eagle-eyed, as he recorded the tally from memory. At least he didn't have to go through this every sodding night, without fail, any more. He'd put his foot down. Now it was just most nights.

When he'd finished the tally, Frank snatched it back and ran a finger down the neat columns of names, addresses and numbers.

'Get the lads around to number fifty-one.'

'It's done.'

'And?'

'Don't worry, Fr— Pop – she'll make the payment.'

'So you say.'

Frank slipped the ledger back behind his belt and tapped it twice for luck. He held out his hand and Doyle handed him a thick roll of banknotes. Frank grunted and shoved it into one of his cardigan pockets. He wore three.

Doyle relaxed. Frank had no idea he'd been growing the market, so to speak, with an injection of capital from his new silent partner. Frank would go mental if he found out, and that was never a pretty sight. On the other hand, it didn't matter what he did, Frank would never be happy. Doyle only ever wanted to please, but it was never good enough. Now he would show his father what he could do. Initiative. Enterprise.

Frank turned away without a word and left the kitchen, switching off the light as he went. Doyle was still sitting at the table. That's that, then, he thought. Another fucking day, another fucking dollar.

'Goodnight, Pop!' he called.

But the only response was a door slamming somewhere at the other end of the house.

8

The Narrow ran not quite parallel to the river, a broken link between the bright, soaring financial institutions that had swept aside the old docks, and the Square Mile, as solid as its name suggested, all squat stone and carved Britannias with lions at their feet. The goddess of passion and war. Narrow is the way, and strait the gate.

Berlin walked into the past often, and always at night. The Narrow delivered her into Wapping, and then into the City of London proper, where a sharp right brought her to Newgate's blood-drenched soil, compost to that sombre edifice of the criminal law, the new Old Bailey.

She turned a corner and gasped. Someone was coming at her, striding, enveloped in a long black coat, a pale face and haunted eyes picked out in the headlights of a passing car. The figure receded with the vehicle and Berlin laughed. Her own reflection in a shop window had spooked her. She knew she was right to be afraid. She was her own worst enemy.

After leaving Mrs Ranasinghe, she had legged it to her flat, stowed six precious ampoules of diamorphine in the bread bin and administered the contents of number seven. Heroin. It was her version of a stiff drink at the end of the day, although she would never claim her use was recreational. Her relationship with the drug was more complex than that, and at the same time a simple matter of addiction.

The prospect of losing her free, legal and pure supply had induced blind panic and a callous disregard for Lazenby. She was a monster. His body had lain in a sticky pool of gore while she stole the prescriptions. Like a common junkie. No better than the junkie who'd killed him.

She hadn't murdered Lazenby, but when it came to her informant, it was a different matter. She wasn't sure what role she might have played in Juliet Bravo's ugly, terrifying end, but she had no doubt she was implicated.

Two bodies in one day. It was a nightmarish coincidence, and whichever way you cut it, there was blood on her hands. Now she had six days to find another doctor to prescribe her heroin. Six days to find Juliet Bravo's murderer. She owed her that much.

Six days because beyond that she had no idea how she would function if she found herself with no doctor, no connections and no dope. What would the seventh day be like if it came to that? The eighth or, God forbid, the ninth? She suspected she would be in no state to catch a cold, let alone a killer. She hoped to Christ she didn't have to find out.

Turning into Dorset Rise she found herself confronting the sculpture of St George and the Dragon. The dragon appeared to be winning.

The Second Day

9

The first bleak hint of what passed for dawn in mid-February streaked the sky as Berlin returned from her nocturnal wandering. She turned the key in the lock of her over-priced Bethnal Green 'studio' and wondered why she had finally joined the real estate stampede. Did she just get sick of people telling her she was mad to rent because it was 'dead money'? Or was it a final, doomed bid for respectability?

It had cost her dear. She'd bought at the top of the market, just before the crash. Now she was sunk deep in negative equity. If they sacked her, how long could she last? She thought about her one hundred and ten per cent mortgage, the spare room at her mother's, and her personal habits. Not a happy combination.

Closing the curtains she crawled under the duvet and switched on the TV. Lazenby had made the local news. An anonymous caller had alerted the police to foul play at the surgery. The doctor, a well-known figure in the locality and among campaigners for the decriminalisation of hard drugs, had conducted an 'unorthodox' practice for more than four decades and had been investigated by the General Medical Council for irregularities. A quantity of drugs had been stolen. Dr Lazenby's patients came from all over London and the South and police were anxious to contact anyone who had attended the surgery yesterday.

Berlin knew the police would pay her a visit sooner or later. They would go through Lazenby's records and conduct interviews with all his regulars. But it would be routine. She hadn't taken the whole prescription pad, just a few scripts; they'd have no way of knowing they hadn't been issued by Lazenby. Her forging of his signature would go undetected. She was confident Mrs Ranasinghe wouldn't say anything. After all, she had done the wrong thing too.

Berlin switched off the TV. All she wanted to do was sleep, but as soon as she closed her eyes the vision that greeted her was the blue flesh of her dead informant bobbing up and down in the lock. She opened them again.

Nestor may have been fishing when he asked her what else she had failed to record about Juliet Bravo, but he was right. They had met on half a dozen occasions, none of which she had logged. Berlin had recognised in the other woman an echo of her own angst. There was at least twenty years between them, but age was irrelevant. Nietzsche warned against looking into the abyss too long, lest it look back. They had both looked, and seen in each other the same response: a taut resolve to be unafraid.

Berlin had been loath to initiate the usual process, which would have seen Juliet Bravo managed by an agency that took a one-size-fits-all approach to so-called covert human intelligence sources. Informants were usually victims of one kind or another. This woman didn't fit the profile of the financially excluded. She'd said she was 'something in the City'. That could cover a multitude of sins.

Berlin touched her throat, choked with the memory of her informant's savage wound. Whatever she was and whatever the demons that drove her to inform, now she was Berlin's demon. Draping the duvet around herself, she got out of bed and sat down at the table with a bottle of Talisker Single Malt.

Was there something in their early conversations that would give her an edge, something that would compensate for her lack of access to the official investigation? She could hear the boiler struggling against the plummeting temperature. Wrapping the duvet around her more tightly, she prayed the pipes wouldn't freeze and burst.

She would go back to the beginning.

When all the standard inquiries came up blank Berlin had called Juliet Bravo and asked her why Doyle was absent from all official records. Her reaction indicated a certain lack of faith in British bureaucracy.

'There must be a stuff-up somewhere,' was all she'd said. Her cynicism echoed Berlin's own.

'Is there anything else you know about him that could help me? Before I can take further action I need something, reasonable grounds, to take it forward.' She couldn't get an authority for surveillance just on the basis of a phone call.

She'd waited for a response but none came. 'Hello? Are you still there?' Berlin had asked.

'I'm here.'

Berlin gave her the company line in her best firm-but-fair voice. It sometimes worked. 'You haven't even given me your surname. We don't act on uncorroborated, anonymous tips. I'm sure you understand.'

The sense of struggle at the other end of the line was palpable. The more she tells me about Doyle, the more she gives away about herself, Berlin thought. That's the real problem here. She tried a different tack.

'Look, why don't we meet, somewhere public, somewhere you're comfortable with, and just have a coffee? Call it a goodwill gesture. Then we can move forward.'

To her utter surprise, the woman said yes.

The informant had described herself as mid-thirties, average height, medium build, shoulder-length brown hair, and said she would be wearing a black business suit and pink striped shirt with white collar and cuffs.

Berlin arrived early in order to take up a position in the café at the Tate Modern that would give her at least some opportunity to assess if the woman was being followed. One-on-ones were a breach of procedure, but Coulthard had broken up her partnership with Delroy under the mantra of 'upskilling'. Her skills or Del's, he had never bothered to explain. She didn't care to work with anyone else and she had wanted to get out of the office, away from Coulthard's smirk. Get the jump on him if this shark turned out to be a great white. A trophy kill. So she had come alone.

The only woman wearing a pink striped shirt to enter the café bore no resemblance to the description she had given. She was taller than average, willowy, with translucent, apricot skin perfectly complemented by a black designer suit. Her gold jewellery was subtle, and her thick, chestnut hair was cut with precision, so it bounced ever so winningly as she walked. She wore dark glasses, although it was the middle of October.

She bought a coffee and sat down. No one followed her in and Berlin couldn't see anyone outside watching her.

Before Berlin could make a move an attractive, tanned tourist, complete with expensive camera and guidebook, approached the woman. He was carrying a tray of tea and scones and seemed to ask if he could share her table. There were plenty of spare seats elsewhere. He was suave, his body language insinuating, his smile confident.

Berlin was astonished when the woman didn't reply or even look up from her coffee, just raised her middle finger in an emphatic, silent gesture. She nearly laughed out loud. So much for British reserve. The man looked shocked, offended and sheepish in quick succession. He scuttled away with a scowl and Berlin took the seat denied the would-be Lothario.

'Bravo,' she said.

The woman almost smiled.

Berlin offered her hand. 'Catherine Berlin. What should I call you?'

The woman hesitated. 'You said it, so how about Juliet Bravo?'

Berlin was surprised by this reference to a TV cop lost in the mists of time – the early eighties.

'You're not old enough to remember the show, surely?' she said.

Juliet Bravo took off her sunglasses. 'My mum loved it.'

She had the saddest brown eyes Berlin had ever seen.

The next time they met it was at Starbucks and official. Berlin scheduled it so that Delroy was the only other investigator available and Coulthard reluctantly had to assign him to go with her. Del was the only bloke on the team that Berlin could trust and Coulthard knew it. Which meant Coulthard couldn't rely on him to do anything other than confirm whatever Berlin logged.

Delroy went along with Berlin's assessment that Juliet Bravo presented as a credible informant, whatever her motivation and despite her reluctance to identify herself. It was worth pursuing. So Berlin submitted the form seeking authorisation for surveillance. Signing off on an obs operation was usually Coulthard's job, but he had just gone on leave, scuba diving in the Maldives. How he could afford holidays like that she had no idea. Nestor signed it off in his absence.

There were only two bodies available to watch Doyle – two of Coulthard's boys, who shared a brain. Both were white, heavily built and had shiny shaved heads. They'd sit in a nice clean vehicle with tinted windows in a predominantly poor Bengali neighbourhood. Like that was going to work.

And it didn't. Someone called the local cop shop and reported perverts on the manor. The boys had failed to log their presence with the Control Room Supervisor at the police station. They blamed each other for the oversight, but Berlin strongly suspected that they hadn't wanted to sit in the car freezing their bollocks off for the likes of her, so hadn't followed procedure on purpose. Maybe they weren't as stupid as they looked.

Whatever the reason, the surveillance was blown. By then Coulthard was back and she couldn't get it started again, try as she might.

Coulthard said there were bigger fish to fry than her target. She was trumped. Berlin couldn't log Doyle's movements, identify his associates or find his victims, which meant she couldn't turn them with the attractive proposition that if they gave evidence he would go to prison and their debt would be wiped.

There was a glaring gap in the intelligence because of the failure of the surveillance. But it was immaterial, because the next thing she knew Nestor had closed the file. She tried to raise it with him but he waved her away, told her to refer operational matters to Coulthard.

Instead of just informing Juliet Bravo that it was over, Berlin continued to meet her, in the bars at Waterloo or Euston, busy railway stations where they had conversations she never wrote up. They both had a taste for good Scotch. But it was more than that. Berlin rarely made a connection with anyone, and she was reluctant to lose it.

They talked about growing up in London and the bonds of prejudice, myth and history that ensnared them. The conversation was never domestic. There were no references to husbands or children as yardsticks of achievement. Their exchanges were genuine, unsentimental. It was a relief.

Finally she was forced to tell Juliet Bravo the investigation was dead on its feet. The ferocity of her informant's reaction was a surprise: she insisted Doyle mustn't be allowed to get away with it. Berlin pushed back and told her it was down to her: she had to come up with hard evidence, something Berlin could use to kick-start the investigation again, something that her boss couldn't ignore. Juliet Bravo said she would get it.

The next time Berlin saw her she was floating in the Limehouse Basin.

10

Berlin stood opposite the block of flats where Doyle supposedly lived. Number fourteen: a former Council flat bought by the original tenant in the eighties under the Right to Buy legislation. The right to make a fast quid for anyone in London. The flat had been sold a number of times since. Now it was owned by a company and Doyle wasn't listed as a director.

Dumb and Dumber had managed to fire off a few grainy shots of the flat's occupant with the telephoto before they had been rumbled. The photos were still on Berlin's phone, ready for Juliet Bravo to confirm the ID when they met at the lock. That was also when she was to hand over the hard evidence that Berlin had demanded. A demand that had apparently proved fatal.

Berlin's problem now was that she could stand in the street until kingdom come, shivering in the dim morning murk, and never see anyone enter or exit number fourteen. It was on the second floor. She could hardly hang about on the landing. The angle from the street was too acute and on her own she couldn't cover the stairs at each end of the building. Surveillance had never been Berlin's strong suit. She gazed around and tried to assess the layout.

The flats overlooked Weaver's Fields, in the middle of which was the children's playground. There would be a direct line of sight from there to the landing and the front door of number fourteen. A morning stroll around the park was in order, followed by a go on the swings. Better than the gym, and cheaper.

Chilled to the bone, two hours later she was listening to the traffic build up on Bethnal Green Road and watching two dog walkers and one little old lady brave the cold. The old dear was bent double over her sholley, a hybrid of shopping trolley and Zimmer frame. Berlin, now sitting on the kids' slide, clocked her shuffling along the nearby path and expected her to just shuffle on past.

She fixed her gaze on the second floor of the flats across the park, trying not to yield to boredom and distraction. But the squeak from the sholley stopped and when Berlin looked back, the old lady was standing directly opposite her with her head twisted as far round in her direction as it would go.

'Chilly, isn't it?' offered Berlin.

The old lady's mouth worked for a while, lining up her false teeth. 'Fuck off out of here, you junkie cunt!' she finally managed to spit out.

Berlin stared at her, impassive, and said nothing. The old lady clung to the sholley, her body shaking with the effort.

'Fucking kids' playground! I'm sick of you lot hanging around here, leaving your fucking needles everywhere. So fuck off!'

Before Berlin could respond to the old dear with a suggestion as to where she might like to shove her sholley, she caught a movement at the flats. The front door of number fourteen had opened. A fat figure sallied out along the landing into the brisk morning.

Berlin took off towards the park gate. She would follow him, identify his victims and get them to confirm he *was* Doyle, then find the connection between him and Juliet Bravo. She was a civilian investigator and didn't have the luxury of just arresting him.

The old lady watched her go, amazed and delighted. She lined up her teeth. 'See, they just need a good talking to!' she congratulated herself, and stood a little straighter.

Berlin sprinted for the gate, her eyes fixed on the landing. The man raised a hand to greet someone and the pale sun glinted off his heavy gold rings. She realised she'd seen those hands before; the fat face in the photos hadn't rung any bells, but the fat fingers banded with sovereigns, signet rings, antique wedding bands and snake rings were unforgettable.

The man disappeared for a moment as he turned into the stairwell. Berlin slowed down and craned to see him appear on the next landing. It had to be Doyle.

She didn't notice the three hoodies barring the gate until she was nearly on top of them. She kept going, expecting them to step aside, but they didn't move. She was forced to come to a sharp stop.

'Excuse me, lads,' she said, breathless.

Their eyes were dull pinpricks as they peered out from deep within their hoods. They closed in on her, no taller than she, but wiry and street hard. And there were three of them.

'Give it up,' growled one.

'What?' asked Berlin, in a tone that conveyed no fear.

'The cash or the smack or both. Whatever you've got. You're not out there freezing your fuckin' arse off having a fuckin' swing,' he said. 'So hand it over, bitch.'

Their hands were thrust into their pockets and she wondered if they had knives. But she was so intent on not losing Doyle she abandoned caution.

'Fuck off,' she said, trying to shove her way through them.

One kicked the back of her knee and the other two jumped her, punched her in the head and dragged her to the ground. The kicker sunk his boot into her while the others went through her pockets. When they came up with an old mobile and a fiver they weren't happy. They stomped on the phone and kept the money, then ran off, swearing about the wasted effort.

Berlin rolled over and threw up. A couple in matching lycra jogged around her into the park. She tried crawling, without success, and lay there in a puddle of freezing puke, semi-conscious.

After a while she became aware of a pulsing blue light. A police car. Amazing. Someone must have called it in. She waited in vain for a kind police officer to assist her. Eventually she managed to turn her head enough to be able to see two constables emerge from the flats. She heard one bark into his radio, 'Looks like we just missed him, sir.'

You and me both, she thought.

11

The cut above Berlin's eye was bleeding sporadically and the bruising was coming out nicely. Her back hurt like hell and her right knee was already swollen. Muddy, bloodstained, she had limped home, dumped her shattered mobile on the table, and gone straight to the bread bin. It was breaking her usual routine, but this was an emergency. Heroin was, after all, a painkiller.

Now she was in that comfortable, clear space she inhabited in the first hour after a hit. It was a holiday from anxiety, but the package came with strict terms and conditions. Years of effort and self-control, not traits that most people associated with addiction, had gone into stabilising her dose and the fix routine. The rush had gone out of it long ago and she had resisted the temptation to seek it out again by increasing her dose. Tolerance. Which, after all, was all that she asked.

Some of her colleagues believed she was a diabetic because of her regular doctor's appointments. She let them. It was a strategy that kept nosy parkers at bay. She used a variety of injecting sites to avoid tracks, although her puncture marks didn't constitute tracks in the conventional sense.

Years before she had learnt to switch between intravenous, intramuscular or subcutaneous administration. It was part of her strategic approach to managing her dependence. Sometimes it just depended on her mood. She didn't use blunt picks or get infections because she always used a fresh kit, courtesy of Mrs Ranasinghe.

Berlin had felt little in the way of emotional attachment to other human beings in the last twenty years. But her sense of belonging to the dead was strong. When the backwash had roiled Juliet Bravo's body it had exposed more than just the violent wound at her throat; it had exposed Berlin's vulnerability. A crack in the carapace. She could still feel.

But that was then. A hit and a hot bath and she didn't feel anything except a sublime lack of concern about her suspension, her informant, her doctor, or Uncle Tom Cobley and all.

Everything drifted away on a gentle sea of indifference. Only one tiny worry tugged at the corner of her consciousness. She had only five ampoules left. Five days. She closed her eyes and that too faded to nothing.

12

Doyle couldn't be arsed driving out to bloody Chigwell. The first flakes of snow settled on his shoulders, merging with the dandruff, both tinted yellow by the sodium streetlights. He thrust his hands deeper into the pockets of his camel-hair overcoat and stamped his feet. Rings on his fingers, bells on his toes. It had been a bloody long day.

Word had got out that the law was looking for him, which gave some of his clients a notion that if they kept out of his way, he might get banged up and they would be home free. So he was avoiding the police, while his creditors were avoiding him.

It had all begun a few weeks back with those bald geezers in the motor. They didn't look right. He'd got Ahmed in the drycleaners to ring up the Police and Community Support Officers and report two men sitting in a car near the park gate at the bottom of the flats, watching the kiddies. The PCSOs had been down there like a shot and Doyle had stood on the landing, watching the argy-bargy with these blokes.

Ahmed caught most of the row and reported back to Doyle. Any law enforcement types on the plot were supposed to notify the local nick and get some sort of code number to quote in just these circumstances. These blokes had forgotten to get their code.

Later, Ahmed made a cup of tea for the PCSOs, who told him the numpties were from some government department. Doyle guessed they were from that bloody interfering Financial whatsit Agency, intent on disrupting the wheels of commerce. It turned out he was right. He'd made a call. That's all it took. After that he had been pretty sure they wouldn't be back. Now he was bloody certain, because the grass who'd started all this aggravation was dead. It was sorted.

But just to be on the safe side, he'd swapped the Audi, the car he used for shopping, for a modest Mondeo he kept registered to one of his clients – a deaf lady who couldn't drive and wouldn't dare give him up if anyone inquired.

He stood beside the shitty little car now, cursing that he'd been reduced to this. He'd never had any trouble with the law before; he was a community service and he was sure most local coppers would take the view that while his clients were borrowing money from him it meant they weren't stealing it. A result all round.

But there was no point just standing there freezing his bollocks off. He struggled to open the car door with a key. The bloody thing didn't even have electronic locking.

Doyle crashed through the unfamiliar gears and wondered if the problem he was having with the bloody government was related to his move into commercial lending. Maybe getting mixed up with the banker wanker Fernley-Price had been a mistake.

Doyle had been minding his own business in The Silent Woman when a City gent had approached him and asked if he could sit down. Suit yourself, he'd said. There were plenty of spare tables, so he knew the geezer wanted something. He had thought it would be the usual. Money.

It was only when they were well into the drink and the conversation, about the state of the nation and the decline of the robust entrepreneur, that he had realised this Fernley-Price didn't want to borrow, he wanted to lend. He'd seemed to know a lot about Doyle's operation, and after a bit of a pitch, had proposed a joint venture, giving him a bloody economics lecture in the process.

'SMEs!' he'd exclaimed.

Doyle hadn't wanted to sound ignorant but the look on his face must have given it away.

'Small and medium enterprises. That's where the crunch has bitten hardest. No excess labour to lay off and they've got cash flow problems because the banks aren't lending. In fact they're calling in overdrafts. So these small firms are owed money by creditors who can't pay up because they're going broke too. No line of credit either. A vicious circle.'

He had sounded convincing. Bigger loans and more of 'em, with more juice. No crying housewives to contend with or desperate gamblers who would put up with a broken leg. Doyle's usual sphere of operations was messy compared to the cold logic of the higher echelons of the market. He'd liked the sound of it, and taken Fernley-Price up on his business proposition. That was nearly three months ago and it had all gone beautifully. For a while.

*

The road was icy, the tyres were crap and the windscreen was opaque with condensation. Doyle tried to rub it clear with his glove as he pondered Fernley-Price's reaction when told about the geezers in the car. They'd been having one of their conflabs in The Silent Woman when Doyle mentioned he'd seen off surveillance. Fernley-Price nearly choked on his pint.

'What? What the hell? How do you know they were watching you?' he'd spluttered.

'Calm down, mate, it's sorted.'

'That's not the fucking point. Mate.'

Doyle had noted the edge of sarcasm. The wanker had better shut up. But he didn't.

'How did they know about you and how did you know about them? That's what I want to fucking know. I've got a lot of cash tied up with you now. Serious money invested in your local SMEs!' exclaimed Fernley-Price.

'Yeah, yeah, okay,' replied Doyle. He was used to the bloody jargon by then. SMEs meant the Indian grocers, the tobacconists, the real estate agents, the accountants and the builders' yards. They were all doing it tough in the crisis. All except him and Fernley-Price.

'Maybe one of our new clients got a little bit uppity. Perhaps these geezers from the SMEs don't understand the rules yet. I'll find 'em and make an example. Don't worry, it won't happen again. Anyway, those blokes have gone.'

'But you can't guarantee they won't be back!'

Doyle put his glass down and gave Fernley-Price the dead eye. 'Yes I can, mate. I'm all about risk management. And I'm not the Bank of England, so you can trust me.'

Fernley-Price had gone on and on that night about the bloody surveillance. The bloke had a temper and it got on Doyle's nerves, so he had made further inquiries, just to shut him up. He had told Fernley-Price for the umpteenth time that it was nothing to worry about. Turned out it was some narky bitch, according to his contact. Anyway, it was over.

He fiddled with the Mondeo's heater, but the bloody thing couldn't handle these temperatures. Something else to worry about. He was sick and tired of Frank's demands and the endless nights waiting for another miserable dawn. He hadn't had a decent sleep for bloody years. Since Nancy left, if he was honest with himself.

He intended to keep Fernley-Price happy so he would deliver more supermarket bags of cash, capital for the well-oiled Doyle system. 'Oily Doyley'. He had to chuckle.

The prick was supposed to be a silent partner, but he hadn't been silent enough for Doyle's liking. All Doyle wanted was a bit of peace and quiet. For Fernley-whosit to stick to his end of the bargain and keep his nose out of Doyle's end of the business, and for Frank to give him a break once in a while. Was that too much to ask?

He took a sharp right onto a pub forecourt, causing havoc in the traffic behind him. He gave the hooters the finger. Fuck it, he needed a drink. Frank would have to wait.

By the time Doyle got to Chigwell there was a foot of snow around the premises and the place was in darkness. He clambered out of the Mondeo and wrestled with the gates, his fingers numb with cold. He got back in the car as quick as he could, drove through the gates and kept going, not bothering to get out and shut them again. Bugger Frank and his bloody rules.

When he got to the end of the drive and turned off the motor the soft silence of the snow was eerie. The front door didn't open.

A bit unsteady on his feet, he stumbled up the steps and grasped the knocker. The door was ajar. He released the knocker and it swung open.

'Fr— Pop? You there?'

He spoke softly. He was a bit late and maybe the old fella had fallen asleep. He took a step over the threshold and a voice came out of the darkness.

'What time do you call this?'

Before he could reply, Frank came flying at him, a fucking banshee, wielding his thick leather belt. Doyle heard it whistle through the air. The next moment it struck him across the shoulder. He staggered under the blow. Before he could recover Frank struck again, this time at his head. He felt the buckle catch his cheek and the blood trickle down his neck. Suddenly he was fifteen again. He cried out.

'Pop! Pop, don't!'

Frank's face, scarlet with rage, seemed to glow in the dark, his eyes enormous white orbs protruding from their sockets. He struck again and again until Doyle sunk to the floor, his arms over his head, weeping.

'Pop! I'm sorry! I'm sorry!'

As suddenly as it had started, it stopped. Frank fastened his belt around his trousers, walked back down the hall and left him to it.

The Third Day

The Third Day

13

Berlin woke with a pounding headache, a raging thirst and an overwhelming sense of her own stupidity. She swung her legs off the couch and as she put her feet to the floor her right knee shrieked with pain. Her back was stiff and one eye puffy and difficult to open.

The first thing she did was check the bread bin. Five ampoules remained in the brown paper bag. After the belting at the park gate and her resort to 'analgesia' she had done precisely bloody nothing. She swore.

She should have been sorting things out, trying to find Doyle, preparing her defence for the suspension hearing and finding a new doctor who would prescribe her heroin.

She went into the bathroom and looked in the mirror. What a bloody mess. She needed to get her head on straight and get down to business. Fast. An app downloaded her voicemail to the computer; she would listen later. A bath, breakfast. But first, a quick check online to try to allay at least one of her anxieties.

The National Health Service homepage boasted 'Your health. Your choices.' Except not in Berlin's case. The website made it clear that registered addicts were prescribed methadone and required to participate in counselling and other so-called therapeutic activities, with the ultimate aim of being drug-free. Whatever that meant. She trawled through the government portal and pages offering advice on substance abuse, but came up with the same result every time.

Lazenby had regarded himself as a doctor, not an instrument of social policy. It seemed Lazenbys were few and far between. There was no easy route to a general practitioner who was licensed to prescribe heroin and who actually did so. It would take time and luck to find one. She was running out of both.

*

Pellicci's on Bethnal Green Road was famous. It was built in 1900 and had been run by the same Tuscan family ever since. It had a Grade II-listed interior which dated from 1946 and the Krays used to eat there. But for Berlin it was the chips.

'There you go, darlin'.' Nino garnished her breakfast with a wink.

Tucked into a tight corner, she focused on eggs, bacon, sausage and chips. She knew it would probably kill her, but then, they had said that about heroin. The first crunchy, golden morsel was halfway to her mouth when the door swung open, admitting an arctic blast and a fat man wearing a camel overcoat and a clutch of gold rings.

'Morning, Mr Doyle,' sang out Nino.

Berlin dropped her eyes to her plate and let her hair fall around her face. Of course, this was where she'd seen him before. It was now late morning. Her usual time was before work, and Doyle obviously didn't keep office hours, so their paths would rarely cross.

She couldn't believe the police hadn't got his flat under observation. Unless he had been interviewed and released overnight. It was unlikely. In a murder the magistrate would usually authorise an extended period for questioning. They had her statement that the victim had identified Doyle as a loan shark, which gave them reasonable grounds to hang on to him for a while.

It was barely two days since she had found Juliet Bravo floating in the lock and here was the prime suspect, ordering sausage and eggs. She looked up and saw Doyle glaring at a bloke sitting in the warmest corner. The man took the hint, scooped up his newspaper and corned beef sandwich and found another seat.

Doyle moved gingerly. The plaster below his right cheekbone indicated something more than a shaving cut. He took off his coat, but not his scarf. When he bent over she could see a livid purple streak across the back of his neck.

Perhaps he felt her eyes on him. Doyle turned and looked straight at her. For a fleeting moment he gave her a small, rueful smile, expressing fellow feeling for another human being who had copped a good smacking. She realised that her face was in a similar condition to his. She couldn't help herself. She smiled back.

14

Jeremy Fernley-Price ate a solitary bowl of Bircher muesli while scanning his *Financial Times*. It was telling a story so miserable that he thought he might bring up his breakfast. His world continued to implode. Each page was littered with words like 'disarray', 'turmoil' and 'collapse'. These were not terms with which a Master of the Universe was familiar.

Amid the chaos of subprime meltdown, credit default swaps and contracts for difference, Fernley-Price had watched his capital, which wasn't his anyway, disappear. It took with it his self-esteem.

He was a massive, gleaming product of privilege. His thick, flaxen hair was swept back, coiffed but nonchalant, accentuating the patrician brow and clear, blue eyes. His hands could only be described as meaty, but manicured. His suits and shirts were bespoke.

His father had been in the City, a broker, but had retired about the time they abolished the distinction between brokers and jobbers, and computer systems had begun to replace the judgement of human beings. This was Mrs Thatcher's Big Bang. The Iron Lady was a class warrior with a very hefty handbag.

He tipped the rest of the muesli into the sink, turned on the tap and ran the garbage disposal unit. A shrieking sound was succeeded by the grinding of metal on metal, then the whine of a seized motor. He had left the fucking spoon in the fucking bowl. Enraged, he smashed the bowl down on the granite bench top, shattering the translucent china. Fine needles of porcelain penetrated his palm. Blood bubbled up from the embedded slivers, a tattoo of exquisite agony.

It was the last fucking straw. His mind buckled.

He was caught between his housemaster's knees, a vice to prevent him squirming as Matron dug black splinters from his fingers with a hot needle. He screamed.

Be a man, commanded his housemaster.

Fernley-Price made a fist of his bleeding palm and struck the granite. Rage smothered despair.

Twenty minutes later he stood in his German Rainmaker shower beneath an expensive mix of water, air and light, and tried to think how it had come to this. The problem was people were less reliable than a well-structured financial instrument. His colleagues across the globe would no doubt share his sentiment.

He recalled his first encounter with The Silent Woman. She was a dull pub that squatted on the border of Canary Wharf and Poplar and lived up to her name. The landlord could guarantee the CCTV cameras at each end of the street were always broken. Despite this, there was never any graffiti. The local hoodies knew better.

Fernley-Price had strolled in, leant against the bar and had been about to order a gin and tonic when he'd realised that a G & T wasn't really on in this environment.

'A pint of London Pride, mate,' he'd said, keeping it chummy.

'Coming up, sir,' said the barman, feigning deference. You couldn't miss the mocking edge in his voice.

Fernley-Price felt again the prick of that humiliation. Fuck them. Once, he could have bought and sold the decrepit establishment. He'd decided at the time that if the new venture flourished, and there was every reason to think it would, he would shut down The

Silent bloody Woman and reopen it as a gastropub. Revenge. He had experience in that area.

He stepped from the shower, grabbed a towel from a set that had cost the same as a holiday in Spain, and reflected on the fact that he had always been ill-used. Though he could still come out ahead if he played his cards right. But at this moment he had no fresh shirts and the place was rapidly becoming a pigsty. A very expensive pigsty.

At the window he gazed down at the river. The apartment overlooked the wharf that was said to have been Execution Dock. He wondered for a moment if he had made some poor choices, then resolved to put that thought behind him and move on quickly from breakfast to lunch.

He would contemplate matters over a drink at The Prospect of Whitby, where they had a gallows. It would suit his mood. He would pull himself together, find a halfway clean shirt and get out of the apartment. There was no point in hanging around. He prided himself on being a man of action.

15

Berlin left Pellicci's without exchanging any more fond glances with Doyle, who was hoeing into double sausage and egg on toast. She hobbled across the road and ducked into The Shakespeare, where the landlord was just putting up the optics.

'Eye-opener, madam?' he inquired.

'Talisker,' said Berlin, without thinking.

'I beg yours?'

'Scotch. Whatever you've got. Make it a double, please.'

She took her drink to a window seat with a view of the café and settled in to wait for Doyle to finish his breakfast. By rights, she should call DCI Thompson and alert him to Doyle's location. But after the way she had been treated at the initial case conference she wasn't inclined to do him any favours. They weren't going to brief her on their inquiries, so why should she keep them informed of hers? Fuck them. She sipped her Scotch and waited.

The sound of sirens was routine in Bethnal Green, but when a police car and an unmarked vehicle pulled up outside Pellicci's half of the locals stopped to watch while the other half made themselves scarce. Berlin noticed the Chinese bootleg-DVD sellers were the quickest off the mark.

Craning to see around the number eight bus, which had pulled up so the driver and passengers could get a good look, Berlin saw uniforms clearing pedestrians out of the way as three suits went inside. Moments later two of them walked out again, frogmarching Doyle. One of them was that little toe rag Acting Detective Sergeant Flint, the other a black detective she didn't recognise. They got in the back of the unmarked car with Doyle between them.

A couple of minutes later DCI Thompson emerged, bacon roll in hand. He paused and nodded at a couple of people in the crowd. Berlin used the moment to appraise the man heading up the Juliet Bravo investigation.

In his late fifties, about five ten in his socks, which, she guessed from the look of him, had holes in them, Thompson had probably joined the Met when that was the unofficial minimum height for recruits. The legal minimum was actually five foot eight until the nineties, when they'd abolished it altogether. Before that most forces had set their own. Yorkshire had been infamous for requiring six footers with good right hooks.

Flint was a good couple of inches shorter than Thompson. Short-man syndrome there, she thought, and then realised that this was a prejudice she had inherited from her mother. 'Short men have dangerous egos,' she would intone. Berlin's father had not been tall.

Thompson seemed in no particular hurry to leave. He stood on the pavement munching and staring across the road at the pub. He couldn't possibly see her, but he could see the shape of someone watching. She wondered whether he had staked out Pellicci's and had a report of her entering and leaving. Great instincts. A man in tune with the manor. He gulped the last of his roll, wiped his mouth and fingers with a large, snowy white handkerchief, then got into the front of the waiting car.

It took off, sirens wailing. No doubt this was Flint's contribution, putting on a show for the locals. Berlin waited until the other police car drove away, then finished her drink and left the pub.

Time would start to run as soon as Thompson got Doyle to the station. Did they have enough to charge him? She considered various scenarios as she headed for home.

The custody officer would authorise detention so they could question him, but it would get harder to justify as the hours ticked by, particularly if his brief turned up and directed him not to answer any questions. She doubted Doyle would rely on legal aid. Too many forms to fill in. If he went 'no comment' the case could stall before it got started, unless forensics had come up with something.

How could she find out what sort of case they were building against him? The truth was, she couldn't. The police had arrested Doyle and her mission had evaporated before her eyes. With it went the sense of purpose that had helped to distract her from her other problems.

The future opened up before her, a yawning chasm of listless boredom and the chill void of methadone. A wave of anxiety engulfed her and she realised that the sweet cushion between her and a deep sense of loss was dissipating. Lazenby. Could she make it without him? In four days she would find out.

*

Berlin's flat, like Doyle's, was only a ten-minute limp from Pellicci's. On the way she dropped in at Poundsavers and bought a pay-as-you-go mobile. The SIM card in her phone had cracked under the heel of the hoodie's boot, but everything on it was synchronised with her computer and she could download her contacts and voice-mail. It was a lesson learnt growing up in a borough with a rich heritage of cutpurses and highwaymen.

Her father had passed on her grandfather's tales of the East End mobs in the nineteen hundreds, coalitions of villains who went by exotic names: the Bessarabian Tigers, the Odessians, the Yiddishers.

In the fifties the Blind Beggar Gang and the Watney Streeters ruled. It was their offspring who had tested Berlin's mettle in the gravel playground. Those hot, sharp stones buried in her kneecaps were the childish equivalent of a soldier's old war wound. The pain still lingered.

The latest youthful crews to run cocksure through the streets, the Brick Lane Massive and the Roman Road Bloods, were just the contemporary versions of familiar foes. But equally feral.

Berlin turned into her road and crossed the courtyard of the block of flats. At the bottom of the stairs she reached for her keys. She was so preoccupied that it took her a moment after she looked up to realise that the Metropolitan police officer swinging a manu-ally deployed battering ram, commonly known as an enforcer, was aiming it at her front door.

Despite her dodgy knee, she took the stairs two at a time. 'Hey!' she shouted.

Two burly coppers, one male, one female, were watching the of-ficer with the enforcer. They turned at the sound of her voice.

The door gave with a crack at the second swing.

Berlin arrived on the landing and kept going, until the female copper put a straight arm-bar take-down on her and she hit the concrete.

The officer kindly kept her there to give her a chance to regain her composure, during which time Berlin managed to lift her head a couple of inches off the ground, just enough to be able to see boots marching into her flat.

'What the fuck is going on here?' she screamed.

The coppers lifted her back onto her feet.

In her doorway stood a tall, cadaverous man in a charcoal suit that was too small for him. His arms hung loose at his sides, the too-short sleeves exposing knobbly wrist bones. Everyone else had about four thermal layers on, but he just stood there in his cheap suit and thin cotton shirt, oblivious. He looked as if he was in charge, so she asked again, as politely as she could.

'What the fuck are you doing?'

He didn't say a word, just nodded at the uniforms.

'If you'd just like to come this way, madam,' said the male officer.

They dragged her back down the stairs.

'Let me go, you bastards, there's no need for this!'

She should have known better than to resist, but the adrenalin had kicked in and she put up a spirited struggle. To no avail. They threw her in the back of a police transit van and the woman slammed the door on her ankle. Then they got in the front and the woman got out her notebook while the bloke intoned a litany Berlin knew all too well.

'You do not have to say anything, but it may harm your defence if you do not mention when questioned something which you later rely on in court. Anything you do say may be given in evidence.'

Berlin collapsed into a corner of the van. She had nothing to say.

16

At the station one of Berlin's two officers went to the canteen and brought back tea in small plastic cups for the three of them. She sat on a bench against an institutional green wall, the last in a long line of miscreants. They were all waiting to see the custody sergeant. Her officers hung about, along with all the other arresting officers who had to wait their turn with their glad bag of shoplifters, muggers and joy-riders.

A girl of about fourteen at the other end of the bench eyed Berlin, then started to whine.

'Can I have a cup of tea?'

Everyone ignored her, so she tried again, louder this time.

'I said, can I have a cup of tea? She's got one, why is she so special?' She pointed at Berlin.

The custody sergeant didn't look up from his keyboard. 'Shut it, Chrissy.'

Chrissy's arresting officer put a finger to his lips, shushing her. Chrissy wasn't having any of it. She leapt to her feet and shouted.

'I want a fucking cup of tea!'

Before the officer could shove her back onto the bench, Chrissy, clearly familiar with the station facilities, hit the panic bar. The alarm was piercing, almost painful. There was a thunder of boots as officers from all over the station ran into the custody suite. Pandemonium broke out.

The bloke in the thin charcoal suit chose that moment to arrive. He glided through the chaos towards Berlin, touched her on the shoulder and mouthed 'Follow me.'

Obviously he had realised they'd made a mistake and he was now going to grovel so that she didn't make a complaint. She noticed her two officers scowl as he led her away. She gave them two fingers.

The interview room was the size of a broom cupboard. The bucket and mop in the corner and the smell of disinfectant suggested it still had a dual function. Charcoal suit closed the door and offered Berlin his hand.

'Detective Chief Inspector Tony Dempster,' he said.

She took his big red hand, surprised that it wasn't cold at all. The devil would have warm hands, she thought.

'Catherine Berlin,' she said.

He gestured that she should sit, and they each took one of the broken office chairs that had been placed either side of a small table. He was so tall his knees nearly touched hers. She noticed he didn't switch on the tape machine.

'You didn't ask why you'd been arrested,' he said.

'I've not been processed by the custody sergeant,' said Berlin.

She noted his faint Newcastle accent. A Geordie. That's why he didn't feel the cold. His hair was the same colour as his suit. Berlin found it difficult to pin an age on him. He could be a wrecked thirty-five or a fit fifty.

'Sorry about your front door. I've sent someone round to fix it. But it's good for your reputation with the locals. If you know what I mean.'

She did. Her stocks would rise if she was seen to be an enemy of the state. But it didn't mean she had to enjoy it.

'What the hell is this about? Do you know who I work for?' she said.

'*Worked* for,' he said.

'I'm suspended pending an inquiry. That's all. So if you think I'm going to have a cosy chat with you now that you've had your bully boy and girl soften me up, you've got another think coming. I'm not just another punter and I want to make a complaint,' she said, rubbing her ankle.

Unmoved, he checked out her battered face. 'Looks like you've got quite a few pre-existing injuries,' he said.

A smart-arse. She sat back in her chair and folded her arms.

He reached into his pocket and tossed a small brown paper bag onto the table. She heard the five ampoules chink against each other. There was a silence.

'I'm a registered addict,' she said finally.

'I know what you are.'

From his inside pocket he produced Lazenby's prescription pad, secured in a plastic evidence pouch. She registered that the brown paper bag and ampoules were not sealed in a similar manner.

Mrs Ranasinghe, thought Berlin. But she was wrong.

'Home Office database,' said Dempster. 'All those scripts have to go to a central collection point. A spike in the number from one GP raises a red flag. When they inquired they were told the doctor in question was recently deceased.'

'He signed them before he died.'

'I don't think so. The indentation of his signature went straight through the pad. You just had to trace over it. Made it easy for you, but hard for us.'

She waited to see where he was going with this.

'But not that hard for a forensic guy, as I'm sure you're aware.'

'So what's the charge? Forgery?' she snapped.

He gazed at her for a long moment. 'No. Murder.'

Berlin shot out of her chair so fast it would have tipped over if the wall hadn't been right behind her. 'You're fucking joking! Why would I kill the goose that lays the golden egg?' Her mouth was very dry, her heart racing.

'You could have a point.' He shrugged.

He was too relaxed. He hadn't brought a file, wasn't recording the interview, wasn't even using his notebook. If he was going to charge her with murder he would have stuck rigidly to procedure, leaving no openings for a clever-dick lawyer to exploit on appeal.

The whole thing was a set-up. She took a deep breath.

'Okay. I get it. What do you want from me?'

He laid it out.

Berlin followed Dempster back down the corridor towards the custody suite, where he intended to deliver her into the arms of her arresting officers – who by now would no doubt be very pissed off.

He moved briskly. She had told him to stick his so-called deal where the sun didn't shine, so she would be charged for forging the prescriptions and processed by the matching pair of surly constables. Maybe she shouldn't have given them a two-fingered salute. She was walking into a dead end.

Dempster was about to key in the security code to open the door on her less than rosy future. She decided it was worth trying to up the ante.

'Hang on.'

He turned, his fingers hovering above the keypad.

'What you're asking of me is worth more than just a walk on these minor offences,' she said.

'A conviction would finish your career. And I could always add a few charges if these are too trivial for you. How about obstruction of justice and resisting arrest, for starters?'

'In your dreams,' said Berlin, although she was afraid he might be right.

'So what else do you want? Apart from what I've already put on the table,' he asked.

'You have someone here in custody. A bloke called Doyle. DCI Thompson brought him in. I'd just like to know what's going on, that's all.'

'That's the case you were working on, right? Your informant. The floater?'

She nodded. He hesitated and she thought she'd pushed her luck.

'Wait here,' he said.

He loped back down the corridor and disappeared around the corner. She heard a door open, close, then open again. Then he stuck his head around the corner and beckoned.

17

Dempster ushered Berlin into a dark room, illuminated only by a monitor high on one wall. On it she could see Doyle facing two detectives across a table. Their backs were to the camera, but she knew it must be DCI Thompson and DS Flint. A woman in a smart suit was sitting beside Doyle, taking notes.

The image was grainy and the whirr of the tape machine in the room was a background to the scratchy sound of their voices. It was like watching a film from the fifties. Or maybe from the nineties, but on a knock-off DVD.

'Honest, guv'nor,' said Doyle. 'Would I lie to the law? Not a bit of it. I'm a great respecter of law and order. I voted for Mrs Thatcher. A great lady.'

'How was that then?' said Flint. 'When you're not even on the fucking electoral roll?'

Doyle felt he was winning. The young detective was coming on with his best hard-man persona, and he was deflecting it with a hurt, reproachful demeanour.

'I put it to you, Mr Doyle, that you were identified by this woman, now deceased, as operating a moneylending business without a licence,' said Flint.

Doyle spread his hands out on the table in a gesture of submission and innocence. The young bloke was leading the interview and Doyle knew that if he addressed his responses to the other detective, it would irritate the shit out of him. So that's what he did.

He focused his wide-eyed look on the older man. 'Guv'nor, I'm not denying I'm an entrepreneur, but I don't know anything about moneylending. On the night you're asking about I was at the Romford Dogs.' He sighed. 'I had fifty quid to win on Dicky's Mentor and he came second. I'm clean, I've got nothing to hide. Happy to help with your inquiries.'

Flint reacted as Doyle knew he would. He thumped the table and shouted.

'You're a loan shark and we know it, you know it, the whole fucking manor knows it!'

Doyle affected a look of shock and spoke very quietly. 'Language, please, detective. There's a lady present.'

Flint flushed. The lawyer smirked. Thompson raised his hand a fraction in a gesture of restraint. Flint slumped back in his chair. Satisfied, Doyle clasped his hands in his lap, patient and relaxed.

Thompson opened a file and with care extracted a bunch of ten-by-four colour prints, which he laid out on the table in front of Doyle. Doyle knew this trick. He didn't look down. Thompson was all business, his tone even.

'For the purposes of the tape I have displayed on the table before Mr Doyle four post-mortem photographs of the victim. Mr Doyle, would you please look at the photographs and tell me if you recognise the deceased?'

Doyle was a bit squeamish, but he knew this would work in his favour. It would look odd if he didn't react to photos of a dead girl who'd just been fished out of the lock. He took his reading glasses out of his pocket, slipped them on, then glanced down.

The shudder that shook him was violent, uncontrolled. He took off his glasses, dropped them on the table and picked up one of the head shots. His hands were trembling.

'Mr Doyle?' barked DS Flint. 'Do you know her?'

Doyle didn't understand Flint's question. He didn't know what was happening. He looked back at the photo. He was shaking so much that the photo of the girl on the mortuary slab was juddering in his hands. His tongue stuck to the top of his mouth. A band of steel tightened around his chest.

'I don't understand,' he managed to get out.

Flint looked as if he was about to shout but Thompson raised a hand to restrain him. He leant towards Doyle.

'Who is she?' he said, very softly.

'It can't be,' said Doyle. 'It looks like her but it's been so long.' He felt the band of steel snap. He sprang to his feet and emitted a guttural cry.

'It is, it's her. My girl! My daughter! That's Gina!'

18

Dempster took Berlin out the back way, to avoid her arresting officers. He said he would sort it with them later.

'Jesus Christ. So Juliet Bravo was actually Gina Doyle,' said Berlin. 'It was clear she knew a lot about Doyle's operation from the inside, but I had no idea it came from as close as that. She grassed up her own father.'

Stunned by Doyle's revelation, her mind raced with the possibilities.

'If he was acting, he deserves an Oscar. He looked genuinely shocked,' said Dempster.

'But if it wasn't him that killed her, or someone working for him, who the hell was it?' asked Berlin.

Dempster released the steel door that opened onto the car park. He shrugged. 'It's not your problem,' he said. 'Leave it to the professionals. Just because I gave you a heads up this once doesn't mean it will be an ongoing thing. It's not part of our deal. It was a demonstration of good faith, that's all.'

Berlin hesitated in the doorway. 'Good faith? This so-called deal between us is serious for me. I'm not just a pawn in some copper's game, am I?'

He handed her a business card.

'I can count on you, right?' she asked.

'Cross my heart and hope to die.'

She glanced at the card and frowned. 'Homicide Task Force, New Scotland Yard. Which means?'

'We support the taskings of the local Murder Investigation Team,' came Dempster's neutral reply.

'I bet they love that.' She held out her hand, palm up.

'Oh. I nearly forgot,' he said with a grin.

Berlin didn't smile. He put the brown paper bag in her hand. She slipped it straight into her pocket, turned on her heel and walked out into the biting wind.

'I'll be in touch,' Dempster called after her, but she didn't look back.

She kept walking until she heard the door close and then began to jog in an awkward limping fashion, anxious to put as much distance as possible between her and the police station. She kept one hand in her pocket, holding on tight to the brown paper bag.

She slowed down as she emerged from the alley that led to the car park and turned onto Commercial Road. She was just in time to see Doyle stumble down the worn granite steps of the station and run towards a black Merc parked on the other side of the road.

A young bloke got out of the Merc, clearly alarmed at the sight of Doyle running. His cigarette fell from his lips as Doyle shirt-fronted him and thrust him back against the car, shouting. The wind whipped away his words, but the youth was obviously frightened.

Another lad had jumped out of the back of the car and wrestled the distraught Doyle off his mate. Doyle practically collapsed into his arms, and the lad steered him into the back seat and got in after him. The other one gave the police station a quick glance and got back into the driver's seat. The Merc took off.

It was a genuine display of grief and fury. Berlin was now convinced that Doyle hadn't killed his daughter, and if he was somehow involved, he hadn't known the identity of the target. Thompson had no doubt come to the same conclusion, and had to release him. She was also certain that Doyle would try to find out who had done it and why.

She made a note of the Merc's number and descriptions of the two lads. Old habits die hard.

19

Doyle couldn't stop shaking. He curled up in the back seat, his arms clenched around his body, trying to hold in his feelings.

'Turn the fucking heater up!' he wailed.

'Where to, boss?' asked one.

'The lock! I want to go to the fucking lock!' screamed Doyle.

The Merc did an illegal U-turn in the middle of Commercial Road, back towards the Limehouse Basin.

Doyle left the lads in the car while he walked to the final lock on Regent's Canal before it reached the Basin. The lock was a hundred feet long and thirty feet wide, with a fall of eight feet. It opened in 1820. Frank had taught him all this. Jesus, Frank.

How was he going to tell the old man that his granddaughter, his only grandchild, was dead? She had been the only thing Doyle had ever got right in his whole miserable life, according to Frank. Gina had blamed him when her mum left, then when she ran away, Frank had blamed him for that. Probably they were both right.

He tried to clear his mind, get the sequence of events right. First up, he had spotted those bald blokes in the car watching his block of flats. After he'd spoken to Ahmed he knew the fucking Financial Services Agency were onto him.

There'd been a crackdown of sorts recently on the activities of unlicensed moneylenders. He'd seen posters in the bus shelters encouraging people to ring a hotline and grass up so-called loan sharks. Someone had noticed that blokes like him were competition for the corporate tally men and high street payday lenders. It was just big business fighting back.

Him and Frank had been at it for over twenty years without any trouble. Until now. It made him sick. The government made a big song and dance about protecting people from sharks but Fernley-Price had told him the UK was the only country in Europe with no legal limit on interest rates. He'd said it was a truly free financial market.

The price of freedom was proving steep, thought Doyle. It was bloody toe rags like Fernley-Price that had got the country into this mess and now it was blokes like Doyle that were getting it in the neck. He'd been going along nicely until he got mixed up with that prick. It was a thought that gave Doyle pause.

He gazed down into the filthy water, flecked with yellow foam from some toxic shit. His little girl had lain in that muck. His tears stung as they coursed down his squirrel cheeks and dribbled into his mouth. They were bitter. Someone would pay.

20

The atmosphere at the Agency was toxic. It was the sort of environment in which Senior Investigator in Charge of Operations Johnny Coulthard thrived.

Coulthard had jumped before being pushed from a regional force where he'd been a wooden top, a common or garden constable, for thirteen years without advancing in rank. He had worked with probationers, king of the kids, and had taken his coaching duties with a female trainee very seriously. Hence his move to the Agency and civilian waters, which he found gave him more freedom to get the job done without a lot of nancy-boy lawyers breathing down his neck.

An action man who didn't like much action, he was a smooth talker with a charming northern accent that perfectly complemented his self-deprecating, 'I'm a no-bullshit, genuinely nice guy' persona. Coulthard's delivery would be the envy of many a sociopath. He had honed it to compensate for a face that not even his mother could love, and a beer belly he seemed to have been born with and which grew with him, no matter how long he spent in the gym. A real prince.

The tension in the office of late suited Coulthard. He would reassure his lads, give them little treats, turn a blind eye to their weaknesses. Love, not fear, was Coulthard's weapon.

Delroy Jacobs didn't feel the love. Although his sole ambition was to lead a quiet life, he was cursed with a strong sense of fair play. His placid temperament and desire for tranquillity were a reaction to his heritage: his mum was Jamaican, his dad was Jewish. They had opinions.

Against his own better judgement Delroy had felt compelled on occasion to express concern about the team's dubious operational methods. This hadn't endeared him to Coulthard.

Del was at his workstation, but could see what Coulthard was up to out of the corner of his eye. He made sure he never turned his back on him. Coulthard had been on the phone for some time, talking in a subdued tone. He wasn't usually that quiet. Now he hung up, clicked his mouse and sat staring at his computer. He didn't usually sit still that long, either.

When Coulthard stood up he went straight to the glass box that was Nestor's office and strode in without knocking. Delroy saw him gesticulate, apparently urging Nestor to look at his computer. Nestor did as he was told.

While they were busy, Delroy slid his chair along to Coulthard's desk. He jiggled the mouse as he dialled 1471 on Coulthard's phone, then 3, ringing the last number to call Coulthard. No one could see him over the desk partition. The screen saver melted away to reveal a post-mortem photo of a woman. Delroy stared. He was startled when his call was answered.

'Detective Sergeant Flint speaking.'

Delroy hung up and rolled his chair back to his desk just as Coulthard emerged from Nestor's office.

'I'm to conduct an inquiry into Investigator Berlin's unauthorised activities,' Coulthard announced. The rest of the team exchanged glances. Delroy was gobsmacked.

'Boss's orders,' said Coulthard, smirking at Delroy. He glanced at his watch, then grabbed his jacket from the back of his chair. 'Drinks on me!' he said.

Delroy watched as the other blokes scuttled out of the office after Coulthard. Finally he got to his feet to follow them. He couldn't afford to get any more offside with Coulthard than he was already. When he glanced back, Nestor's door was shut and the blinds were closed.

21

Berlin walked from Limehouse down to the Ratcliffe Cross Stairs. It was a quiet stretch of the river. She stood at the top of the ancient watermen's slipway and watched the tide rise. The masonry was slick with ice. One slip and you could disappear under the freezing mould-green water or break your neck with a snap that no one would hear.

She had agreed to assist Dempster with the Lazenby investigation by conducting covert inquiries. In other words, by becoming his snout. She was perfect for the role: a heroin addict with the necessary professional skills and experience.

Her first distasteful task was to approach Lazenby's other patients and see if anyone had pharmaceutical-grade heroin for sale. Dempster thought it possible one of them had got greedy. She knew it wouldn't end there.

In return, Dempster had said he would forget about the forged prescriptions and would let her keep the heroin. She thought he would have trouble making the forgery case against her anyway. She had worked with the Crown Prosecution Service, and it was highly likely that if he took it to them, they would live up to the more popular version of their acronym, CPS: Can't Prosecute, Sorry.

But she couldn't afford to take the chance. It was blackmail, pure and simple, a reliable investigative method employed by the police every day.

Dempster hadn't returned the five ampoules out of the goodness of his heart, either. It was to keep her functioning while she did his bidding. He'd promised to help her find a suitable doctor. Jesus Christ, she came so cheap.

Something chirruped. It took her a moment to realise it was an alert signal on her new mobile. She fished it out of her pocket with numb fingers. It was a text from Delroy, one of the few people who had her new number. It was the first time she'd heard from him since she was suspended. The message was stark: 'JC = discip inq.' It meant Coulthard was going to run her discipline inquiry. Surely things couldn't get any worse. She made for the nearest pub.

The Grapes claimed to be the oldest hostelry in London. It was a crowded field. Berlin sat nursing a double and reflected on Coulthard's role in her demise. He'd had her fooled at first, but after he'd dropped her in the shit once too often, the big smile and the 'sorry about that, mate, nothing personal' failed to convince.

Coulthard had a problem with people who didn't listen to his war stories. And with anyone who had a better idea. When Berlin first started in the job she'd had a lot of better ideas. Like, how they could work legally. She soon learnt that these initiatives did not sit well with Coulthard's predilection for the 'tricks of the trade'.

But instead of keeping to the moral high ground, she had joined Coulthard in a race to the bottom. Meeting an informant alone was *verboten*. There were too many risks. Informants were usually borrowers in trouble, and loan sharks frequently had people watching defaulters to make sure they didn't do a runner. Or go to the police. Not that this was very likely.

The police weren't interested in loan shark victims until they actually suffered violence, after which it was too late. Berlin had known police officers to send away victims who reported threats by moneylenders with the advice that debt was a civil matter.

Coulthard manipulated Nestor, who was supposed to be in charge, by relieving him of operational decisions. Nestor couldn't make a decision if his life depended on it, preferring to write memos and fire off emails. So had he really made the call to close the Doyle file? Or was Coulthard behind it? It had his paw prints all over it, but it would be difficult to determine if it was just to get at her, or if he'd had other motives.

If she'd had the support of a team maybe it would have been different. But she was not a team player. At least that was one thing she and Coulthard could agree on.

She swallowed her self-disgust with the dregs of her whisky and went home for something stronger.

22

Nestor at home was a very different creature from Nestor at the Agency. Chez Nestor, he had aspirations to be the suave, witty bon vivant: a man at ease at table. A raconteur, even. This fantasy had now fled, along with most of his other delusions. He was drinking in his cellar among a collection of vintage burgundy that was probably his last remaining asset.

He could hear his wife upstairs, clattering her French copper-bottomed pans about in her designer kitchen. She would make him eat something unspeakable, a dribble of brightly coloured jus on an enormous white plate topped with a sliver of braised celeriac and a niggardly dressed chop. Appearances were everything to her. She knew he would give his right arm for a steak and kidney pie.

Women could be so cruel.

His own mother, a leggy debutante in her day, had laughed at him and told him he was a chinless wonder and it was lucky his rugger bugger of a father hadn't lived to see how his pusillanimous son had turned out.

Good God.

Now he was in the wilderness. The wine was his pride and joy. He preferred the full, harmonious reds to the complex whites, seeking in the bottle what he couldn't find in life. But he rarely drank it.

Possession gave him pleasure, and anticipation. Deferred gratification was the hallmark of his existence.

Well, those days were over. He pulled the cork on a 1999 Comte Georges de Vogüé Musigny and, with reverence, wafted it under his nose. Heaven.

Halfway through the bottle it occurred to Nestor to check his mobile, just in case the bastard had returned his calls. He imagined that all over London, all over the globe for that matter, hedge-fund managers and investment bankers were ducking calls from their clients. No doubt many of them had disconnected their phones, or been cut off by now. But he suspected that this bastard had more reason to duck than most.

Nestor had committed his pension fund, the house, the cottage in Wales. The return he had got was phenomenal – too good to be true, really, but he didn't question it. He just bought more burgundy. When the margin calls came, thick and fast, he didn't even recognise the names of the firms. His options had been bought and sold, bundled with other derivatives, then sold again. His debts had been sold too. At least, that's what he'd been told. But it all went wrong. He'd lost everything and then some. How could that be?

He considered himself an intelligent man but he just didn't understand what had happened. Yet he occupied a senior – well, senior middle-management – position in the agency whose precise role *was* to understand. He took another mouthful of delight, drained the Riedel glass and reached for a fresh one. This he would fill with a Grand Cru, he decided after some reflection.

The problem, the real problem, was that after the meltdown, after the catastrophe that had wiped him out financially, he'd been offered a one-time-only, 'ask no questions, be told no lies' opportunity to recoup his losses. A devil's bargain, no doubt.

It took the very last drop from his cash account, but he had taken the view that if he was hung for a penny, might as well be a pound. There was something in there about sheep and lambs, too, but the burgundy was playing havoc with his metaphors. Anyway, he had taken the opportunity offered, thinking he couldn't sink any lower. How wrong one could be. He drained his glass.

'Jing cring we'll all be rooned,' he sang out, laughing.

'Ludovic? What are you doing down there?' a querulous voice called from above.

His laughter turned to tears. It wasn't the money. It was love that had ruined him. His mother was right. He had aspired to punch above his weight. Now he was out for the count.

He put his glass down and tottered out of the cellar, up the stairs and down his classic Victorian black and white chequered tile hallway, past the open door to the dining room, where his wife was preparing to serve avocado-wrapped ceviche with tomato pearls.

'Nestor! Where are you going?' she asked, astonished.

'To see a man about a fucking dog,' he replied, and stumbled out into the night.

23

Early drinks at The Prospect of Whitby had turned into lunch at The Gallows restaurant in The Captain Kidd. Fernley-Price had sensed a theme for the day, which he decided he might as well continue at his club.

There were plenty of pirates there, all avoiding each other for fear they'd bump into someone to whom they owed money, which could be anyone. In this climate, no one really knew who owed what to whom. The club was full of 'em, whey-faced, miserable City types crying into their Krug. They were all in the same boat, so what the hell.

One more drink and he would have another go at contacting that fat weasel for an update on their fortunes. He had to look forward, not back, keep his chin up and expect – no, demand – a positive return. After the sacrifices he'd made and the risks he'd taken he mustn't show any sign of weakness now.

It hadn't been Fernley-Price's idea to move into the black economy, although if he ended up making a motza he would claim it had been. No one would be around to argue the toss on that score, or share in his triumph, which rather took all the fun out of it for a chap, now he thought about it. Perhaps he'd get two more drinks in and save the waiter a trip.

Three drinks later he decided that if the bastard wasn't returning his calls, there was no point in ringing him. Sod it. He was ignoring calls himself, a dozen since lunch time, all from the same party. Sod that too. He would sort it later. But in the meantime he would go and beard the lion in his den.

Staggering out of his club, Fernley-Price found a black cab conveniently waiting for the likes of him to pour himself into the back.

'Poplar!' he commanded.

Another City gent, thought the cab driver, who had just lost his savings to some fucking Viking bank. He accelerated sharply, throwing the drunken git to the floor.

The Silent Woman was quiet, even for her. Doyle sat at his usual table, alone, knocking back pints before driving out to deliver the bad news to Frank. Word had got around about Gina, and the atmosphere was respectful. He knew that some would say she was a grass who had got what was coming to her. But not in his earshot.

The police wouldn't release the body. It was more than he could bear to think of his little girl lying on that cold slab in the mortuary, being poked about. They wouldn't tell him how she died.

They were going to make him come back when the doctor was at the station to give blood and prove she was his. It wasn't the last that would be spilt. He gestured for another pint.

The door swung open and Fernley-Price staggered in, clearly three sheets to the icy wind.

'It's cold enough to freeze the brass balls off a monkey!' Fernley-Price announced loudly, leaving the pub door open behind him.

'Shut the bleeding door, you pillock,' cried the old man in the cloth cap, who had been sitting there since 1956. The belligerent scowl Fernley-Price turned on him vanished in the face of the sudden silence and the watchful, threatening postures of the other patrons. 'Right you are, squire,' he mumbled.

Doyle sighed as Fernley-Price caught sight of him.

The drunken sod kicked the door closed, stumbled over, slumped into the chair opposite and put his hands flat on the table to steady himself. 'Mate, you haven't been returning my calls,' he said. He dragged out his mobile and waved it at Doyle, ignoring the flashing symbol which rebuked him for failing to respond to his own messages.

Doyle didn't respond.

'I said —'

'I heard you,' said Doyle.

'Well it's not friggin' good enough,' said Fernley-Price, apparently oblivious to Doyle's mood. 'We need to keep the channels of communication clear.' He smacked the mobile down on the table. 'How's business?'

Doyle answered quietly. Fernley-Price leant forward to catch it, knocking the table and slopping Doyle's pint.

'What? Whadyasay?'

Without warning Doyle reached out and grasped Fernley-Price by the throat, squeezing his Adam's apple between his thick thumb and two precisely placed fingers, so Fernley-Price

73

couldn't swallow or gasp for breath.

'I said I've had a fucking death in the family!'

Eyes wide, Fernley-Price raised his hands in a gesture of mute surrender and Doyle released him. 'Fine, I'm sorry, I had no idea, fine, of course, I'm so sorry. In your own good time, old chap. Do what you have to do and get back to me, whenever,' Fernley-Price croaked, rubbing his throat.

Doyle stood up and put a hand on the banker's trembling shoulder.

'No hard feelings, mate. I've a lot on my mind.'

Fernley-Price nodded. As Doyle turned on his heel and walked out, the landlord leant over the bar and addressed the dazed Fernley-Price.

'You'll be settling Mr Doyle's bill then, sir?'

The little contretemps with Fernley-howsyourfather had set Doyle up nicely to deal with Frank. He wasn't going to take any shit. Frank would blame him for Gina's death, like he blamed him for bloody everything. Nancy leaving, for example.

It shook Doyle to think that Nancy was out there somewhere and didn't know about Gina. Unless Gina had found her since, or maybe Nance had kept in touch with Gina all along and they'd cooked up this business between them, grassing him up to get back at him.

He hadn't told Frank about the surveillance because Frank would have blamed him for that, too. So he certainly wasn't going to tell him the full story now, about the Agency and everything, then tell him Gina had grassed them up. Frank would just get abusive and start on about what a useless piece of baggage he was and how Gina would never have left home if it wasn't for him. He wasn't going to stand for it.

It was only ten miles from Poplar to Chigwell, but as he took the

Green Man interchange Doyle thought, not for the first time, that it was like another bleeding country once you got through Leyton-stone. At the next roundabout he took the exit onto Hollybush Hill. It even sounded like something out of Enid Blyton. He didn't like it, all that open space, playing fields, horses even; it gave him the willies. Miles between fish and chip shops, and the curries were shite out here.

When he pulled up at the premises his courage almost deserted him. The place was in darkness. He sat in the car for a moment, listening to the engine tick as the cold seized it. He got out slowly.

Frank opened the door in his pyjamas and cardigan, a pair of finger-less gloves encasing his enormous hands.

'I'm in the middle of one of my programmes.'

Doyle stepped past him into the hall. 'Sorry to disrupt your viewing, Pop,' he said.

Frank shut the front door and followed him down the hall into the kitchen.

'Put the kettle on, Pop,' said Doyle.

'One of the customers acting up? I've told you before, come down hard and early.'

Doyle raised his hand. 'It's not the business. Sit down, Pop.'

He really wanted him to sit down so that he would have an ad-vantage if Frank lashed out. Doyle had decided that if he did, he was going to give the old man a wallop. He wasn't going to wear it. Not tonight of all nights.

Frank didn't move to put the kettle on and didn't sit down, just stared at Doyle, apparently confused by his tone.

'Look, Pop, it's Gina,' Doyle said.

'Who?'

'Gina, my —'

'I know who she is. What about her?'

Doyle's heart was thumping in his chest.

'She's dead, Pop.'

'What? No she's not, she's just run off, young girls are like that, flighty. What are you talking about?'

'I was at the police station today, Frank. She's grown up now. But she's gone.'

Doyle shifted his feet slightly and planted them squarely, bracing himself for the onslaught.

Frank took a step forward, his fists working, clenching and unclenching at his sides. Doyle was ready.

'No. She's just a little girl.' Frank seemed to be miles away, talking to himself. 'How?' he whispered.

'Murdered.'

Frank fell on him, sobbing. Doyle was more shocked than if he'd thrown a left hook. He put his arms around Frank's shoulders. He's an old man now, he thought.

Father and son stood locked in an embrace, heads together, tears mingling.

24

Dempster was as good as his word. When Berlin got home she found someone had been around and replaced her front door, complete with a new deadlock. The locksmith's card was tucked under the lintel. She took the card and walked to the shop in Roman Road. It was well after closing time but there was a twenty-four hour bell.

The locksmith came down from the flat above the shop. She held up the card and her ID and he ducked behind the counter, retrieved a key, opened the door and handed it to her.

'Courtesy of the Metropolitan Police,' he said with a grin. It was obviously lucrative work.

She thought the flat would be an absolute tip, but when she got inside she found the police search hadn't left that much of a mess. Maybe Dempster had exercised a restraining hand, wary of alienating her while she could be useful to him.

She took one ampoule from the paper bag and put the rest back in the bread bin with some reverence, acutely aware of how precious they were now that she had come so close to losing them. A bread bin seemed a banal treasure chest, but it was intended for the staff of life.

Inserting the needle of the disposable syringe through the ampoule's rubber seal, she drew up the colourless fluid inside. She could barely remember a time when she had had to cook it up, then force a dull hypodermic into collapsing veins. With Lazenby's assistance she had gradually stabilised on a daily dose. His approach had been all about choice, control and risk management.

Without hesitating she pushed the needle into her thigh. It slowly released its exquisite chemistry. She wondered how she would cope if she had to return to the street, a world where death was an ever-present possibility. Serenely she reflected that it wasn't so very different from this one.

It was the coldest night in London for forty years. Black ice sheeted the roads, pipes froze then cracked, the homeless crawled into Council grit boxes and suffocated. Rooms sealed against the air became tombs as faulty heaters stifled the occupants. The frigid silence claimed its victims. Seven million shivered in their beds.

Berlin, oblivious to the cold, walked through the deserted streets of the City. The heroin was near the end of its metabolic process and was about to exit her system, leaving only a ghost in her veins. She turned into Newgate. In the rose garden of Christ Church Greyfriars an old man, shrouded in newspaper, sought warmth from the earth, beneath which four queens were buried.

The ruin of the West Tower was all that stood of the original church, the empty Gothic perpendicular window framing not heaven, but the sheer glass face of an office building that loomed over it. Berlin heard the gentle sigh of a last breath exhaled. The queens claimed their own. The old man had lost his struggle, just as the poor of London had lost theirs for centuries. She kept walking, always trying to discern the direction that would lead her out of her own past.

The Fourth Day

25

Night was still resisting day as Berlin arrived home, exhausted from her nocturnal wandering, longing for sleep. She struggled with the stiff new lock, cursing. The landing light had been smashed again and her fingers were frozen. She dropped the key as footsteps approached. A figure loomed out of the dark, one arm extended towards her. A black face was barely visible between a black beanie and black puffa jacket.

'What the fuck, Delroy?' she said, rattled.

'Nestor's dead.'

Delroy had never been inside Berlin's gaff. He was surprised at how normal it seemed. It was just one big room really, but comfortable, a few paintings, a polished table and a yellow vase filled with bright, cobalt irises. One wall was taken up with bookshelves. A small, sleek, high-end computer was balanced on a pile of old hardbacks beside the couch. The palette of the room, as they would say in the Sunday papers, was blue and yellow.

Berlin poured him a mug of coffee.

'What happened to you?' he asked, pointing at her face.

'What happened to Nestor?' was her reply.

Delroy shrugged. Fair enough. It was none of his beeswax if someone had taken a pop at her. They were probably trying to get a rise out of her, he thought, then immediately felt guilty about having such an uncharitable reaction. That was the trouble with Berlin: you never knew what she was thinking, but she always seemed to know what *you* were thinking. He gulped his coffee to cover his disloyal thoughts.

'They fished him out of the Limehouse Basin earlier this morning,' he said.

'You're joking,' said Berlin, astonished.

Delroy shook his head. 'Our liaison officer at the local nick gave me the heads-up.'

'How did he die?' she asked.

'They don't know yet if he jumped or was pushed.'

He watched as Berlin tried to take it in. 'That's no bloody coincidence, turning up in the same spot as Juliet Bravo. Gina Doyle, that is,' she said.

'She wasn't using that name anyway,' muttered Delroy as he finished his coffee.

'What? Gina Doyle?'

'Yeah. They can't find any trace of her under that name,' he said, holding out his mug for a refill.

'How do you know?' she asked, pouring a shot of Scotch into her own coffee and ignoring his empty mug. Delroy noticed she was immediately distracted from the fact of Nestor's death. He got up and poured his own coffee.

'Coulthard's always walking away from his desk without logging off.' He looked sheepish, a kid caught peeking through the keyhole. 'He keeps getting email from someone calling themselves Tinderbox.'

'Flint. The weasel-faced DS working the murder,' said Berlin.

'Oh yeah, I hadn't thought of that.' Del laughed. 'Of course, it has to be. Yeah, he called Coulthard yesterday. And here's the strange thing. Tinderbox emailed him a post-mortem photo of Doyle's daughter.'

'Jesus, Del, this is too fucking much. Why would Coulthard want a photo of my dead informant?'

'Yeah,' said Delroy, 'I can't get a grip on it all. That's Coulthard for you.' He took a mouthful of the strong, aromatic coffee. He was usually a Nescafé man; but this stuff was dynamite.

'I heard about that doctor in Hackney,' he said.

Berlin didn't react.

'He's the one, isn't he?'

'The one what?' she challenged.

'The one who treats your diabetes,' said Delroy, his tone measured.

'He's the one, Del,' she said, resigned.

'How's that going then, getting your treatment sorted?'

She gave him a small smile. 'It's in hand, Del, thanks for asking.'

Delroy nodded. He put down his mug. 'I'd better get going. It'll be chaos at work today.'

She followed him to the front door. 'So what are they saying about Nestor?'

'Not much. He was pissed. Went back to the office late. They're not giving anything away. Early days in the investigation, I suppose.'

'I suppose.' She paused. 'Del,' she said.

'What?' he said, instantly on guard. He knew that tone.

'Ever come across a DCI called Dempster in your former life?' She said it casually.

Jesus Christ, he thought, she's moving right on. She knew that before he joined the Agency he'd worked as a civvy with Police Complaints. Her reaction to Nestor's demise was like her reaction to everything: it had gone missing. He loved her to bits; she was fierce, loyal and smart. At work she had often covered for him, borne the brunt of Coulthard's hostility. But she was so fucking weird.

'Why do you ask?' he said.

'He's supervising the investigation into my doctor's murder.'

Delroy sighed and offered her some heartfelt advice. 'Mate, you are already in a world of trouble. Coulthard has been tasked to prepare a report on your shenanigans with the dead informant. Now Nestor goes off the edge in the same location. Just try to keep your head down, yeah? Don't go getting mixed up in another investigation.'

He gave her a brief peck on the cheek and left.

Too late, mate, she thought, I'm already in it up to my neck.

It was still dark but there was no way she was going to be able to sleep now. She poured herself another Scotch. If Nestor was murdered, there must be a connection to the Doyle operation. Why else would you leave the body in the same location? Likewise if it was suicide. Why do it there?

She thought about the impact Nestor's death might have on what was laughingly referred to as her career. Coulthard would probably step up into his job and then there would be no holding him. Seized with a sense of foreboding her gaze fell on the bread bin. She grabbed her coat. Maybe she was just hungry.

26

Preoccupied, Berlin didn't notice Doyle until he cleared his throat. She looked up and he pointed to the empty chair at her table.

'Do you mind?'

She looked around Pellicci's. There was plenty of room at other tables.

'Suit yourself,' she replied.

He took off his coat and scarf, hung them over the back of the chair and sat. Nino brought him tea and toast. Berlin watched and waited.

Doyle sipped his tea. He looked terrible. She thought about Juliet Bravo, the way she was so intent on bringing this man down, urging Berlin to pursue him at all costs. Her own father. Berlin wondered what he had done to make his daughter hate him so much.

Doyle put his cup down with a sigh.

'I hadn't seen my daughter since she was sixteen, Miss Berlin.' He looked up at her. 'It is Miss Berlin, isn't it?'

'How do you know who I am?' she asked.

'Your firm leaks like a sieve, Miss.'

Berlin wasn't surprised and saw no point in pretending outrage or walking out. 'I'm sorry for your loss, Mr Doyle,' she said.

'Thank you. Much appreciated,' he said, and seemed to mean it. But it was clear he hadn't sat down just to exchange pleasantries.

'So what can I do for you?' she asked.

Doyle hesitated. 'What was she like?' His face was soft, vulnerable. 'Gina, I mean.'

Berlin was taken aback. This was the last thing she'd expected from him. 'I... look, I hardly knew her. She was my CHIS, a covert —'

'I know what it means,' he said, and reached across the table to grip her arm. It wasn't a threat, it was a plea. 'Miss Berlin, I know she was grassing me up. You must have wondered what a father could do to a daughter that she would stoop so low.'

She was surprised again, this time by his perspicacity.

'I think I know why,' he continued. 'She always blamed me for it. It must have been because she thought...'

He choked up. Berlin could feel his clammy palm through her coat.

'She thought I was responsible for her mum.' He hesitated. 'For her mum leaving that is, without taking her.'

The investigator in Berlin kicked in. 'And were you?' she asked.

Doyle raised his hand to God and shook his head. 'On my life.'

Berlin had the feeling he thought she knew more than she did. This gave her a tactical advantage.

'So if you know what her motivation was, what do you want from me?'

'I just want to know what she was like, as a grown-up.'

Berlin couldn't think of a reason to deny him this simple, sad request. 'She was smart, confident, well turned out. She said she was something in the City.'

Tears welled up in Doyle's eyes. 'That was my Gina. Sharp as a tack. I always knew she'd do us proud. But why did she wait all these years to have a go at me? That's what I don't understand. Why now?'

It was a bloody good question, thought Berlin. Maybe the Agency's campaign had given her the opportunity she had been waiting for; Gina had probably realised illegal lenders weren't a priority for the police. She would have done her homework. But a dedicated team and a hotline would make all the difference.

Berlin pushed her plate away. 'I'm sorry, Mr Doyle, I really can't discuss it with you any further.'

She rose to go, but he held on to her arm.

'Miss Berlin, I want whoever killed my girl. Never mind what she was trying to do to me. I think you want that too, because in a way, see, we're both responsible. So maybe we can help each other.' Doyle searched her face.

She glanced at his hand on her arm.

He let go.

Doyle waited for her to say something, for a flicker of emotion. It never came.

He took out a pen, wrote a mobile number on a newspaper lying on the table and nudged it towards her. She didn't touch it, just pushed in her chair, went to the till and paid Nino.

As she opened the door to leave, Doyle spoke again. 'You're local. Berlin was the jeweller. Used to be just down the road.'

She closed the door and walked back to the table.

'It was Berlinsky once,' he said.

'You've got the wrong Berlin,' she said.

'My father knew yours,' said Doyle, very quietly.

He spread his fingers, displaying his rings.

She picked up the newspaper and walked out.

27

Walking home along Bethnal Green Road Berlin felt as if something or someone, or perhaps fate, was snapping at her heels. It was all getting too close. The shop was still there, but no longer a jeweller's. They had lived above it. She crossed over so she didn't have to pass by; the business had been her father's, and before him her grandfather's. He had scraped together the key money after he arrived from Russia.

Community. A warm, suffocating web. Doyle had invoked her father, and with him the dead weight of a shared history. She walked past the Underground station and there was the plaque on the wall. There was no escape.

Berlin had heard the story so often it felt like a memory.

It was 1943. People were heading down into the station, which was being used as an air-raid shelter. It wasn't even finished yet and no trains stopped there. The crowd was quite orderly until they heard the boom of unfamiliar explosions. New artillery was being tested by the army in Victoria Park, but the crowd didn't know that. They thought it was an air raid and panicked.

A woman carrying a baby fell, but the crush behind her pushed forward. The stampede down the steps left one hundred and seventy-two dead at the scene, including sixty-two children. One casualty died later in hospital. You could say they were killed by friendly fire, thought Berlin.

Her father's recollection had remained vivid. He was fifteen when it happened. He had just started work in his father's business. A skinny kid, a 'runt', was how he described himself.

He was halfway down the steps when the stampede began. Halfway between heaven and hell, as he put it. He would tell her he felt the suffocating pressure on his chest, a sensation of sinking beneath a great, irresistible weight as the oxygen was squeezed from his lungs.

As he spoke he would rest his hand lightly on his chest and breathe more deeply and as a child, she would place her own little hand on her own chest, fearful that she might run out of air. Even now she felt her chest tighten.

Then he would raise his arms above his head and describe how his arms were outstretched as he sank beneath the wave of bodies. It was at this moment in the story that, as a child she had realised that if he had kept sinking, she wouldn't be sitting there listening to him. Her first intimation of not being.

But he didn't sink. He had felt a hand grasp his. It came from above, became two hands which slid down around his wrist, gripped and pulled with such might he feared his shoulder would leave its socket. Her father had kicked and thrust his way up, using the bodies beneath him for purchase. The hands didn't let go until they had dragged him over the railings and he lay gasping for breath on the pavement.

When he looked up, he saw his saviour was a tall, rough-looking boy, probably not much older than himself. The lad was inspecting his own stomach. The spikes of the iron railings had dug deep into his flesh as he'd hung over them, pulling her father to safety. Blood seeped from the livid gashes. The lad tugged his shirt down and grinned at Berlin's father, still lying at his feet.

The din of the chaos around them seemed to come from far away.

The cries of those trapped beneath the dead were fading. The siren wailed, and the lad was gone.

She unlocked her front door, stepped inside and slammed it behind her. But she didn't feel safe. She'd flown under the radar for years, now suddenly everyone wanted a piece of her. Coulthard was on her case, Dempster had her at his mercy, Doyle knew her family. Christ, Dempster might even have a key to her bloody flat.

She turned around and walked out again.

28

Dempster read through the witness statements a third time. They all basically agreed. The woman had stood up, levelled the gun, shouted 'murderer', then fired. The thing everyone remembered most clearly was the sound of her neck breaking as she hit the oak table. She was Merle Okonedo, recently released from a psychiatric ward. It was her other connections that interested Dempster.

He leant over the crumbling brick parapet of the Limehouse Police Station. A station had stood in West India Dock Road since 1897, when the manor belonged to dockers and seamen from every corner of the globe. Hard as nails. Heirs to a maritime tradition of piracy and mayhem on the high seas. The police could barely hold the line.

Nothing much had changed. The current station reminded Dempster of a truncated version of Soviet constructivism. It had been started in 1940 and finished after the war. Just in time to meet the post-war tide of crime from East End gangs that reached its zenith in the sixties with the Krays. They had set a standard in dress sense, manners and loyalty that the current denizens of Poplar could only aspire to. But in terms of cruelty, they had well caught up.

The narrow balcony he was standing on was a refuge for smokers now that the pubs and cafés were smoke-free zones. He was freezing his bollocks off out here. They'd given him a broom-cupboard sized room on the top floor, well away from the Lazenby Incident Room. They didn't know him and they didn't trust him. The feeling was mutual.

The DCI leading the team had told him point blank they weren't going to pursue any connection between Okonedo's death at the town hall meeting, which they regarded as an accident, and Lazenby's murder. They weren't exactly sweating over that, either. Their attitude was that Lazenby was a maverick doctor pandering to junkies and should have been struck off years ago. What a bunch of numpties, thought Dempster. The DCI had as good as told him that Lazenby was bound to get it sooner or later from one of his scumbag patients. You reap what you sow.

The Lazenby team had already lost two detectives to the suspicious death of an infant: his smacked-out mother had decided to warm up his bathwater by putting the tin bowl on the cooker. With him in it.

Dempster watched a young mum across the road. She looked to be about fourteen, with a toddler in a pram. She'd stopped to talk to a mate and the kid was making her pay by chucking his teddy out on the ground, then wailing if she didn't pick it up and give it back to him.

He sucked the smoke deep into his lungs and felt it stirring his brain. He tried to put the pieces of the puzzle together. A dead woman clutching a fake pistol and a doctor killed with a real one. She died during a struggle to disarm her, but he died during a robbery. There was no sign of a struggle. Someone walked in, blew him away, took the drugs and went out the back.

The body had blocked the door from the waiting room, but whoever did it knew they could get out fast through the room used by the addicts to shoot up. It had been left to Catherine Berlin to push the door open and move the body.

He contemplated Berlin's role in all this. It was clear from the get-go that she hadn't killed Lazenby, unless she had the presence of mind to run out of one door and then back in the other, to establish she had arrived after his death. Then there had been the hand print. No killer ever stepped over a body to leave their mark in blood spatter on the wall.

But it had been useful to let her think, if only for a moment, that she might be in the frame. It had put her off balance just long enough for him to push her in the direction he'd wanted her to go. By reputation, she wasn't easily moved.

His thoughts drifted back to Merle Okonedo. He couldn't believe it was sheer coincidence that had brought her to the public gallery of the town hall the same day Lazenby was murdered. The debate was about the management of addicts in the area. Bonnington was campaigning hard to have Lazenby shut down once and for all. If Okonedo was so hostile to Lazenby's practice, why didn't she just wait until after the Trust voted? If he lost, it would all be over.

Okay, she hadn't been thinking straight. After all, she'd been treated for – he flipped back through the file – severe depression, following the death of her junkie brother. But she was thinking straight enough to know that waving a starting pistol around at the town hall would get her cause, which was Bonnington's cause, maximum publicity.

Dempster didn't think Merle had anticipated a dummy gun would lead to her death. A dozen eye witnesses had seen Bonnington engage in a heroic struggle to disarm her and in the mix she'd toppled over the balcony. It was an accident.

He watched the baby in the pram throw the teddy out again and this time his long-suffering mother plucked him from the pram and hoisted him onto her hip. The baby smiled. He had a result. The dodge with the teddy bear was just a distraction. Who's the dummy?

Of course, he thought. Dempster dropped his fag and ground it into the concrete, cursing. *I am.*

29

Berlin's mobile rang. She answered, the wind whipping her hair into her eyes.

'What's that noise?' asked Dempster.

'Waves breaking on the shingle.'

'So I'm guessing you're not in Bethnal Green?'

'Correct,' she said.

'Brighton?' he asked.

'I thought I'd get some fresh air and do some of your dirty work at the same time.' She picked up a smooth black stone and tossed it into the grey sea. 'Kill two birds,' she added.

'What time will you be back?' he said.

Berlin held out the phone to capture the hiss and crunch of wind and waves. She hung up. He didn't own her.

He could imagine her. A wasted figure shrouded in black, head down, shoulders hunched, hands in the pockets of her Lenin overcoat, tramping across the pebbles at the shoreline, her knee-high Cossack boots marked with a salt tidemark from the breaking swell.

He realised he was listening to the static of a broken connection, not the sound of the sea.

He put the phone down.

Berlin had always thought of the man who answered the front door as Pink Cheeks. For years they'd exchanged polite nods and nothing more. She guessed he was in his early sixties, well-preserved and, of course, pink-cheeked. He was apparently in the middle of cooking something because he had a wooden spoon in one hand. It smelled wonderful. He took a moment to put Berlin's familiar face into the right context, then stepped back.

'You'd better come in.'

Berlin followed him down the hall into a large, homely kitchen. He gestured to three saucepans bubbling on the cooker.

'I've got people coming later. This evening actually,' he said, flustered.

Berlin looked at him. She'd bet he'd been up half the night cooking because he couldn't sleep. His agitation oozed from every pore.

'How did you find me?' he asked.

Berlin had a sudden flash of Traitor's Gate, but ignored it and went into her spiel. 'I'm sorry for this intrusion. I know it must be disconcerting to have me turn up on your doorstep like this.'

She paused to give him an opportunity to put her at ease. He didn't take it, so she went on. 'You had an appointment that day. Just before mine. I know you would have kept it, but when I got there the waiting room was empty.'

He stared at her, aghast. Berlin watched the pink drain from his cheeks.

'Christ. You're not a police officer are you? I've already been interviewed. I can't believe they'd employ someone like you. Someone like us, I mean.'

Uninvited she sat down at the beautiful scrubbed deal table. He turned off the gas under the saucepans and sat down too. Now she could see the tremor in his hands, the sweat at his temples. He was doing it the hard way. He put his head in his hands.

'When I saw you at the front door and realised who you were, I thought perhaps you had come to, well, that is, I thought perhaps you were connected to…'

Berlin recognised his desperation. Dempster could take him off the list.

'You thought I'd come to sell you heroin. You hoped that I had the stuff that was stolen from Lazenby,' she said.

He didn't look at her, just nodded.

'And if I had – if I was "connected" to whoever killed Lazenby, or if indeed I had killed him, a man who did the right thing by us for decades – you wouldn't have said a word to the police, just paid the price and hoped and prayed that I would call again? Right?'

His head hung in shame.

'Am I right?'

He nodded.

'You disgust me,' she said, thinking *I disgust me.*

'You know what it's like!' he protested. 'I went to a local GP who just palmed me off on a methadone clinic. I can't use that poison. I tried it years ago. The list of heroin-prescribing doctors is closed pending a Home Office review. Someone told me it's been going on for seven bloody years. I'll end up buying on the street. I'll lose everything!'

Berlin tried not to let her sympathy overwhelm her. She smacked her hand down hard on the table and Pink Cheeks sat bolt upright.

'Now, you're going to tell me everything you didn't tell the police and when you're finished, if I'm satisfied that I've got the truth, I might be able to help you out.'

He licked his lips – from fear or anticipation, she couldn't tell. Berlin felt like shit, sitting in his kitchen, holding out the inducement of a salvation she couldn't deliver. But Dempster was right. It takes one to know one. They weren't called 'users' for nothing.

Pink Cheeks took a deep breath and gave it all up.

30

Flint checked out the bloke's 'Who's Who in Business' entry and made a few phone calls. The target's club was listed in his biography because membership in itself was an indication of status. The club did the right thing by refusing to confirm or deny his presence. But Flint knew if he hadn't been there they would have just said so.

Fernley-Price woke up in a single bed with clean sheets, all tucked in tight. He felt the strange peace that he used to feel at boarding school, knowing his life was completely out of his hands. A moment later he remembered. The peace left him, and he knew it would never return. Never.

He lifted his head from the pillow, which set the room spinning, but once it settled down he realised he was in one of the rooms at his club. He had no memory of returning here after that god-awful scene. The porters must have put him to bed. He ran his hands over his face and throat and winced. He was losing it.

His life had turned to shit. The ship was sinking fast and he had no idea how to save himself. He withdrew further into his high-thread-count cotton cocoon.

There was a soft knock at the door. He ignored it. The next knock was firmer.

'Enter,' he said.

The door opened and the porter peered in at him.

'Sorry to disturb you, sir. There are two gentlemen to see you downstairs.'

'What, at this hour?' blustered Fernley-Price.

'It's nearly lunch time, sir,' he said.

'I'm aware of the time,' said Fernley-Price, although he wasn't. 'Who is it, then?' he asked with trepidation. It was probably some of his former colleagues who had seen him in the bar and knew he was holed up here. People he owed money to, no doubt.

'Two police officers, sir.'

The porter, who had been working since six a.m., was about to lose his job because rubbish like Fernley-Price had trashed the economy and club membership was falling off. He padded away down the corridor and with each soft tread imagined the faces of the arrogant twats beneath his leather soles.

31

Gazing out of the train window Berlin realised the sea air had done her good. It had reminded her why she never left London. The moment the express pulled into Victoria Station she was on her way to the British Library.

The BL had good coffee, free wi-fi and, most importantly, it was a secure public place where it was unlikely you would encounter a target – or a colleague, for that matter. And Berlin didn't want Dempster to start feeling at home at her flat.

He slid into the booth opposite her. He was late.

'What's with this place? Are you implying I need an education?

We have a book in Newcastle,' he said.

'I heard that book had never been returned to the library.'

He laughed. Then he got down to business. He passed a bunch of documents to Berlin and summarised while she leafed through them.

'The woman who died at the town hall, Merle Okonedo, was a psychiatric inpatient until three days before she died. She had been admitted with depression after her brother died of an overdose. In prison.

'One of those documents is a ballistics report. The gun that killed Lazenby was a converted starting pistol – same as the gun that was used to threaten him at the town hall. The only difference was that this one had been modified to fire real bullets.'

Dempster kept talking. Berlin wondered why he had bothered handing her the documents if he was just going to tell her everything anyway. This bloke loved the sound of his own voice and obviously no one else would listen.

'It was an Olympic BBM 9 mm revolver,' he said. 'Easily converted to the real thing, if you know what you're doing. You sand off the orange paint and drill out the barrel so it can fire short ammo. Weapon of choice for London gangs fighting turf wars.'

Berlin leant back and folded her arms. 'There's no link between Okonedo and Lazenby except the type of gun, which you've just said is very common. And why would a gang want Lazenby out of the picture? Because they didn't like him providing free heroin to potential customers?'

She could see her deadpan attitude irritated him more than it should have.

'I never said it was a gang. There is another connection between Okonedo and Lazenby.' He paused. Waiting for a drum roll. 'Bonnington.'

'What? They said on the news he was anti-drugs. It was someone who wanted Lazenby's drugs bad enough to kill for them,' said Berlin.

'You're looking at this all wrong,' he snapped. Dempster leant across the table and retrieved the reports. 'He didn't want the drugs to sell; he wanted them out of circulation.'

Berlin raised an eyebrow. 'Are you serious? You think that Okonedo was working with this Bonnington? The bloke who struggled with her, defending Lazenby?'

'Suppose he knew her gun was a dud?'

Berlin worked her way through the implications. Dempster stayed quiet.

'Okay,' she said slowly, with more than a hint of scepticism.

Dempster couldn't help himself; he had to give her a nudge in the right direction.

'He wanted Lazenby out of the way. It's the perfect cover. Be a hero and save a man's life at lunch time so no one suspects you of killing him after tea. Anyway, who tackles a deranged woman with a gun? Someone who knows it's not real,' he expostulated.

'You've been watching too much television,' said Berlin.

Dempster snorted. She could see he was pissed off, probably because she didn't ooh and ah in the right places, awed by his superb powers of deduction. In his irritation he seemed to have forgotten they'd met so she could brief him on the outcome of her recent 'mission': that which others might call blackmail. Dempster was obviously something of an expert in that field himself, although he would probably prefer to call it leverage. She took her time, wanting it to play out on her terms.

'Yeah, it's a nice theory. There's just one problem with Bonnington as Lazenby's killer,' she said.

'And what's that, Sherlock?'

'It was a woman.'

*

The combination of cold, wet bodies and not enough space turned the Underground into a fetid sauna. Jammed between two enormous Australian backpackers, Berlin reviewed what Pink Cheeks had told her. She'd left a peeved Dempster in the BL, digesting the same information.

According to Pink Cheeks, when he'd arrived at the surgery there was a woman in the waiting room he'd never seen before. It struck him as odd because he'd seen very few women there over the years, apart from Berlin herself. Also, the regular appointment before him was usually someone he'd described as a tall gentleman with 'Mediterranean looks'. Whatever that meant.

The woman, enveloped in a hoodie, was standing by the consulting-room door, gazing up at the green light, clearly anxious to get in. Pink Cheeks had sat down and got out his newspaper before he heard the click that meant that Lazenby had released the lock. The green light came on. The woman shot straight into the consulting room without looking at him.

Sound didn't travel well through the heavy door, but Pink Cheeks was aware of a sort of thumping: more a vibration in the floor. Like a couple of heavy steps. Then he heard a bang, like a whip cracking, and another heavy thud.

Lazenby hitting the floor, thought Berlin.

Pink Cheeks said he was startled and froze for a moment until he heard the door of the self-administration room slam. He caught a glimpse of a man running down the hallway. On the way out people usually moved more sedately. Whoever had been in there had felt compelled to get out, fast.

Pink Cheeks was pretty sure the running man was Mr Mediterranean, the patient before him. He had no doubt recognised the sound of a gunshot and bolted. So far this man had eluded Dempster, having gone to ground, perhaps, after seeing news of Lazenby's demise. But anyway, it was unlikely that he had seen the woman.

While he was running away, she was still in the consulting room, presumably cleaning out the drug safe that Lazenby always stupidly left open to save time between patients.

The routine was that after a brief chat with Lazenby the patient would take the ampoule into the other room, do the business, then leave. Lazenby would give them about ten minutes before he switched on the green light to summon the next in line. These people were experienced users, stabilised on a maintenance dose. They didn't experience the rush any more, throw up or nod off on the spot.

Lazenby also gave a few of them the privilege of taking ampoules home, if they lived at a distance or had other commitments. This was in breach of the Home Office guidelines and one of the reasons Lazenby had been constantly harried by the GMC. He'd argued it was a clinical decision and nobody's business but his and the patients'. In other words, up yours.

When the man ran past the open door of the waiting room Pink Cheeks took this as a bad sign and decided he should also scarper. He didn't see the woman again. His description of her – 'ordinary' – wasn't helpful. Her back had been to him, it was only a minute and he'd been anxious to get in and see Lazenby for what he referred to as his 'little helper'. Berlin reflected that this euphemism was reminiscent of drinking a full bottle of red while preparing dinner, then describing it as a 'cook's nip'.

She extricated herself from the backpackers at Bethnal Green and gratefully ascended from the pit into the freezing air, weaved in and out of the beggars on the corner and made her way home.

Her key was in the lock when the sound of footsteps thundering up the stairs behind her made her turn defensively, her heart pounding.

The postman was taken aback by the fear in her face. 'It's all right, missus. Just me,' he said.

'Sorry,' she said, her shoulders sagging with relief.

'I don't blame you. Around here I keep looking over my shoulder, too,' he said, thrusting a thick brown envelope into her hand.

'What's this?'

'Registered, innit.' He handed her a stylus and held out a touch screen.

She signed.

'Thanks, missus,' he said, and took off down the stairs.

She tore open the envelope and took out a letter from work and a pamphlet. The letter summoned her to attend 'an initial interview in relation to allegations of serious misconduct'. There was a long list of her infractions, and the associated penalties should she be found guilty.

Suspension without pay for six months was the best result, termination the worst. She could bring a support person, but not a lawyer. The pamphlet explained the Agency's disciplinary process and her rights.

The final paragraph warned in sombre tones that if she failed to attend without a reasonable excuse the inquiry would proceed without her. The interview was scheduled for five p.m. the next day. A time, she noted, when the office would be emptying out. A one on one. The letter was signed by John Coulthard, General Manager (Acting).

She had barely turned the key in the lock and pushed open the front door when her landline rang.

'Oh, fuck off,' she said. It was probably Dempster with another wild theory. He seemed intent on this Bonnington, one way or another. The phone kept ringing. Or it could be her mother. She picked up.

'Hello?'

'Cathy, how are you? Roger Flint here.'

'Acting Detective Sergeant Flint,' she said. Her voice was tight.

The over-familiar little prick.

'We've been trying to get hold of you,' he said.

Berlin glanced at the pieces of her old mobile on the table. Flint didn't have her new number.

'Inspector Thompson and I would like another word,' he continued when she failed to respond.

'I've already made a statement.'

'We would like further clarification on some matters.'

'Such as?'

Flint's tone hardened. 'It would be in your interests to attend.'

'When?'

'There's a car downstairs.'

She crossed the room to the window and looked down. A bored-looking woman got out of an unmarked car and looked up.

32

When they drove past the police station Berlin had a bad moment. The woman driving hadn't spoken a word, just opened the back door and gestured for her to get in. She knew the doors were locked automatically by the driver.

'Where are we going?'

'Not far,' came the oblique response.

Talk about a little power being a dangerous thing. Unfortunately, a lot of power was an even more dangerous thing, and once the police had you in their grasp that's exactly what they had, despite the oft-heard complaint that the villains had more rights than police. Until you'd been banged up in a cell you couldn't appreciate the enormity of powerlessness and the fear that went with it.

From the moment Berlin got into the car she had wanted to get out again, but when they pulled up and the car door was released she was strangely reluctant to make a move.

The Limehouse Basin. The water was as still and grey as it had been that morning when she came to meet Gina. Berlin could see Thompson and Flint waiting for her on the other side, just beyond the footbridge across the cut where the Basin ran into the river. Their hands were plunged into the pockets of their overcoats, their shapes indistinct against the granite sky and leaden water. Wraiths.

Flint smiled as she approached. A bad sign. Thompson was bent over the rail, staring into the water.

'What's this about and why the hell are we down here?' she asked, trying not to sound nervous.

Flint ignored the question and gestured at the lock. 'No accident that they both went in here.'

'Who?'

'Don't play smart with me, Berlin. Doyle's daughter and Ludovic Nestor. What do you think the connection was between them?'

'I've no bloody idea.'

'But you agree there must have been one?'

'I don't believe in coincidence.'

Flint cocked his head and widened his eyes in mock admiration, as if she'd said something clever. 'So what was the link?'

'Come on, Flint, enough with the games,' she snapped.

Flint shrugged and pointed at her. 'You. You're the link.'

'What? What are you talking about? She was an informant and he was my boss. If you call that a link.'

She could see that Flint was having the time of his life. Thompson was still gazing into the water as if he could read the flotsam and jetsam like entrails.

'He never met her or spoke to her?' persisted Flint.

'Not to my knowledge. He could have got her mobile number from the log, I suppose, but why would he want to talk to her?'

Detective Chief Inspector Thompson slowly straightened up, his hand in the small of his back. His tone was mild. 'You tell us. He made one hundred and twelve calls to her in the week before she died. But the last call he ever made was to you.'

A small hollow feeling invaded the soft area beneath Berlin's ribs. 'No,' she said. 'He didn't.'

Flint extended his hand. 'We'll need your phone.'

She took a step back. 'Get a warrant. Or arrest me. But you'd better be bloody clear why or I'll have you for false imprisonment and harassment before you can say Police Complaints.'

Flint took a step forward.

'And assault,' she added.

Thompson smiled and put a restraining hand on Flint's arm. 'We're not here for a confrontation. We're just running an investigation and no one's being straight with us. Including you. We didn't do this at the station out of professional courtesy.'

He was a reasonable man who'd become tired, she thought. Weary not just because he was working long hours, with two bodies on his whiteboard now, but worn out by the constant lying and perfidy of the human race. Especially those members of it who were supposed to be on his side.

Seagulls skimmed the surface of the lock, alighting on the rafts of rotting garbage that hung in the water, squabbling over morsels of decay. Their raucous, mocking cries were an insult.

Berlin realised she had no alibi for the nights that Gina and Nestor died. From some distance she heard Flint's voice. 'We have evidence you met Gina on a number of occasions that you didn't log. Nestor was obviously also involved with her in some fashion. He shut down your investigation and you were angry about that. Any comment?'

A bleak future yawned in front of her. She turned and walked away as fast as she could without running.

'Miss Berlin,' Thompson called after her. 'Please come back.'

She stepped onto the iron footbridge and felt the vibration as someone stepped onto it behind her. Even as she picked up speed she knew it was a stupid thing to do, but her legs seemed to have a will of their own. She ran.

'Hey!' shouted Flint. She heard the disbelief in his voice, then the sound of feet pounding across the bridge behind her.

The adrenalin surged through her and she flew off the bridge and around the Basin towards the Narrow. She was aware that Flint was gaining on her and that her heart was about to burst, when ahead she saw the passenger-side door of a parked car swing open.

A voice she recognised shouted 'Get in!'

She did as she was told. The car took off at such speed she had to hang out and grab the door to stop it swinging. She dragged it shut and fell back into the seat. She turned to look at her knight in shining armour.

'You bastard,' she gasped between gulps of air. 'You knew they were waiting for me!'

'Yeah. Well they can have you when I've finished with you,' said Dempster.

33

Dempster was unlike any policeman Berlin had ever met. Intense, tossing wild theories about with scant regard for the evidence, and making rash moves. Like snatching her from the street while other officers were in pursuit.

He said he had driven back to her flat from the BL and waited for her to arrive. He hadn't bothered to pretend he was doing anything except keeping an eye on her. Very trusting. He had watched her go up, then almost immediately come back down and get into the car. It had to be a police vehicle because the driver put her in the back. He just followed.

She sat on his couch and watched him pacing up and down on the tiny balcony, phone pressed to his ear. His free hand swooped and darted through the air, an angry red-necked bird, as he harangued the poor sod on the other end. She suspected it was Flint.

Finally he hung up, slid the glass door open and stepped back into the studio, one of hundreds in a new complex south of the river, near Waterloo. It was compact, and that was being kind. London rents were worse than Tokyo. The only place more expensive than either was Moscow, so she'd heard.

'That's sorted,' he said with satisfaction, slipping the phone back into his suit pocket. 'They were just trying to put the frighteners on you. They haven't even got Nestor's cause of death yet, let alone evidence to charge anybody. The Council invested with some Icelandic bank which has gone belly up, so there's a freeze on postmortems.'

He paused and gave her a wry smile to see if she had picked up on the clever pun. She had, but she wasn't going to give him the satisfaction.

He continued, disappointed. 'Plus, the pathologist's on holiday and they can't afford a locum. Borough Command has just cut DCI Thompson's budget, so he hasn't even got the resources to put someone onto hassling the telco for your voicemail. SCD4 and Met Forensics have laid people off and say they can't find the disc with the dump from Nestor's phone. They think someone might have taken it home. Nestor left it at the office, by the way. His phone, that is. Did you know that?'

He barely paused for breath, while she was still catching hers.

'How can you get away with this?' she asked him.

'What exactly?'

'Snatching me from the grim arms of the law.'

'Apart from Flint giving me an earful, what can they do? They were in the wrong dragging you down to the lock for questioning. Thompson knows that. If they go after me, that will come out, then we'll all be in the shit. What have they got to gain?'

'So it's the pot calling the kettle,' she said.

Dempster laughed.

She laughed too. Now I know I'm going off the deep end, she thought. Laughing. It'll be crying next.

He stood there looking at her, expectant. She knew he was waiting for her to check her phone messages. There was no point. It was the wrong SIM card. Anyway, Nestor was none of his business and she had always stuck to the 'need to know' principle when it came to sharing. He didn't need to know.

Dempster shrugged and moved on. 'By the way, I've got something for you,' he said, retrieving a battered grey file from behind the couch Berlin was sitting on. He dropped it into her lap.

In the top right corner a steady hand had written in perfect copperplate 'Doyle, F. DOB. 6 Sept. 1928'.

She opened it while the unstoppable Dempster rattled on. 'They're a very interesting family. When she was eleven your informant walked into Bethnal Green Police Station and informed them her dad had murdered her mum. So you see, she had a history of dropping her old man in it.'

That explained a lot, thought Berlin. How would you cope with believing such a thing? She must have carried that burden for years – the conviction your father was a murderer and the ignominy of not being believed. Perhaps she'd finally seen a way to get him. Berlin had been right all along: demons had been driving her.

The file contained a yellowing sheet of lined foolscap, half a dozen typed reports, liberally spotted with white-out, a couple of handwritten index cards and some carbon copies. One of them bore the name 'Georgina Doyle'.

Christ, thought Berlin, it's like looking back into the Dark Ages. There was a slight change in her expression, which Dempster picked up on. Maybe he was getting used to her.

'Yeah, it's hard to believe it was 1986, not 1936, isn't it?' he said. 'No computers. The quality of local records was down to the collator. This file was buried deep in the basement at Bethnal Green, along with stuff from 1888 on the Ripper inquiry.'

'You're kidding me.'

'Yeah, I am, actually. The Ripper files all went to the National Archive years ago, but there's boxes and boxes of documents down there I bet no one's ever gone through. Wonderful stuff on the Krays, Jack the Hat, the Bethnal Green Disaster even, remember that?'

'I'm not quite that old,' she said, without expression.

'I meant had you heard of it. It was a stampede down at Bethnal Green Station —'

'I know what it was,' she snapped.

Rebuffed, he shut up. Offence showed in his face.

Jesus, he really is a romantic, thought Berlin as she flicked through the file. 'Nothing on the current systems about the Doyles?' she asked, business-like.

'No. CRIMINT didn't get going until the nineties, and I guess a lot of bods thought it was easier to dump files than enter them into a new system. There was a lot of resistance to computerisation.'

The report Berlin held in her hand said it all. On 5 March 1986 a Senior Constable Marks had taken little Georgina Doyle home after her visit to the station to report her mum's murder. Her father had explained to the copper that her mum had left him a few weeks before and his daughter was having difficulty accepting that she had been left behind.

It was pretty much the same story Doyle had given her. Had Gina been right? Doyle was a murderer? Or had she just been a confused child lashing out at her father? She certainly hadn't come across as a confused adult.

The report noted that when the constable tried to reassure the girl, she swore at him in an 'unbecoming fashion', kicked him in the shins and went to her room.

It turned out the mum and dad weren't married, but their daughter didn't know that. The report stated that the girl was 'well nourished' and the home 'clean and tidy'.

Berlin could see it all. Doyle grateful to the officer for bringing her home, a cup of tea, chocolate bourbons and a man-to-man about the heartless woman who would abandon her child.

There was a postscript to the report. The mum, Nancy Baker, was known to the police. The report didn't say how. But on another piece of paper Berlin found her record: convictions for soliciting, shoplifting and receiving.

The senior constable's report was signed off by a sergeant, who'd initialled it 'NFA'. No Further Action.

The last time Berlin had seen that acronym it was splashed across the policy log she had opened on Doyle. Nestor's digital signature was beneath it and he had entered 'Insufficient evidence to proceed' under 'Reasons'. Now they could engrave 'NFA' on his gravestone.

She glanced up from the file. Dempster was standing over her with a cup of coffee. She didn't know how long he'd been standing there, but he looked amused. She took the coffee and he plonked down on a stool at what she supposed would be described as the breakfast bar.

'So there you go, the father's got form too,' he said.

'The father?' She was confused. Doyle didn't have a record.

'The grandfather, I should say. Archie Doyle's father, Frank.'

Berlin paused. She looked again at the name on the file. This was the man who supposedly knew her father. 'His name didn't come up in my inquiries,' she said.

'Yeah, well, he's a bit of a recluse these days, apparently. A wide boy from an early age, worked his way up to robbery and GBH in the sixties, quietened down in the seventies, then went off the radar completely in the eighties.'

'He must be an old man now,' she said, wondering about his connection to Doyle's sharking operation. Was it a family business?

Dempster clapped his hands together. 'Right! You've got your intel on the Doyles and I've got Thompson off your back, for the time being at least. So let's get back to business. Actually, I've done you another favour, so this isn't going to be too hard.'

Here we go, thought Berlin.

34

The receptionist was pleasant but edgy. Her name tag read 'Polly Poh Li' but Berlin could see the invisible writing underneath that said 'In Recovery'. Polly thrust a clipboard and pen at her, and Berlin sat down to scribble her personal details on the form clipped to it. She was late.

The soft cushions and pastel walls screamed 'calming environment' but the smell of sweat and fear hung in the air. A door opened and an open-faced young man in jeans and a Gap sweater emerged. He approached Berlin, his hand extended.

'Hi. I'm Daryl Bonnington. Pleased to meet you.' His grip was firm and warm, his smile genuine.

Berlin's first instinct was to run.

Bonnington's office was even more calming than the reception area. She could detect a whiff of incense. Bonnington sat on a beanbag and gestured for her to do the same. No chairs. She chose a purple one.

'Okay. Ms Berlin, you have been referred to this facility by the Home Office, via the Metropolitan Police Service Witness Liaison Service, following the tragic death of your GP. You're here for urgent assessment pending transfer to detox and/or a methadone programme.'

'Or another GP with a heroin-prescription licence,' she said, shifting her weight, trying to get comfortable on the beanbag. It was bloody demeaning, being sprawled on the floor.

Bonnington smiled, indulgent. 'May I call you Catherine?'

'Berlin.'

'Fine. Berlin, may I ask you a personal question?'

As if she could say no.

He glanced at the open file on his lap. 'I understand you found Dr Lazenby's body. That must have been a terrible shock. How are you coping with that?'

Berlin composed herself. 'Pretty much the same way you're coping with the death of that woman at the town hall, I should imagine,' she said.

Bonnington was good. He didn't react, just made a note on his pad. Berlin would have bet it was 'Defensive'.

'That was a very sad accident,' he said. 'And one I'll have to live with for the rest of my life.'

Berlin could have sworn he meant it.

'Anyway, Berlin, we're here to talk about you, not me.' He read from the file. 'Stress exacerbated by the murder of an informant. Feelings of guilt. Question mark. Unresolved until case closed. Question mark.' He looked at her with the steady, non-judgemental gaze of the professional.

'So. What sort of outcomes are you looking for from a programme?'

She looked into the abyss and cursed the man who had put her at its edge.

Bonnington showed Berlin out, pausing at the desk to ask Polly to make another appointment for her.

'We need a little more time to thrash out these issues before we can agree on a way forward,' he said.

Polly offered a rueful smile with the card for the next appointment. She'd been there.

Berlin tried to slam the door behind her as she left but it was controlled by a heavy-duty door closer and she just jarred her shoulder. Striding away she felt her feet slip on the ice but she was not about to slow down. Fury drove her on. She ignored the man in the vehicle kerb-crawling beside her.

'Get in,' he said.

'Fuck off, Dempster.'

'Come on. Get in.'

She stopped, leaning in at the car window. 'Do you know what you've done? You've left me at the mercy of a man who is pathologically opposed to heroin on prescription. He won't support a referral to another licensed GP under any circumstances. He wants me on methadone, for fuck's sake.'

'Yeah. Well, that is his job,' protested Dempster.

'You are an utter shit, Dempster. You said you had arranged an urgent appointment with someone who could help me.' She kicked out at the car door.

'Hey!' he shouted.

She strode on. He drove up beside her.

'Come on! I needed someone to get near him. It's perfect,' he said.

She stopped dead and stared at him in disbelief.

'Perfect? You selfish prick! I suppose you think while you've got those scripts as collateral you can do what you fucking well like with me!'

A couple on the other side of the road had stopped to watch, concerned. Dempster got out of the car and gave them a wave. 'It's okay. She's emotional. You know how it is,' he called.

The man nodded and tugged at his wife's arm. They kept walking.

'Well, I'm over it!' shouted Berlin. 'Do your fucking worst! You can keep your so-called favours. Whatever happens next, on your head be it!'

She reached out and snapped one of his windscreen wipers, then marched into the traffic as if there wasn't a car on the road. A road which was slick with black ice. The driver of a Vauxhall Cavalier was unimpressed. His muffled shouts of abuse included the words 'stupid' and 'bitch', accompanied by a horn blast. Berlin made it to the other side, turned and gave him the finger. She could see Dempster watching her. He looked frightened. Good. She strode on.

He ran across the road and caught up but didn't touch her. She kept walking, forcing him to trot alongside. 'Look, I'm sorry. I realise now it was a stupid thing to do. I should have told you it was Bonnington. I'm not used to working with someone else,' he said.

'There's a surprise. And you're not working with me, you're blackmailing me.'

'Listen to me. I promise I'll find you the sort of doctor you want,' he said.

'Why should I believe you?' She stopped dead and got in his face. 'I've got four hits left! What happens then?' she hissed.

'I'll sort something out. Trust me.'

His great red, bony hand touched her arm, ever so lightly. But she felt it.

He wanted to make it up to her, so he drove her out to a pub in Essex for dinner. It was modern, warm, and they served Talisker. Berlin found th?e ahistorical ambience strangely comforting. She didn't have to sneer at faux Tudor fittings or a Disneyfied past that had been gussied up for tourists.

Her sensibilities, which grew out of her visceral connection with the past, weren't outraged by the King William IV. She almost relaxed. She hadn't said a word on the way out there, but once she was on her third Scotch, she thawed a little.

Dempster had been his usual garrulous self during the drive, going over again why he needed someone to get close to Bonnington. Someone trained to manage a conversation. Bonnington would never suspect she was working on a professional assessment of him while he was supposed to be assessing her.

'The woman who got pushed over the balcony at the town hall, Merle Okonedo. Her brother died of an overdose in prison,' he said.

'I know that,' she said.

'Bonnington was his CARAT worker.'

'His what?'

'Counselling, Assessment, Referral Advice, Throughcare.'

Berlin wasn't impressed. She knew verification bias when she saw it. You make up a story and then go looking for the facts to fit it. It was a trap that was very difficult to avoid once you'd got a scenario fixed in your mind, no matter how hard you tried to keep it open. Dempster's mind was now firmly closed.

'Have you got any evidence he knew the sister?'

'I'm working on that,' he replied, slightly peeved. 'The connection shouldn't be too hard to make.'

'So the theory is that Bonnington set up a mock hit so he could save Lazenby from the mock gun and thereby distance himself from the not-mock murder? Using Merle Okonedo as a sacrificial stalking horse. That's pretty cold.'

'She was collateral damage. A martyr for the cause, if you like, chosen by Bonnington,' suggested Dempster.

Berlin thought it was an odd choice of words. 'You're forgetting about the woman Pink Cheeks saw at the surgery; how do you account for her?' she said. 'What's Bonnington's alibi for Lazenby's time of death?'

Dempster shifted in his seat and picked at his french fries. 'He was with a couple of kids. The sons of one of his outreach clients.'

'And?' she pressed him.

'The times are a bit rubbery. It's difficult to get anything definitive out of a pair of kids,' he hedged.

'In other words, Bonnington's alibi checked out,' she said. 'Give it up, Dempster, it's a dead end.'

Dempster was unusually subdued as they walked through the car park and got into the car. I've hurt his feelings, thought Berlin with satisfaction. He drove out of the car park and turned right onto Hainault Road.

'Where are we?' asked Berlin. 'I mean, I recognise the wilds of Essex but where exactly is this?'

'Chigwell. I thought you might like to see the place where Doyle's father lives. We can swing by his house. I haven't forgotten Gina Doyle.'

She gazed out of the window at the flat, windswept fields, aware he was still trying to make amends.

'I'm focused on Lazenby's murder; you're focused on her. I know that. I said I would help and I will. I got you that file, didn't I? It's all intel.'

God, what a sweet-talker, she thought, as they turned into a narrow lane. Bare hedges towered over the car on both sides. She suspected Dempster found her silences difficult to take.

'You're too hard on yourself, you know,' he said.

'Is that right?' she muttered.

'Drugs don't necessarily make you selfish. It's just an excuse. Gina Doyle's murder got to you and you're afraid that without heroin you won't be able to paper over the cracks. Finding her killer won't fix it.'

She was astonished. Had he been managing their conversations? She stared at him.

'It's fear that rules you, not the drug.'

The silence was palpable.

'Stop the car!' she shouted.

Shocked, Dempster slammed on the brakes and she leapt out.

She thrust her way through the brittle hedge and into a barren landscape, a blur of earth and sky melding in the dark. Stumbling across the glacial furrows, she turned her face to the icy gale. Perhaps it would freeze her rage.

Frank heard the car approaching. He cocked an ear when the motor cut out, but after a while it started up and he heard the whine of the reverse gear as it backed down the lane.

Repelled again. Try as they might they couldn't get near him. It would be a sorry day for them if they ever did. He was ready.

35

Doyle, sleepless, tried to take his mind off things by running through his mental tally, ready for Frank. He actually had to keep two sets of figures in his head now, because he had to give that pillock Fernley-Price a regular update on his end of the business.

The banker knew all about dicky figures, or he wouldn't have come looking for investment opportunities with Doyle. He had kept on asking for a list of clients, or amounts lent, or repayment schedules or whatever. He said any type of documentation would do. He must have thought Doyle was born yesterday. He would just tap his bonce and tell him it was all up there.

Doyle sighed. Nobody gave a flying fuck about him. He just had to get on with it. At least it didn't look like the Agency was going to come after him now. Given the state of play, they probably wanted to sweep it all under the carpet and give him a wide berth. They weren't going to get out of this smelling like roses. And the police weren't interested in illegal moneylenders. They wanted to be real thief-takers. Plus, all the paperwork involved in a financial case didn't appeal to them. They could put in a lot of legwork and then the legal eagles would knock the case back.

So it looked like it would be business as usual.

He'd ignored all Fernley-Price's attempts to make contact since he'd fronted him in The Silent Woman. He doubted the prat would show up unannounced like that again. The less contact the better. He didn't want whispers getting out about their joint venture. God forbid that Frank found out. He was sure there was no way he would, all the way out in his Chigwell castle. Well, almost sure. The old man's paranoia was getting out of control lately and Doyle didn't want to give him any more reason to be jumpy. He was still sharp.

Frank's business model was simple and had the virtue of being transparent and self-financing. The punter knew exactly what was going on and you didn't have to borrow to lend, which appeared to be what banks had been doing. Doyle could have told them it would end in tears.

Frank had drilled the basics into him. You take a hundred quid and lend it to someone who can't borrow from the bank or anywhere else in the high street. You tell them they have to pay the hundred quid back to you eventually in a lump sum, but until they can afford to do that, they can just pay ten quid a week. A tenner a week sounds good to them; they can manage that. But they'll have trouble ever putting a hundred together.

After a year they've paid you five hundred and twenty quid, and they still owe you a hundred. Of course, you had to come up with the hundred first – your little bit of capital, as Frank put it. But you hang on to the tenners you collect until you've got a hundred, then lend it out again. Now you've got twenty quid a week coming in and two punters who each owe you a hundred quid. Magic.

The beauty of this model was that it didn't require tricky interest-rate calculations and there were no contracts with five pages of small print, which no one ever read anyway. The small print was 'pay up or else'. Something everyone could understand. The back end of the operation was just a couple of fit lads. No overheads.

If the punter couldn't pay the tenner one week you didn't thump him, you treated it as a business opportunity: you offered to lend it to him. The upshot was that he would have to pay you eleven quid a week until he could put one hundred and ten quid in your hand.

Worst scenario, he paid you out. This was bad for business and you would want to know how he managed it. You would then reveal administration costs, like an exit fee, which he still owed you. It was standard business practice.

If he stopped paying the tenner and wouldn't borrow to cover it, then the small print would kick in, literally. The word of mouth from that wouldn't do you any harm either.

Frank had honed his financial skills during World War Two. At the tender age of thirteen he'd become a sort of broker, at least that's how he described it. If you wanted something like petrol, mixed fruit for your daughter's wedding cake or a nice bit of cloth, Frank was the go-to lad.

Unfortunately the government didn't reward enterprise with tax breaks in those days. The Ministry of Food inspectors nabbed him and he was sent to the naughty boys' home for black-marketeering. Frank described it as the educational opportunity of a lifetime.

Doyle drained his delicate bone china cup and returned it to the saucer with care. It was from an antique set his mum had left behind. When he was a nipper she used to hold one of the cups up to the light and show him how you could see right through it. He thought it was marvellous. She'd say, 'You see, that's how a man should be. You should be able to see right through him. There shouldn't be any dark secrets between him and the light.'

Then she'd clasp him to her and sing, 'All things bright and beautiful, all creatures great and small, all things wise and wonderful, the Lord God made them all.' She wasn't religious, but when she sang that old hymn the weight of the world seemed to lift from her thin shoulders and the black eye she always seemed to have didn't mar her beauty.

Doyle blew his nose and realised his cheeks were wet. Blimey, he was falling apart, crying like a big girl's blouse.

Frank had chucked all his mum's stuff in the dustbin after she'd gone, including the tea set. Doyle was just a little kid, but he'd carefully taken it out, piece by piece, and hidden it in a box under his bed. He wasn't allowed to mention her ever again and if he forgot Frank would give him a back-hander and mutter 'that bitch'. He couldn't even whistle 'All Things Bright and Beautiful' without Frank flying off the handle.

Christ. What a family. His mum walked out on Frank, Nancy walked out on him, then Gina walked out on the both of them. He and his father were a right pair. Doyle wiped his face with his handkerchief. He had a feeling that he hadn't really grown up to be the sort of man you would compare with a bone china tea cup.

36

Berlin closed the curtains and got out her kit. She and Dempster hadn't exchanged a word on the way home. She had stood in the bone-cutting wind, hands and face scratched and stinging from her tussle with the thorny hedge, waiting for him to drive off and fulfil her fantasy of abandonment. But when the car continued to idle and it was clear Dempster was going nowhere, she shrugged it off and got back in.

She lined up her four ampoules, hands trembling, the back of her neck damp with cold sweat. It was late and she was well overdue.

She thought of Pink Cheeks and wondered how he was coping. It was clear from his sorry story that it was going to be impossible to find a doctor in the time she had left. How was Dempster going to help her? His promises were vague, but she had wanted to believe him, so she had bought into his deal. Perhaps he could get her some decent junk that had been seized by the drug squad. At least twenty per cent of it always came back into circulation. The problem was Dempster didn't seem to be bent, just unorthodox.

She subdued the panic that threatened to overwhelm her by choosing an ampoule and injecting its contents. A sense of calm soon prevailed.

She considered her options. She could try going private. At least if she was a paying patient she might find a GP who would prescribe her some strong tranquillisers. She'd have to prepare her system for the shock of withdrawal, if it came to that. But if she lost her job, where was the money going to come from to pay for the doctor and the drugs?

The alternative was even bleaker. An NHS doctor would run her number through the system and up would pop her status as a registered addict. Then they would palm her off on a detox programme or insist their lists were closed. Junkies were high maintenance and a bloody nuisance around the surgery. The judgement of these doctors and their approach to prescribing was moral, not clinical. Heroin bad, benzodiazepines good.

But currently there was no room for concern in her system. Any imperative she had felt to listen to Nestor's voicemail dissipated. She was physiologically incapable of anxiety, while retaining absolute clarity about her situation. She was coherent and calm, safe in an embrace that would never disappoint.

The three ampoules that were left in the line glinted in the soft yellow light. Three days before she descended into hell. Her mother would retort that Jesus rose from the dead in the same time. Her father would wink and tell her not to take that too literally. The ties that bind. She nodded, smiled.

Somewhere in the distance a woman screamed. A face flew at her out of the darkness, the head lolling at an acute angle because half her neck was missing. Berlin woke up with a start. The screams were her own.

The Fifth Day

37

Berlin's metabolism was reeling from the change in routine. Dragging herself out of bed, she stumbled to the computer. On top of it lay the old Doyle file. The file had given her a lead, but first things first. She pushed it aside. She'd like to do the same with Dempster.

According to Thompson, Nestor had made his last call to her old mobile. It would have been among the voicemails she'd downloaded from the carrier after her phone was smashed by the disaffected youths at the park gate.

She clicked through her messages. She had missed a number of calls, some with blocked ID. Probably Flint or Thompson. Only one message had been left late the night before last. She selected 'listen'.

The abuse at the beginning was clear enough, although Nestor's delivery was slightly slurred and breathless.

'Berlin, you think you know everything, you arrogant bitch, but you never knew Juliet Bravo. When I said no further action I meant no fucking further action. Now look what you've done.'

It was a shock, hearing such language from Nestor's usually pursed lips.

There was the sound of buzzing, an entry phone maybe, then the lift doors droned.

'So glad you could make it,' said Nestor to his visitor in his familiar, perfectly clipped, unctuous tone. Coming hard on the heels of his venomous outburst it gave Berlin the chills. It was as if he was suddenly seized by sober malice.

The visitor mumbled something Berlin couldn't catch. Then there was a thud, as if Nestor had dropped the phone. Everything after that was indistinct.

Berlin realised Nestor hadn't just left her his last phone message. He had left a record of what was probably his last conversation.

38

The Central line was beset with the usual tangle of dramas, great and small, that plagued the Underground: security incidents, bodies on the line, drivers on strike. Like most Londoners Berlin neither knew nor cared which it was; she just wanted to get where she needed to go, get the information she wanted and get out again, fast.

She peered at her reflection in the glass of the double doors and tried to straighten herself up a bit. She needed to create a good impression.

The walk from Barkingside Station took her to a row of pretty cottages that had the great good fortune to be within a stone's throw of a Sainsbury's. There was a pub on the corner and a Chinese take away about a hundred yards further on. A perfect location.

The herringbone brick path had been cleared of snow, which lay quite thick out here, and grit had been laid. The path wended its way through a garden that was pristine white. A modest, immaculately clean Ford was parked in the drive, also clear of snow. Someone was home. The brass knocker gleamed. After she'd used it she was tempted to give it a rub with her hanky in case her fingers had sullied the shine.

The door was opened by a tall man with a heavy build wearing a crisp checked shirt and grey flannel trousers. His slippers were brown corduroy and not the slightest bit worn.

'Senior Constable Marks?' inquired Berlin.

'Retired. I was intrigued when I got your call,' he responded, taking a step back and inviting her to cross the threshold. 'Always happy to help with inquiries.'

The array of horse brasses on the living room mantelpiece was dazzling. She could hear Marks in the kitchen, the clink of tea cups, which were no doubt coming out of the top cupboard. It was to be the best china then, not the old mugs he used for every day.

He hadn't asked, and she hadn't volunteered, just let him assume she was there on official police business. She prayed he wouldn't want to see ID. It made her feel uncomfortable. It was the sort of underhand technique Coulthard used.

Sympathy cards were arranged on the sideboard and a sneaky look at them alerted her to the fact that Letty Marks had passed on just before Christmas. The truth was that Marks would jump at the chance to talk to anyone.

He returned with a tray of tea and chocolate bourbon biscuits. Her favourites.

'So you're interested in the Doyles,' he began. He put the tray down with care on an occasional table and produced coasters to protect the French polish.

When his wife had done this he would have told her not to fuss, thought Berlin.

'You don't forget that family in a hurry. Your phone call brought it all back. It's not every day an eleven-year-old girl walks into the station and accuses her dad of murder.'

Berlin sat on the edge of her armchair, trying to find the balance between saying too much, and not enough.

'Got a cold?' Marks asked.

She realised she was sniffing.

'It's that time of year,' she said.

'You should try Lemsip,' said Marks, solicitous. 'I swear by it.'

Maybe it is a cold, she thought. But somehow I don't think Lemsip will quite crack it. She brought out a soggy tissue and blew her nose.

'I've seen your report in the old file,' she said. 'I wondered if there was anything else, Senior? The sort of thing that an experienced copper like yourself might notice, but wouldn't put on paper because it was based on instinct, not on facts.'

Flattery will get you everywhere.

'Call me Harvey,' he said, and dunked his biscuit. 'I was in the job twenty-five years. Didn't get beyond Senior. Didn't want to. I was content to work my shifts and go home. Unlike some.'

He wasn't going to be rushed through this. He sat back in his chair, his gaze drifting to the sympathy cards. Berlin raised an eyebrow, interested, encouraging him.

'Is this something to do with that girl who turned up in the Limehouse Basin?' he asked.

He was still a canny copper, thought Berlin. 'Why do you ask?'

'The lock down there, at the Basin, was one of Doyle's stomping grounds. Quite literally. Frank Doyle, that was – the patriarch, if you like. He's probably dead.'

This was what Berlin had come for, the history that was written between the lines. Marks was on a roll now.

'I knew the family pretty well, although Frank's wife had left him before my time. Frank lived with his son, who for some reason was only ever known as Doyle. He was always Doyle and his father was always Frank Doyle, as if his son was just a piece that had been snapped off him.'

He sipped his tea and glanced again at the sympathy cards.

'Nancy lived there too, of course, Doyle's wife – common law, that is – and their little girl. Or rather, they lived with Frank. The flat was council then and I think Doyle's mum was the original tenant.' He sighed and shook his head, rueful. 'I knew Nancy the best. Nance. She was a very nice woman, but she had her flaws. Issues, I suppose they would call them these days.'

'She was on the game,' said Berlin.

Marks nodded. 'She wasn't out every night. But she made a bob or two around the Haymarket at the weekends, bank holidays, that sort of thing. She was very careful with her money, didn't drink or splash it around. She told me once she was putting a bit by, a nest egg like, so that one day she and Doyle could get their own place, somewhere with a bit of garden for Georgina to play in.'

He stopped suddenly, perhaps aware that he was turning into one of those geezers that bang on about the old days. 'You're not interested in all this trivia,' he said quickly.

'No, I am. This is very important background. Please go on, Harvey.'

She reached for another chocolate bourbon to demonstrate her commitment. 'May I?'

'Help yourself,' he said. 'I always had trouble believing that Nancy would run off and leave her kid behind. On the other hand, who knows what drives people? Doyle seemed okay, he kept a low profile, although none of them ever had any visible means of support. You never know what goes on behind closed doors.'

'Do you think he was living off immoral earnings?' asked Berlin.

Marks shook his head. 'I doubt it. He was a weak character, always in Frank's shadow, but he didn't strike me as that type.'

'What was Frank like?' she asked.

'Now he was a violent man, very free with his fists.'

'Did you ever receive any complaints about Doyle, from his clients?'

'Clients?'

'People who'd borrowed from him. The loan-sharking business.'

Marks looked confused. 'It doesn't ring a bell. I'm sure I would have heard if he'd been standing over anyone, that sort of thing. I would have been first in line for a loan.' The joke was half-hearted. 'No. He definitely wasn't into loan sharking in those days. Neither was Frank. He was just a run-of-the-mill villain. Thieving mostly. They must have got into the lending lark a bit later, after my time. I was moved to another station not long after Nancy disappeared. I heard Frank had moved out to Chigwell. Turned into a bit of a recluse, by all accounts.'

Berlin noticed Marks's tea had gone cold.

'But I'll tell you one thing,' he said, leaning forward to make his point. 'Doyle didn't move a muscle without Frank's say-so. Anything illegal, Frank would be at the bottom of it.'

Marks regretfully saw her out.

'Sure you won't stay a bit longer? I could whip you up an omelette. You look like you could do with a good feed.' He smiled. She had eaten the whole plate of chocolate bourbons.

Berlin was almost tempted to stay, but she was going to be late for her appointment if she didn't get going. It was one she couldn't afford to miss.

She also knew that sooner or later Marks would ask her what her rank was and where she worked. Then it would get awkward. She didn't want to lie to him. It had never been awkward for Coulthard, who would dissemble and mislead punters and police alike by always referring to himself and other members of the team as 'Inspector'. She'd even seen him sign into a casino on a covert operation as Inspector Coulthard. Lying wanker.

'Another time, Harvey,' she said and shook his hand.

She was halfway down the path when he called to her.

'Catherine!'

She rarely heard her first name. As she turned around she half expected to see her father standing there. She shuddered.

'Yes?' she said.

'Don't forget the Lemsip.'

39

Fernley-Price had been astonished the police had found him at his club. He didn't know the old bill were that efficient. He knew he had acted like a guilty man, but who wouldn't, confronted by two detectives? Everyone has something to hide.

He'd had a few drinks to steady his nerves after they'd gone, and kept ringing Doyle, but as per, the bastard wasn't answering his calls.

He had stayed in his room all day, drinking and weeping in a welter of fear and despair. He dreaded the night, and when it came his childish terrors had returned. He had made a hell of a noise, members complained and there was a tussle with the porter. The last thing he remembered was being sick and blubbing in the porter's lap.

Today would be a different story. He had to find Doyle, although really this was the last thing he wanted to do. The man was a monster. But it was either that or walk away penniless. Time was running out and he had to salvage something from this nightmare.

He would scour London until he tracked Doyle down.

The traffic was gridlocked. The cab had crawled half a mile in fifteen minutes. He tapped on the glass partition and urged the cab driver on.

'Can't you find a way through this mess?'

The driver glanced at him in the rear-view. 'What do you want me to do, mate? Fly?'

Fernley-Price slumped in his seat. Jesus Christ, what was the country coming to? There was no respect any more. Once upon a time people like this bloody cab driver had put on a suit and tie to keep an appointment with people like him. The City had been important, revered even. Deference was expected, and forthcoming. Now they asked you before you got in if you had the cash for the fare.

Something had gone terribly wrong.

*

Doyle felt he might have taken his eye off the ball a bit lately. Returns were slipping; he was going too easy on the customers. He had such a lot on his mind.

Fernley-Price wouldn't take the hint when Doyle didn't answer his calls or respond to his increasingly hysterical messages; he just kept on ringing. No manners. But when Doyle got a text from the publican at The Silent Woman saying the wanker had been in there looking for him, he decided he couldn't afford to have him running around town. He caved in and rang.

Fernley-Price had sounded half-pissed. He'd demanded to see him immediately 'on a matter of the utmost importance'. The geezer was in a cab roaming all over the bloody East End on the hunt for him. He must be unhappy with his cut, thought Doyle. Wouldn't meet at The Silent Woman either, wanted to get together on neutral ground.

Doyle swore. He'd never get a parking space near Liverpool Street Station. It was inside the ring of bleeding steel and the Congestion Charge Zone. They had built the original station on the site of the old asylum, the Royal Bethlem Hospital, and it certainly carried on the Bedlam tradition.

He didn't want the lads dropping him off there either, in case they caught sight of Fernley-Price. It would be a disaster if it got back to Frank. Fuck it, he would walk: it wasn't that far from home. It would do him good to stretch his legs.

40

By the time Doyle found the right café at the station he was nearly frozen to death. He'd put on his sheepskin driving coat, which
might have kept the sheep warm but was seriously inadequate in
these arctic conditions. He wasn't happy. He spotted Fernley-Price
at a corner table and raised his hand in greeting. The numpty pretended he didn't know him. What, did he think they were in some
bloody James Bond film?

Doyle plonked himself down and picked up the menu. 'What's
up with you, mate? You look like you've lost a pound and found a
penny.'

Fernley-Price glared at him. 'I've lost a bloody sight more than
that, I can tell you.'

Doyle could smell the liquor on his breath across the table. 'Yeah,
but none of it was yours, was it?'

Fernley-Price flushed.

Doyle looked at him steadily. The prat didn't like that; didn't like
being reminded that he had taken a lot of people's savings down
with him. He dropped the menu on the table and when the waitress came over he didn't look at her.

'Cup of tea and an Eccles cake, love,' he said. The waitress slunk
off.

'I want my investment back,' Fernley-Price said.

'Beg yours?' said Doyle.

'I want my cash.'

Doyle leant back in his seat and folded his hands in his lap. He
could see Fernley-Price was coming apart. He was sweating, despite
the weather.

'Steady on, mate. What's brought this on?'

Fernley-Price's voice broke as he leant across the table. 'Look,
I've had a visit from the law,' he said.

'You better tell me all about it,' said Doyle.

'One of my clients died in unusual circumstances.'

'Why did they come to you?' asked Doyle.

'He phoned me,' said Fernley-Price.

'Is that all?'

'A number of times, okay. The day he died,' said Fernley-Price. He ran his fingers through his hair, which Doyle noticed was matted.

'So? What's that got to do with me?' asked Doyle.

'I got the Agency off your back, didn't I? It was business as usual for you, right? But it's all getting a little too close for comfort. I've done a risk analysis and this is a good moment for me to exercise my options.'

Doyle was getting seriously pissed off. He'd walked miles, at least three, in the freezing cold, to sit in this shithole and listen to a load of crap from this twat. Outwardly he remained calm. 'I don't know what you're talking about.'

Fernley-Price was trembling like a girl. Doyle was a pretty good judge of character and he knew when someone was close to the edge. He'd pushed them there often enough. This bloke wasn't just scared, he was bleeding terrified. Of what?

Fernley-Price struggled to keep the hysteria out of his voice. 'When you told me about the surveillance operation I pulled some strings at the Agency and got the bloody investigation closed down.'

The waitress put the Eccles cake and a cup of warm liquid that was supposed to be tea in front of Doyle. 'Thank you,' he said, but didn't move. Just sat there staring at Fernley-Price.

'What? For God's sake why are you looking at me like that?' said Fernley-Price.

'The op was cancelled, courtesy of my contact in the Agency,' said Doyle.

'No. It was my man, Nestor. Ludovic Nestor.'

Doyle remembered how frantic Fernley-Price had been when he'd told him about the two blokes in the car outside his flat. He couldn't believe he had taken it into his head to interfere. Bloody amateurs.

'But I told you it was sorted,' said Doyle, through gritted teeth.

'Well, I'm used to managing my own risk. I don't outsource it,' snapped Fernley-Price.

Doyle reined in his temper. 'So what are you telling me? What's the connection here? This Nestor was one of your clients and worked at the Agency, is that it? Is that how you managed it?' he asked in the most reasonable tone he could muster.

'He didn't just work there. He was the boss,' said Fernley-Price, and snorted.

The snort spoke volumes to Doyle. It said, as if I would have had anything to do with the lower echelons.

It seemed to go very quiet in the café. Something in the pit of Doyle's stomach felt like lead. He tried to recall the chain of events. After he'd spotted the two pillocks in the car outside the flats, his contact had confirmed there was an operation on him. But all he could say at that point was that the informant was a woman going under the alias Juliet Bravo. The bloke owed him five grand. Doyle had told him to get the op shut down and he'd write it off.

As an added incentive he'd implied that if he went down, this bloke was going with him. The geezer was cocky and gave the impression he could do pretty much what he liked at the Agency.

No problem, he had told Doyle. I can sort it. He personally would guarantee that Doyle was protected.

Now here was Fernley-Price telling him that this Nestor was the boss, not the wally in Doyle's pocket. So if Doyle's bloke was just another shitkicker, what did he do to stop the investigation?

Doyle felt dizzy. He was overcome by a terrible feeling that his contact might have gone the time-honoured route and got the investigation shut down by getting rid of the informant. He swallowed hard and made sure his tone was the right side of reassuring.

'Let's just take this down the road,' he said to Fernley-Price. 'There's a nice little pub down there, just beyond the bridge.'

Doyle knew better than to smash someone's teeth in before you'd got all the information you wanted. He stood up and started to walk out, then turned back, picked up his Eccles cake and put it in his pocket.

'Get the bill, will you?' he said.

Fernley-Price was surprised at how fast a man of Doyle's proportions could walk. He followed with reluctance as Doyle took a sharp right off Liverpool Street into a narrow lane that ran between a building site and an office block. It was not the sort of place he would have ventured alone.

'I thought we were going to a pub just past the bridge,' Fernley-Price said, nervous.

'Shortcut,' said Doyle amiably.

Doyle slowed to a stroll halfway down the lane and they walked side by side. There was only just enough room. No one was coming the other way. A couple of junkies crouching in a doorway looking to mug someone appeared to think better of it when they saw Doyle, and took off.

'So what happened when the police came around?' asked Doyle.

'They told me that Nestor had drowned.'

'They looked you up just because he was a customer?'

'We were at school together, then went on to the same university, although he was a few years older than me. We socialised on occasion. Anyway, they said it looked like suicide and they were talking to everyone he knew about his state of mind. He'd made some calls to me from his mobile the same day he...'

Doyle's pace slowed another notch and he nodded sympathetically. 'It must have been a shock.'

'It was terrible. Terrible. I don't know how they found me so fast.'

Doyle realised Fernley-Price was more shocked by the visit from the law than by the death of his old school chum. He came to a complete halt and put his hand on Fernley-Price's arm. Fernley-Price flinched.

'And it was this Nestor who you had persuaded to get off my case?'

Fernley-Price nodded.

'How?'

'Everything he had was tied up with my firm.' He broke off and tried to tug his arm away from Doyle, who tightened his friendly grip. 'See here, Doyle, I've got to get going, appointments et cetera. Let's just agree to dissolve our partnership. Settle up. No hard feelings.'

'None whatsoever,' said Doyle, with an expression of concern.

Fernley-Price gabbled. 'I really appreciate it, old man. My life's in the crapper at the moment. I need to move on. You know how it is, exposure. One can only manage it with cash.'

Doyle glanced up and down the deserted lane. He knew all about exposure.

The next moment Fernley-Price gasped as Doyle's knee connected with his groin. He doubled over as Doyle delivered a swift uppercut, smashing his rings into the soft place under the chin. Doyle felt the lower jaw crack nicely.

'Fuck!' Doyle exclaimed, and flexed his fingers. He should have taken his rings off.

Fernley-Price was on the ground, throwing up. He didn't seem to be able to open his mouth properly and the vomit was backing up.

'Mate,' said Doyle. 'That money has gone out to the market. Your bit of capital's tied up. Be patient. Pull out now and there will be significant penalties. You understand this principle, don't you?'

Fernley-Price gurgled.

'Good. This is not a gentlemen's agreement.'

His knuckles still stung, so he delivered a few swift kicks to the kidneys and stomped on Fernley-Price's head.

Fernley-Price's screams died in his throat. Doyle heard, with satisfaction, the gentle chink of teeth tumbling onto cobblestones.

'No hard feelings,' he said as he walked away. He took the Eccles cake out of his pocket and bit into it savagely. Could he have set up his own flesh and blood without knowing it? Good Christ, what had he done?

He wished he'd never met fucking Fernley-Price. He'd told him that the problem with the surveillance was sorted. Why the fuck had the wanker taken it on himself to interfere? He had got at this Nestor bloke and opened up a second front.

Doyle stopped short as it struck him: could Nestor have killed Gina, then topped himself out of guilt? No. He kept walking. It didn't make sense. If Nestor was the boss then all he had to do to protect his investment was stop the investigation. Why bother to murder the informant?

It was doing Doyle's head in. He had to get hold of his bloke at the Agency. He would know by now the dead informant was Doyle's daughter. God help him. God help them all. He threw the rest of the cake into the gutter. Let the rats have it.

41

Detective Chief Inspector Thompson returned from the canteen just in time to witness Acting Detective Sergeant Flint slam down the phone.

'You won't believe this!' exploded Flint.

Thompson thought that he probably would; he was accustomed to disappointment.

'I've just got off the phone after twenty minutes arguing with some cow who is supposed to be Law Enforcement Liaison at the telco. They got the RIPA authority, oh yes!' He brandished a photocopy of the form required by the Regulation of Investigatory Powers Act. 'But there was a technical problem and a whole lot of stuff got dumped. They just didn't bother to tell us! I said, what about the bloody EC Data Retention Directive?'

'And what did she say?' said Thompson mildly.

'She said "so sue me" and hung up. Jesus Christ! What can we do, boss?'

'Nothing,' said Thompson.

It was obvious Flint was gutted. Thompson also detected contempt; he knew Flint thought he just rolled over when they faced this sort of obstacle. Flint had been all for reporting Dempster to Professional Standards after their run-in with him over the Berlin woman. Thompson had been forced to remind him that they had been operating outside the guidelines themselves and it would only open up a can of worms. He had suggested they move on to their next target. But he knew Flint thought he was a spineless old fool.

'Their logs show that Berlin deleted all her messages, and now their back-up has gone. So that's that? Fuck me! Why do we bother?' said Flint.

Thompson knew that eventually Flint would stop asking, and

would stop bothering, too. He sat at his desk and woke up the computer.

'Here's a piece of good news,' he said, reading from an email. 'The Poplar Public Mortuary has forty-two fridge spaces and eleven deep freeze spaces. Due to a backlog of post-mortems the mortuary is now full. HM Coroner for the Inner Northern District of Greater London, exercising powers under HM Coroners Act and the Coroners Rules 1984, has directed that in all cases where an inquest has been adjourned pending the outcome of a police investigation the case will be transferred to the Inner West London Coroner's District forthwith.'

'Meaning?' said Flint.

'Meaning our bloke Nestor will be shipped down the road for a P-M so we'll finally know if he chucked himself into the Limehouse Basin or if he had encouragement.'

Thompson looked around at what was supposed to be his senior team in the Major Incident Room. Three empty desks: one detective on long-term sick leave awaiting the outcome of an inquiry into the bashing of a suspect, one on a management course down at Bramshill, and one out in the field re-interviewing witnesses because it hadn't been done properly the first time. Then there was Flint.

Thompson opened up the computer files and checked recent entries in the activity log by the outside team. There wasn't much. He checked the scene log, managed by the Action Allocator, and the policy log, where he was supposed to record the reasons for instigating certain lines of inquiry and discarding others. Not one log was up to date.

'This investigation is at a standstill. We still haven't got anything on Gina Doyle,' grumbled Flint.

'She's as big a mystery as her old man,' mused Thompson.

He remembered Flint's challenge to Berlin at the first case conference concerning the informant's motives. Was the dead woman a good citizen, Doyle's disenchanted squeeze or one of his victims? Turned out it was none of the above. She was his angry little girl.

Doyle had told them she had always blamed him for her mother leaving home. It was plausible. Thompson knew that fury and resentment from childhood, real or imagined, could flourish even in the most mature of adult breasts.

But Thompson wanted more than just Doyle's account before he'd be satisfied. There was an entry in the sparse activity log from the detective assigned to background on the Doyle family. Apparently there was an old paper file relating to them.

So why wasn't it on his desk?

42

Berlin wasn't fronting Coulthard without a union rep, even though the union seemed doubtful that she would keep her job. Failure to obtain authorisation to run a CHIS was a hanging offence, and failure to follow a lawful direction to cease an investigation was where the drawn and quartered bit would come in.

Nonetheless they had grudgingly sent someone to keep an eye on the proceedings, a snotty graduate no doubt slumming with the union to build his credentials for the main game: a shot at preselection in a safe Labour seat. They had met in the lobby at four forty-five precisely, so Berlin could brief him. Now she watched as a stand-off developed.

The union bloke was pissed off when the receptionist at the Agency told them Mr Coulthard had left the office early and wouldn't be back today. He demanded to know why they hadn't been informed via that new-fangled device, the mobile telephone?

No question, he had mastered labour relations.

The receptionist made it clear that she didn't like his tone and she wasn't Coulthard's secretary. He was only 'acting' in the role and she hadn't been Nestor's assistant anyway. All executive assistants had been retrenched in the latest cuts. In fact, her own hours had been reduced and she was only on reception part time now, so maybe if he was from the union he could do something about that while he was here, instead of giving her a hard time?

The union bloke left. Berlin's irritation that he had just walked out, after all the trouble she'd gone to, was mitigated by relief that her discipline hearing had apparently been postponed. Relief was quickly replaced by anxiety and suspicion. What sort of game was Coulthard playing?

The receptionist told Berlin that, just between them, things had gone to hell in a handbasket since poor Mr Nestor passed away. There was a rumour that the government was going to fold the Agency into another department, which meant, of course, that more jobs would go sooner rather than later. People were jumping before they were pushed, although there was nothing out there to jump to. Coulthard probably had a last-minute job interview somewhere. She wouldn't be surprised.

Berlin found it difficult to believe that Coulthard would easily sacrifice an opportunity to humiliate her, maybe even deliver the coup de grâce. She needed to talk to someone who could, and would, give her a heads up on Coulthard. It was a very short list.

Berlin was on her second Scotch by the time Del arrived. He nodded at her while he waited at the bar. She watched him scan the busy pub.

'Don't worry, there's no one here from work,' she said when he sat down.

'Yeah, sorry. You know, we've all been warned off you, and the way things are job-wise I'm trying to keep a low profile.'

'I get it, Del. I know you're risking it by even talking to me. Thanks for coming,' said Berlin.

'No problem, mate,' said Delroy.

'Now tell me about Coulthard,' she said.

'He got a call, went as white as a sheet and left without a word. Just left the troops sitting there, so everyone packed up and went home.'

It was no way for an Acting Manager to behave, thought Berlin.

'After you rang I spoke to his girlfriend, thinking it might be a domestic drama or something,' continued Del.

'And?' said Berlin, anxious to cut to the chase.

'She said he came home, told her there was an op on and he might be late, then went straight out again. She saw him getting into the back of a black Merc.'

'That's it? Did she ask why you were ringing?'

'Yeah. I didn't want her to worry. He's a pillock but she's okay. I told her there'd been some confusion about the debrief. She said she'd get him to call me. He's not answering his mobile.'

Del gulped down his pint. She could see he was nervous just being there with her. 'First Nestor, now Coulthard's gone off the radar. Is it a conspiracy or has Coulthard just taken a package and dumped the girlfriend?' he said.

'Who's in charge when Coulthard's not there?'

'Good question,' said Delroy. 'The rumour is the axe is about to fall, so everyone is scrambling to get a new gig. Apparently senior management are falling over themselves to take redundancy while the packages are still good.'

'No one gives a shit about the job,' said Berlin.

'Never did. It's been flavour of the month for five minutes, but it won't last. There wasn't a prosecution for illegal moneylending for donkey's years before our team was set up,' said Del.

'Yeah. You were more likely to get a medal for services to the

Empire or a seat in the Lords,' she said. 'Do you want another drink?'

At least he had the decency to look embarrassed.

'Look, er, I better get going. You know.'

'Yeah, I know, Del. Thanks.'

She watched him leave and decided to have another. She was used to drinking alone.

Berlin thought about the black Merc that had been waiting for Doyle outside the Limehouse Police Station. She ran through the sequence of events: an aborted investigation, a murdered informant, a dead Nestor. Now a black Merc waiting for Coulthard.

Confirming a connection between Doyle and Coulthard would go a long way towards addressing her disciplinary proceedings, and could lead to Gina Doyle's killer. Was Coulthard capable of murder? Maybe Doyle was wondering the same thing.

The phone number Doyle had written on the newspaper was now stored in her contacts as 'Billy Bunter'. She didn't think he would find this flattering. It wasn't his size, it was more his peevish quality that led her to use that name. His was a kind of blind, almost innocent, greed, a sense of entitlement that, when disappointed, would turn cruel. Doyle would cry, Bunter-like, 'Why is everyone always so beastly?' as he yanked out your toenails.

She tried his number, although she wasn't sure what she would say if he answered. Hello, Mr Doyle, can I have a word with Johnny Coulthard? In the event, a robotic female voice invited her to leave a message. She declined.

She knew Doyle would never take Coulthard to his own place, or that of his associates. Men like Doyle always had a neutral space somewhere, anonymous, safe from prying eyes and CCTV. Doyle lacked imagination, so in his case there was one strong possibility. He would stick to what he knew.

*

Nino was surprised to see her so late in the day. 'We're closing soon,' he said.

'Time for a quick pastry and espresso, Nino?' Berlin said, giving him a smile.

He smiled back, indicating she should take a seat. 'I'll bring it over.'

She sat close to the counter rather than in her usual corner. 'Mr Doyle in this morning?'

'Now you mention it, I haven't seen him today.'

She knew Nino had seen them talking recently, so maybe he would think it was a casual inquiry. 'Is his lock-up around here?'

There was nothing casual about that.

Nino put the coffee and cannoli on the table in front of her and folded his arms. 'How should I know?'

'Maybe I should ask your granddad? He must have known Doyle's father, Frank. He was a busy lad, apparently. During the war. He would have kept his stock somewhere close.'

Nino watched as she drank her espresso.

'Everyone around here did business with him, from what I understand,' she said. 'Flour, tea, sugar. All rationed then. Tough for a small café.'

'Leave Granddad out of it,' he said.

Berlin reached for the pastry, but Nino snatched the plate away. Berlin didn't move.

'Granddad upstairs, is he?'

Nino hesitated. Berlin could see he didn't want any trouble.

'Bow Wharf,' he said, and went to the door and opened it.

She took the hint.

'You should look closer to home,' growled Nino as she stepped outside.

She turned to ask him what he meant, but he slammed and locked the door behind her.

The café went dark. It was like watching the lights go down on another era. She would never taste those chips again.

43

Bow Wharf sat at the junction of two canals: the Hertford Union and the Grand Union. As a distribution hub into the East End it would be difficult to think of a better location, particularly during the Second World War when there was petrol rationing, and horse-drawn narrow-boats and barges had made a comeback. Frank must have been involved in a bigger operation than the police at the time realised, thought Berlin.

The wharf had once housed an enormous glue factory. The warehouses around it had undergone the sort of haphazard transformation that went with property developers and gentrification during the boom. In the bust, it had become even more haphazard. The word moribund sprang to Berlin's mind as she worked her way through the high grass surrounding empty 'business studios'. The only signs of recent life were the fresh estate agent billboards.

She was looking for something from the past. Like a bloody archaeologist of crime, she thought, hunting the artefacts of endless generations of London villains. The lock-up must rank as one of the most ubiquitous.

Leaving the flimsy structures of the twenty-first century behind, she moved towards the remnants that slouched in forgotten corners of the site: sheets of corrugated iron, crates that had once held twin-tub washing machines, even an abandoned milk float. They were the first tidemark of development.

She made her way beyond these to an area where strange brick edifices protruded from the ground. She guessed these were the vents for long-abandoned tunnels or air-raid shelters. Beside them were great gobbets of rusted industrial plant that had defied all attempts to remove or destroy them. It was darker here and she trod carefully, wary of potholes and barbed wire. The sound of traffic fell away to a hum as she moved further into the wasteland. The only sound was the plop of rats dropping into the water.

She came to a standstill at a narrow channel that ran off the main canal. On the other side stood a row of concrete buildings, their worn walls revealing a rusted rebar skeleton. Lock-ups. A light bulb encased in a metal grille shone above a steel door, which looked to be of more recent vintage than the shed itself.

Berlin cursed as she realised that there was no way across the channel from this side. The water disappeared into the distance and she might have to walk a long way before she found a footbridge or it disappeared underground.

In the distance beyond the sheds she could just see the faint glimmer of streetlights. She would have to retrace her steps and approach the whole area from another angle, which would take an hour at least. The channel was only about five feet wide. Could she jump it? Not a snowball's chance in hell. And if she missed her footing on the slimy bank it could be very nasty. Was it worth the effort to try to get over there, anyway?

As she pondered her options, the shed door opened. For a brief moment a shaft of light illuminated a black Merc standing a little way off. Then the door closed and it was dark again. Suddenly it was definitely and incontrovertibly worth the effort. Whoever had opened the door to step outside hadn't gone far. She stood very still.

The sound of water splashing on metal told her someone was pissing on a pile of old cans.

As the door opened again and the man went back inside, the sound that came from within made her blood run cold. It was the unmistakable sound of a man in pain. The steel door slammed shut, cutting off an agonised scream.

She picked her way back to the pile of corrugated iron, carefully dragged out a section and, clutching it with both hands, stumbled back to the channel, gritting her teeth and silently swearing every time she made a sound. Kneeling at the edge, she lowered it across the gap. It covered the channel with a foot to spare either side, but now it was suspended above the water she could see it was badly corroded.

On hands and knees she eased herself onto the makeshift bridge, trying to spread her weight evenly. The iron sagged as she reached the middle. She steadied herself and exhaled, as if by so doing she would weigh less. The slimy murk six feet below was visible through a row of holes where once there were bolts.

She kept going, not taking another breath until she'd reached the other side. The shed was close now and she could hear voices and a low, continuous moan. She got to her feet, but crouched low and crept closer. The voices grew louder, carrying across the still night.

The Merc was close to the door. The sheds had been built on a slight rise. A gravel track extended from them into the darkness and, she supposed, across the wasteland to the road. She tiptoed over to the Merc and peered inside. The key was in the ignition.

Inside the shed, Doyle sat in an old armchair nursing a cup of tea, watching the lads bring Coulthard around with a few slaps. He was sitting here freezing his bollocks off and they were getting nowhere.

The lads were bored and listless now, no heart in it. Doyle was willing to bet they'd gotten everything they could out of this numpty, but you never knew. Men reacted in strange ways to pain. Some made stuff up to appease you; some became defiant and wouldn't even tell you what day it was. This geezer was an arrogant prick and fancied himself a hard man. Doyle sighed. Time to bring out the big guns.

Doyle put his mug down, eased himself out of the armchair and went over to the kettle. He filled it up at the butler sink, where in the old days Frank had kept eels fresh. As a little boy, Doyle used to stand on tiptoe and peer at them, horrified but fascinated by the writhing and thrashing.

He put the kettle onto the gas ring and turned to Coulthard, who was watching him nervously.

Coulthard was slumped on a kitchen chair. His shirt hung at his waist, his chest spattered with blood and snot from his broken nose and busted teeth.

'No more Mr Nice Guy,' said Doyle.

The kettle's whistle began to sing. He turned off the gas, wrapped a dirty tea towel around the handle and picked up the kettle. He nodded at the lads, who grabbed Coulthard's arms.

'One more time, Mr Coulthard. Did you kill my daughter?'

Despite the cold, Coulthard was covered in clammy sweat. 'How many times do I have to say it?' he cried. 'No! It wasn't me and I don't know who it was! All I did was make sure the investigator running the job couldn't get anywhere with it.'

'Tell me one more time,' said Doyle.

Spitting blood and struggling to breathe, Coulthard gabbled through his story again. 'After you clocked the blokes doing surveillance – and don't forget I was able to check and confirm you were the target – the investigator wanted to continue the op. But I told her we didn't have the bodies. I knew that wouldn't stop her, she's a stubborn cow, so to make sure I told the boss there was nothing in it, that we should shut the investigation down. So he closed the file.'

'You told me you were the boss. Now I find out from my partner that this bloke Nestor was the boss,' said Doyle.

Coulthard made a sucking sound. Doyle knew his mouth would be dry.

'I never said I was the big boss! I was boss of operations, yeah, but not the whole shooting match!'

'So what you're saying is that you're a wanker and you lied to me about what you could do.'

'No! Yes!' Coulthard was falling apart.

'So what about this bloke Nestor, then, the real boss. He shut down the job on your say-so?'

'Yeah! I was sorting it, just the way you wanted.'

Doyle brought his face close to Coulthard's.

'You lying toe rag. He closed the fucking job down off his own bat.'

Coulthard blanched.

'Well?' roared Doyle.

'Yeah, yeah, all right,' said Coulthard.

'Why?' demanded Doyle.

'He didn't say. And now he's dead so there's no way to find out.'

So Coulthard didn't know about Nestor's connection with Fernley-Price, thought Doyle, and that his dosh was tied up with the banker wanker. How must Nestor have felt, discovering that his money was now invested in Doyle's enterprises? As long as Doyle was doing well, so was Nestor. If Doyle went down, Nestor stood to lose everything. Of course he stopped the investigation.

Was that enough to make the geezer top himself? Guilt? Doyle couldn't stand not knowing. So Nestor was turning a blind eye to the misdeeds he was supposed to pursue – so what? It was the same in every bloody regulatory authority in the kingdom. There must be something else, but Doyle couldn't put his finger on it.

'I'm very disappointed,' he said to Coulthard as he advanced towards him with the steaming kettle.

Coulthard's eyes were wide with fear. 'I looked after your interests, didn't I?' he screamed. 'I didn't know the informant was your daughter and I didn't know Nestor was involved!'

'I can't hear you properly. Who killed my Gina then?' snarled Doyle.

The lads braced themselves and licked their lips. Doyle started to tip the kettle. He didn't want the water to go too far off the boil.

Outside, a motor started. Doyle paused. He looked at the lads and the lads looked back, gormless. The motor roared.

'For fuck's sake!' yelled Doyle.

The lads knew this cue. They ran to the door, fumbled with the latch and finally flung it open.

'The car!' one shouted.

The Merc was bouncing down the gravel incline, headlights ablaze. The lads shot after it. Doyle put down the kettle and ran out of the shed after them, registering on the way out that the light over the door wasn't on.

'Get that fucking car and bring the little toe rags in it to me!' he bellowed, as they ran down the incline shouting abuse at the disappearing tail lights.

From out of the darkness an old-fashioned milk bottle connected hard with the back of Doyle's head and he went down, face first.

Berlin dropped the milk bottle, still in one piece. They don't make them like that any more, she thought, running into the shed and straight to the astonished Coulthard. Plastic ties bound him to the kitchen chair. She grabbed an old knife from the sink and sliced through them with one cut. They were obviously from Poundsavers.

She pulled him to his feet and he hobbled after her, joints stiff from lack of circulation. Shuffling past Doyle's prone form he helped life return to his legs by giving Doyle a good kick in the guts.

'For fuck's sake, come on!' hissed Berlin.

He caught up and followed her across the creaking sheet of iron.

When they got to the other side, Berlin kicked it into the channel. Looking back they could see the Merc had hit a ditch and was hanging at an angle, its motor still roaring. The lads were caught in the glare from the high beams, standing there, staring at it.

Berlin and Coulthard ran like the clappers.

Berlin hailed a cab heading west down Roman Road. It pulled over and she opened the door.

'I'm going to resign,' mumbled Coulthard.

'No, you're not,' she replied. She leant on the cab door. He could see she was trembling with fatigue.

'Jesus, you put Doyle down,' he whispered. He didn't know who he should be more afraid of: her or Doyle.

'I wasn't even there,' she said. 'Some slick joyriders trashed his car and you took the opportunity to snap the ties and belt him. A tough bloke like you, in the gym all the time.'

She was just too smart for her own good. He wondered how much she had heard.

'How did you know they had me?'

When he got no reply he remembered his manners.

'I mean... look, thanks.' He glanced up and down the road, nervous. 'What was going on back there, with Doyle, I should explain. It was a misunderstanding.'

'You obstructed my investigation because you owed him.'

'Something like that,' he stuttered.

'Well, now you owe me.'

Now he knew who to fear most. She gestured and he climbed in the cab, as meek as a lamb. 'What are you going to do, you know, about all this?' he asked, his voice tight with trepidation.

'Bank it,' she said, and slammed the cab door.

44

A hot bath eased Berlin's aching back, but she knew that tomorrow she would feel it in her legs. She hadn't run so far, so fast in years. The contents of an ampoule had finally subdued the tremor in her muscles that she hadn't been able to control. She wanted to believe it was the adrenalin draining out of her system, but she knew it was more likely the onset of withdrawal because of the delay in getting to the heroin. It was a precursor of worse to come if she didn't sort something out.

Her world had been the antithesis of the stereotypical junkie's universe. She had lived an ordered, careful existence according to a strict timetable. Now she was descending into the chaotic lifestyle you'd associate with a rampant illegal addiction. And the real nightmare hadn't even begun.

She feared that Dempster would prove unreliable, but she had to keep that option open as the alternative was high risk. She hadn't heard a word from him since their row, but tomorrow she would be doing more of his dirty work. She had to keep her end of the bargain. Time was running out.

A sense of foreboding threatened to dominate her, but she had to get past it, and fast. Coulthard's gratitude and contrition would last about as long as her bath. She knew him too well. It wouldn't be long before the whole episode would become another one of his stories, where he escaped the clutches of the bad guy single-handed. Still, she didn't regret it. You wouldn't leave a dog in Doyle's hands, let alone a human being. Even if it was Coulthard. And she had eliminated one risk: she wouldn't have to worry about her disciplinary proceedings.

She eased herself out of the bath, wrapped herself in a thick towelling dressing gown and opened her computer. She had 'borrowed' an old version of analytical software from work, and now it would come in very handy.

*

Information is just a collection of discrete facts, perceptions and feelings. Subjecting it to a process produces intelligence: actionable knowledge. This was work that required perspiration, not inspiration. Sift, review, collate, eliminate.

Coulthard owed Doyle and interfered with Berlin's investigation, but where was the evidence to support the proposition that he killed Gina Doyle? He hadn't known who she was, and there was only a mobile number for her in the logs.

Gina wasn't the type to be easily lured to her death. The wound at her neck was very particular too. Berlin had a note from Thompson's description at the case conference: 'A bite or a tear. A wound from some kind of serrated edge or teeth that perforated the neck, almost severing the head.' Coulthard was a wheedler, a dodger, a manipulator. He avoided dirty work. And Gina's death had been dirty.

She had been wrong about him forcing Nestor to shut down the investigation. Nestor had taken the initiative there because . . . the thought took her nowhere. She looked at her charts and realised there was nothing to indicate Nestor's motives or to tie him to Gina.

When Doyle was interrogating Coulthard he said his partner had told him Nestor was the boss. Doyle also knew that Nestor had put a stop to the inquiries 'off his own bat'. Doyle hadn't elaborated on the nature of the partnership – domestic or business – or how the partner had come by his or her information about Nestor. Another broken connection, indicating a line of inquiry.

She had thought Nestor weak, but not corrupt. Nestor could have vetoed her investigation at any time. Why would he need to kill?

She struggled with the connections, but she couldn't tie any of them back to Gina's murder.

She sat back and reviewed her work. She took cold comfort from the fact that she was ahead of Flint and Thompson. She made a note of unresolved lines of inquiry: Nestor's inaudible conversation with an unidentified person who may have murdered him, the Doyle family file and Harvey Marks's account of their history, and now the intel from Doyle's interrogation of Coulthard. She wondered if she should have let the latter go on a bit longer, but dismissed the thought as uncharitable.

She had also known the victim, which gave her some insight into Juliet Bravo/Gina Doyle. It was all progress, of a sort. Logging names, places, vehicles, telephone numbers and all the other myriad facts, significant and seemingly insignificant, that swirl around an investigation was just the first stage. Teasing out the links between them would expose the gaps in her knowledge and provide a rationale for the next stage.

No one would NFA this investigation. She just had to keep her head on straight long enough to see it through.

The Sixth Day

45

Berlin knew she was being kept waiting quite deliberately, even though she was the first appointment of the day. It was a test.

She had woken with a splitting headache and for a brief moment had wondered why the day was so unwelcome. Then she had tried to move. Her knees ached and her legs were as stiff as boards. The one thought that sustained her was that Coulthard must feel much worse.

She wriggled her toes to get the blood moving through her taut muscles, determined to remain calm, to give no indication of weakness. This was one she had to tough out.

Through his office window Bonnington watched Berlin in the waiting room. She sat perfectly still, apparently reading a magazine, relaxed. Too relaxed. She looked tired, but she was alert, able to focus on what she was reading, so she hadn't got her hands on sedatives or tranquillisers. Which she would certainly need if she was in withdrawal.

She glanced up and caught him staring. Bonnington tasted bile at the back of his throat. He tried to tell himself that his anger should be directed only at the establishment that allowed this travesty to continue. It was wrong.

Berlin held his gaze. He felt his rage rising. She was a victim. He mustn't blame her. She needed his help. But it was no good. Her defiance was obvious. Discipline was the answer.

He opened his office door and stepped into the hall wearing his best smile.

'Berlin, would you like to come in?'

Berlin reclined on the purple beanbag and watched Bonnington squirm on his. A thin film of sweat beaded his upper lip.

'This is blackmail,' he snapped.

'I'm levelling the playing field,' she said. 'You think you have the right to make choices about my life, so I'm just taking a little bit of that power back. It's very simple. Dempster is convinced you're a killer and he wants me to help him prove it.'

'And you will if I don't give you a referral to another heroin pre-scriber?'

'Correct,' she said.

Bonnington flushed and sprang to his feet. 'This is all wrong. I'm going straight to the police and having this out. I'm not going to be blackmailed by a crooked policeman and a degenerate...' He stopped himself before he said it.

'Junkie,' she finished his sentence. Now she had him. He'd lost his cool and revealed his true feelings. She adjusted her tone to one of urgent persuasion.

'If you're charged with murder, or just taken in to help police with their inquiries, as they say, the papers will get hold of it. Even if the charges are dropped, you're finished professionally.'

This gave Bonnington pause. He sat down again and regarded her with a cold stare. It was disconcerting how quickly he seemed to regain his self-control.

'So what exactly have you got that you think would convince Dempster to charge me? I didn't kill her.'

Berlin took a moment. Gotcha.

'Her? I was talking about Lazenby.'

46

Thompson disliked this time of year. He arrived at work and left again in the dark. But what he particularly loathed was being kept in the dark all day.

The morning's steady stream of irritations had become an avalanche of frustration: incomplete logs, computer failures, calls not returned. This was the final bloody straw. Yesterday he had sent one of his outside team to find the old file on the Doyle family. Now he was reading an email that told him the file had been signed out of the archives to DCI Dempster.

Dempster was beginning to get on Thompson's nerves.

He stood up and reached for his coat. Flint sprang from his chair but Thompson waved him back. 'Keep at it, Flint. I need to see a man about a dog,' he said and strode out, dialling a number on his mobile.

Dempster had made light of snatching Berlin from Flint and Thompson, but it hadn't been nearly as easy or without consequence as he'd let her believe. The call from Thompson wasn't entirely unexpected. Now they were going to meet in what he hoped would be a damage limitation exercise.

Thompson had made the first move and had chosen the turf. They were going to meet at Becks in Red Lion Street. WC1. Well away from the police station. It wasn't Dempster's idea of lunch, but he had a feeling that Thompson was one of those types who would smirk if he had suggested sushi.

Dempster decided to keep shtum and let Thompson make the running. It would be a struggle for him to say nothing, but when necessary he could deliver the silent treatment. It seemed to work for Berlin. Or he would lie. He didn't have a problem with lying to another officer. He didn't know Thompson from a bar of soap and he had to cover his arse.

*

Thompson watched Dempster examine the menu in forensic detail.

'It better be good,' he said.

'I can guarantee it,' said Thompson. 'Everything's cooked in beef dripping, the old-fashioned way. This place hasn't been Jamie-Olivered.' He chuckled at his own joke, but Dempster didn't seem to get it. He's a queer fish, thought Thompson. He also noticed Dempster only seemed to have the one suit, which didn't fit him anyway.

A harassed waitress hovered over them. Thompson ordered black pudding, bacon, egg and chips, bread and butter and tea.

'I'll have the same,' said Dempster.

She grabbed a couple of plates of ready-buttered bread from a counter and plonked them down, then left them to it.

'What's your interest in Doyle?' Thompson jumped straight in.

'You're aware I'm here to support the taskings of the local Murder Investigation Team who are working Lazenby's murder. There may be a connection to Doyle.'

There was no connection and they both knew it, thought Thompson. He frowned. 'I didn't ask for a quote from operational policy, mate,' he muttered. He waited to see if Dempster would elaborate, but he just sat there. Thompson ate a piece of bread and butter. 'You signed out an old file on Doyle's father, the grandfather of my victim,' he said.

'Yes,' said Dempster.

'So, what's the connection to Lazenby?'

Thompson knew damn well that Dempster must have got the file for Berlin, in exchange for some underhand bit of business they were doing. Dempster didn't reply, so he probed from another angle.

'There was no reason for Berlin to run from us, you know.'

'Your bloke was chasing her.'

'Impetuous youth. He thinks it's a sign of disrespect when you're talking to someone and they run away.' He paused as the waitress returned with two enormous plates of food, each topped with a thick wedge of glistening, marbled black pudding. Thompson fell on it like a starving man.

'You just happened to be handy, did you? To do your Sir Galahad impression. Pass the brown sauce,' he said, mouth full.

Dempster stared at the plate of food as if it were a deadly weapon. 'She's important to my investigation,' he said.

'Yes. I understand you're in a difficult position. No resources, no snouts and no influence with the local team. They tell me you're on a frolic of your own, that the doctor's death was gang-related, if the weapon is any indication, and that they were after his drugs.'

'Look, Thompson, I was keeping an eye on Berlin, that's all. I followed the car you sent to the Limehouse Basin and saw her talking to the pair of you. When she ran, I saw an opportunity to win her confidence. Plus, she's not a suspect, is she, so why pursue her?'

'She hasn't got an alibi for either *her* informant or *her* boss. See the connection there, do you?' said Thompson.

'You can hardly think she's a prospect for the murder of the Doyle woman. And I thought Nestor was a suicide.'

'Most likely,' Thompson agreed grudgingly. 'We're still waiting on the post-mortem. These bloody cuts.' Thompson smiled at his joke, but again Dempster remained deadpan. 'Look, the last phone call Nestor made was to Berlin and that's what we were after – her voicemail. It was deleted, by her and then by the bloody telco. It could be something or nothing, but she's the only one who can tell us what he said.'

'Have you thought of asking her nicely?' said Dempster.

'Mate,' snapped Thompson, 'I don't need you to tell me how to do my job. Like I said, she doesn't have alibis for either of them so I'm entitled to treat her as a bloody suspect, not my best friend. She says she was home alone.'

Dempster sipped his builder's tea and grimaced. 'We both know she's not a contender. You're just looking for some leverage. I'll be straight with you, Thompson, I don't want her in the system.'

'Why not?'

'It wouldn't be good for her health, and that wouldn't be good for my investigation.'

Thompson munched on a chip and stared at Dempster, putting two and two together. 'Dr Lazenby.'

Dempster didn't respond.

'She was one of his patients,' Thompson said.

Dempster remained tight-lipped, which told Thompson everything he needed to know. He burped quietly. 'So now she's implicated in three deaths, not just two. Her informant, her boss and her doctor.'

Dempster poked at the food on his plate.

'You haven't touched your lunch,' observed Thompson.

'I've just remembered I'm a vegetarian.'

This was the final straw. Thompson wiped his mouth with a paper napkin, stood up, got a banknote out of his wallet and dropped it on the table.

'I don't know what your game is, Dempster, but stay out of mine. And make sure that the Doyle family file is on my desk first thing tomorrow morning.'

47

Thirty minutes later Dempster was waiting in the car outside Berlin's flat. He got out as she approached and followed her up the stairs. He's got an unhealthy interest in me, she thought, as she let them into the flat.

'Well?' he said, impatient.

'You're a bloody stalker, Dempster,' she said, and went to the bathroom.

When she came out the kettle was on, which she thought was a bit of a cheek – him acting as if he owned the place.

She handed him the mini recorder and he switched it on and replayed her exchange with Bonnington.

Dempster grimaced. This obviously wasn't the result he was after.

'I keep telling you he didn't kill Lazenby,' she said. 'But there is an issue around Merle Okonedo's death. Otherwise he would have said "I didn't kill anyone," or "I haven't murdered anybody," or even "I haven't done anything wrong." Something like that, not "I didn't kill her." His response was like a "tell" in poker.'

He knew she was right, but she could see he didn't like it.

'I knew it would incense him if a low-life like me threatened him. He recovered fast, but not fast enough. I'm telling you, there's something dodgy about Okonedo's death,' said Berlin.

'But that case isn't going anywhere, with all those eye witnesses saying it was an accident. It's a waste of time pursuing it,' he said, irate.

She regarded him with disgust. 'You're a piece of work, Dempster.'

He gave her a look that warned she was going too far. She tried to rein in her temper by telling herself that he had the upper hand. It didn't work. He was just another bloody copper who was only interested in a result.

'We're done! I'm not playing any more of your games!' She re-alised she was shouting and struggled to bring her voice back to a normal level. That didn't work either. 'I'm not going to be manipu-lated by you because of some stupid competition you think you're in with the local team!'

Dempster shouted back. 'But they're not working it! They're just waiting for the smack to surface and then they'll follow the bod-ies. You should know better than anyone what will happen when pharmaceutical-grade hits the streets: junkies who have been using the adulterated crap will be dropping like flies. Or don't you give a shit about the likes of them? Think you're a cut above the average addict?'

The kettle spluttered and boiled, the room filling with steam. Dempster moved to turn it off.

'Leave it!' she shouted. 'Just fuck off, Dempster! Fuck off out of my life!'

He walked out, leaving the door open.

She strode over and kicked it shut behind him.

Berlin dispatched a Scotch and fumed. Dempster had used her and then dumped her. Or had she dumped him? Now the bastard was on his own with the Lazenby inquiry and she could concentrate on Gina Doyle. 'Concentrate' in its loosest sense, given her current state of mind. Take it easy, she chided herself, you've got two hits left before things go pear-shaped.

She fired up the computer to work on her logs and charts. She must maintain some discipline and keep generating lines of inquiry if she was going to get anywhere.

But the row with Dempster bounced around in her brain. Her hope of a solution to the dope problem went out the door when he did. There was little prospect of Bonnington responding to the blackmail ploy either. It was conversation management, a gambit.

He was no fool and she couldn't see him caving in to some vague threat from a junkie.

At least Dempster had been good for something. He had retrieved the old Doyle family file for her. She reached for it where she had left it, right beside the computer. It wasn't there.

She knew straightaway Dempster had taken it with him. He must have grabbed it while she was in the bathroom. His exit had been planned from the minute he walked in. So he had dumped her. She felt a flicker of disappointment, but then dismissed it and tried to focus on assessing what Dempster's underhanded behaviour implied in her current situation. He wouldn't dare move on the forged prescriptions after what she'd done for him; it could get too messy. That was a result of sorts.

From the point of view of her investigation, the old Doyle file had yielded Retired Senior Constable Harvey Marks and brought her closer to understanding Gina's motivation. But what was the connection between her death and Nestor's? Del had told her that Nestor had shut himself in his office after Coulthard showed him the post-mortem photo and presumably told him she was Doyle's daughter. That night Nestor went off the deep end, literally. It remained to be seen if he had been murdered.

Coulthard owed Doyle, who suspected Coulthard had killed his daughter or knew who had. Coulthard had obstructed further surveillance, at Doyle's behest, but Nestor had NFA'd the file.

That had obviously puzzled Doyle too. He had said that his partner had told him Nestor was the boss at the Agency. So if the investigation was a problem for Nestor, he had dealt with it. He didn't need to kill the informant.

She was going around in circles. There had to be something in the intelligence that she hadn't managed to identify, but she was buggered if she could see it. She poured herself another Scotch and went back to her notes of the exchange between Doyle and Coulthard on this point. She had written:

Doyle (aggressive): So what about this bloke Nestor, then, the real boss. Do you know why he shut down the job?

Coulthard (hysterical): He didn't say. And now he's dead so there's no way to find out.

Maybe there was a way. Doyle had said his partner told him Nestor was the boss. So who was the partner?

If Doyle, Coulthard and Nestor were out of the frame for Gina's murder, then the partner moved in.

She clicked on Nestor's voicemail and played it again. She had slowed it down, speeded it up, cleaned it up as much as she could. It didn't matter; she didn't recognise the voice, couldn't hear what was being said and didn't have the expertise to enhance the audio. But a harsh, mocking laugh and the sound of someone sobbing was unmistakable.

48

Berlin believed in keeping your friends close and your enemies closer. Her friends were few and far between, so the room was never crowded. To accommodate her enemies, she'd have to book the Albert Hall.

She picked up her mobile and called Coulthard. Her caller ID was permanently blocked, so she knew there was a good chance he would answer.

'Acting General Manager Coulthard speaking.'

'So you're back at work then?' she said.

There was a pause. Now that the balance of power between them had shifted, Coulthard had to work out how to respond to her.

'I've been meaning to call you,' he said, adopting his reasonable voice.

'I beat you to it. I need to see you.'

'Where?'

'Here. My flat.'

'I don't think that's a good idea. I can't afford to be seen at your place.'

'Who's going to see you? No one's watching.'

This time the pause was meaningful. Okay, thought Berlin, maybe someone is watching. But were they watching him or her? She looked out the window.

'The BL. Thirty minutes.'

Berlin watched from the mezzanine as security went through Coulthard's bag. Coulthard had once proudly informed her that the tactical expandable baton, known as the Asp, had a high psychological deterrence factor on the street and low potential for tissue damage. A great combination.

It was illegal for civilians to carry them, and he'd obviously taken it with him when he'd left the force, but Coulthard had never quite gotten over the fact he wasn't a sworn officer any more.

The security guard waved Coulthard through. He'd remembered to leave his Asp in the boot of the car then. He scanned the lobby, saw her watching him and limped over to the escalator. The lights picked out his bruises.

'Facelift went well,' she said, as he approached.

'Yeah. Did we have the same surgeon?'

Her own bruises had faded, but the cut from the hoodies' attack at Weaver's Fields had left a scar running through her eyebrow.

She wanted coffee and a fig roll. Coulthard dutifully went off to get them. The BL had the best fig rolls in London. Fly cemeteries, they used to call them as kids. A shiver ran through her. Where was all this stuff about her childhood coming from? She had a sudden image of a blank, whitewashed wall. She couldn't see over it and it extended into infinity in all directions. A web of tiny, hairline fissures on its surface were becoming cracks.

Coulthard moved the coffee and cakes from the tray to the table and sat down.

'Are you okay?' he inquired, almost solicitous.

'Yeah, fine.'

'You've gone a bit pale.'

She reached for the fig roll and took a bite. 'Low blood sugar,' she said, and opened her laptop. 'I want you to listen to something.'

Suddenly distant voices, one of them Nestor's, shouted at airy nothing.

She could see the cogs creaking as Coulthard tried to decide what he was listening to and what he could gain from this situation. But he wasn't a quick thinker.

'Do you recognise the other voice?' she said.

'Er, can you play it again?'

He didn't recognise it. If he had he would have been cockier, believing he now knew something she didn't. But she went along with it, just in case he was hedging his bets. She played the file again.

'You know the senior management team,' she said. 'You've been to meetings with Nestor. Is it one of them?'

He raised his hands. 'Honestly, I'm not sure. Perhaps if I knew the context it would help.'

Typical, she thought. A pathetic and transparent attempt to fish for more information. Knowledge is power.

'Look, Coulthard, if you've got even the slightest idea who it might be, give it up. I'm not frigging about here. I'm already in the shit. I'd love to drop you into an even bigger pile and I'll do it the minute you aren't useful to me any more.'

She spoke with quiet menace. The studious young man sitting across from them reading a book with the title *Why Everyone Owes Everyone and No One Can Pay* picked up his bag and moved to another table.

Coulthard protested. 'Berlin, mate, I don't know.'

She went to close the laptop, but Coulthard reached over and stopped her.

'Look, if I find out for you, can we call it quits?'

'In your dreams,' she said, and snapped the lid down.

'Email me the file,' Coulthard wheedled.

Berlin's expression gave nothing away.

'One of the blokes working on the Doyle and Nestor investigation is a mate of mine,' said Coulthard.

'Flint,' she said.

If he was surprised she knew, he kept it well hidden.

'Yeah. His team has interviewed dozens of people. Maybe one of them will recognise the voice.'

She finished up her fig roll as she thought it through. Coulthard's eyes were bright with expectation. He wants this too much, she decided.

'No,' she said.

Coulthard stood up. 'Fair enough. Anything else?'

'No, fuck off,' she said.

He pushed his fig roll towards her. 'Here, have mine. I can't eat it anyway. My jaw's too sore.'

He limped away. She watched him travel down the escalator. The moment he got to the bottom he took out his mobile. Calling Flint, no doubt.

She already had her own mobile in her hand.

'Limehouse Police Station,' a bored voice answered.

'Detective Inspector Thompson, please,' she said.

'Who should I say is calling?'

When she didn't reply, there was a deep sigh on the other end. 'Putting you through.'

Flint's mobile chirped at the same moment as the landline on Thompson's desk rang.

'DCI Thompson here, how may I help?'

The person on the other end didn't introduce herself, but Thompson recognised her voice. She cut to the chase. 'Do you know The Approach? Can you come alone?'

'Yes and yes.'

'In an hour?'

Thompson glanced over at Flint, but he was intent on his own call, speaking in a low voice.

'Suits me, sir,' Thompson said and hung up.

Flint paused as Thompson stood and put his coat on. 'I'll call you back,' he said and hung up. He stood up and reached for his coat.

'Stay here and check those witness statements again, will you, Flint?'

'What? What for?'

'We might have overlooked something. Police work is all about patience.'

'So where the bloody hell are you off to again?' retorted Flint.

Thompson gave him a look that served as a reminder of the chain of command.

'Sir, look, sir,' blustered Flint. 'What I meant, sir, was – well I feel my skills aren't being properly used in these inquiries. As second in command I feel I should be kept informed.'

Thompson's tone was mild. 'Quite right, Detective Sergeant Flint. I should inform you that I have just received an email with the post-mortem report on Nestor attached,' he said. 'It records that the body showed no signs of defensive wounds, no bruising or other signs of assault, and his blood alcohol was off the chart. Cause of death: cardiac failure due to hypothermia.'

He paused to give Flint time to build up a nice head of trepidation. 'I should further inform you that now we've definitely only got one body – because Mr Nestor either fell while bladdered or took his own life – we'll be regarded as over-resourced. Once I report this to my senior officers, I dare say there will be reassignments.'

The minute the door closed behind Thompson, Flint was back on his phone.

49

Fifteen minutes later Flint put a pint of Guinness on the table for Coulthard, and settled down with his Stella. Coulthard picked up his glass and drank half of it in a single gulp. Flint took in his swollen nose and the livid purple bruises around his eyes. 'So who was it, mate? Your bookie or your dealer?' asked Flint.

'Very funny,' snapped Coulthard.

'Your missus then?' said Flint, without a twitch of humour.

Coulthard was clearly unimpressed. He drank the rest of his pint in silence.

Flint had never seen him like this. He was always smiling, ready with a quick joke and commiserations if things weren't going your way. Whatever had happened to him, the bloke was shaken, no doubt about it.

Flint was under no illusions. Coulthard was a crafty bastard who would put a knife in your ribs with one hand while slapping your back with the other. His charm had obviously worn a bit thin with someone.

'I'm in a bit of bother, mate,' Coulthard said eventually. He wiped his mouth with the back of his hand.

'Come on then,' said Flint. 'Don't keep me in suspenders.'

'It was Doyle.'

'Don't tell me you didn't pay up?' said Flint in disbelief.

'You put me on to the prick,' hissed Coulthard.

'And I warned you! I told you he's well known around the manor as a source of funds, but he takes no prisoners. Don't fucking put this on me!'

'Yeah, well, it wasn't that anyway. That debt was dealt with.'

'How?' asked Flint.

'I did him a favour,' said Coulthard.

'Jesus Christ! At work?'

Coulthard barely nodded.

'You stupid prick! How did he find out where you worked?'

Coulthard shrugged.

'You told him, didn't you?'

Coulthard looked away.

'You and your big mouth,' said Flint. 'What happened?' he asked, wondering if he really wanted to know.

'He thinks I killed her. The informant. His daughter.'

Flint didn't miss a beat. 'And did you?'

'Leave it out. That's not even funny.'

'Doyle must have his reasons. You better tell me what they are,' said Flint, and picked up their empty glasses. 'I'll get them in.'

Flint didn't want another drink, but he needed an excuse to get away from Coulthard for a minute to think about how he was going to handle this. Evidence about what Coulthard was going to tell him would be inadmissible unless he was cautioned. Coulthard knew that. But if Flint cautioned him, Coulthard would just tell him to fuck off and leave.

They'd stayed in touch since the uniform days, but Coulthard had left the force under a cloud. He was too free with his fists and his tackle. Flint was doing okay in the Met, taking a degree they were paying for to improve his prospects. He needed to stay sweet with Coulthard: he knew a lot of people and his way around other law enforcement agencies, which was always handy. There were also one or two things Flint had done when he was in uniform that were best left buried. And Coulthard was a grave robber. It was tricky. He was caught between a rock and a first-class prick.

Flint put the fresh pints on the table.

'Took your time,' said Coulthard, and gave him a look that said he understood exactly what process Flint had been going through at the bar.

Flint almost blushed. 'You've put me in a difficult position, mate.'

'That's nothing compared to how difficult it will be if you don't help me out of this mess,' Coulthard replied with his first smile. Flint noticed it was crooked.

'What can I do? I've got my own problems. I'm going to be off the Murder Investigation Team and back to volume crime if the old bastard has his way,' moaned Flint.

'Happy days, mate,' Coulthard said as he raised his glass.

They sat and drank in morose silence for a few minutes.

'I blame that meddling fucker,' said Coulthard suddenly.

'Who?' asked Flint. The list of Coulthard's enemies was long, and growing all the time.

'Berlin. Who else?' replied Coulthard.

Flint was surprised.

'It was her that started this whole mess,' said Coulthard bitterly.

'Like she twisted your arm to borrow five grand from Oily Doyley.'

'That was a straightforward business transaction and would have stayed that way if she hadn't decided to play Lone Ranger after the investigation was shut down.'

'Business transaction? That's rich, coming from the man whose job it is to protect the financially excluded from these vicious predators.'

'Look,' said Coulthard, 'do you want this intel or not, and what are you going to do for me if I give it to you?'

'How do I know until you tell me what it is? You sound like a fucking snout.'

Coulthard sighed. 'Okay. We're mates, aren't we?'

Flint raised his hand and they executed a weak high-five.

'I tell you what,' said Flint. 'If it helps me get one over Thompson, you can name it. Whatever you want.'

Coulthard raised his glass and drank to that proposition. 'She's got the voicemail that Nestor left on her phone the night he died,' he announced.

'What? Impossible. The telecommunications company said it had been deleted by her and them.'

'The smart bitch had downloaded it onto her computer.'

Flint hadn't even known such a thing was possible. He felt like an idiot. But if he hadn't known, he was fucking sure that Thompson wouldn't either.

'How did you come by this information?' he quizzed Coulthard.

'She played it to me. Well, edited highlights. She doesn't know who the other geezer is and wanted to know if I could identify him.'

Flint was suddenly sceptical. 'What other geezer? And what do you mean by edited highlights? Did she tell you it was Nestor's voicemail?'

'Mate, I would stake my life on it. It was him and someone else going gangbusters.'

Flint saw a world of possibilities open up. 'My round. Fancy something a bit stronger?'

*

Flint and Coulthard walked out of the pub into the bone-jarring chill. Suddenly they were very pissed. Flint noticed Coulthard peering about.

'What's up, mate?'

'That bastard Doyle could still be on my case. I dunno where he is or what he's doing. Could be round any fucking corner.'

'Tell you what, mate,' said Flint. 'Let's go and find my snout. He's well in touch with all forms of pond life around here and he might have something on Doyle we could use.'

50

Thompson watched Berlin at the bar. They were in what would once have been called the snug. Most pubs served tea and coffee now, so you could meet someone in a boozer at any time of the day or night without appearing to be an alcoholic.

Berlin put their drinks on the table. Thompson squinted up at the malts on display over the bar.

'A decent enough selection,' he said, taking a sip of his Ardbeg and savouring the pungent aftertaste. He'd heard someone say it was like drinking surgical spirit, but that was an immature palate speaking. Berlin's palate was obviously very mature. 'This drop is certainly more than acceptable.'

'You're a committed Scotch man then,' she said.

'Wife took me up there for my birthday,' he explained.

They drank in silence while he waited for her to say her piece.

'I'm sure you understand why I feel a sense of obligation to Gina Doyle,' she said.

'And I'm sure you understand why I don't like civilians poking around in my investigations,' he responded.

'You're swimming against the tide there, Thompson. Of all the experts you use, how many are warranted officers? There are tens of thousands of civil enforcement jobs encroaching on what was once police turf, from benefit fraud to child protection. Even prisons have been privatised. Law and order has been outsourced.'

Thompson knew it was all too true. When they'd introduced Police and Community Support Officers, then Volunteers, it was like watching the Metropolitan Police go into reverse gear.

'It was ever thus,' he sighed. 'It will be back to the tithing-man and the Shire-Reeve next,' he mused. He sensed that Berlin's attitude towards him was softening. The Scotch wouldn't hurt in that respect.

'I want to help, not hinder,' she said. She got out her laptop and fired it up, then double-clicked a file and unfurled a diagram of symbols and coloured lines.

Thompson peered at it. 'A powerful bit of kit that,' he said, impressed.

'I borrowed the software from work,' she explained.

In other words an illegal copy, thought Thompson. 'I've never been able to get a handle on it,' he said.

'A visual representation throws up options that may not otherwise have been considered,' she said, bringing up more charts on the screen. They were populated with icons for telephones, cars, premises, locations and people, the data listed beneath each graphic linked by different coloured lines. 'Especially where there are gaps.'

She pointed to an empty box beneath the icon labelled 'Victim'. 'It struck me that no one has reported her missing.'

He didn't respond, reluctant to give too much away.

'Have they?' she pressed.

'No,' he admitted. 'The national bureau's got the photo. In the event someone walks into a nick and reports a missing woman fitting her description, we should get the alert straightaway. Or when someone gets around to it.'

Thompson reflected ruefully that if he had officers half as efficient as Berlin he would be happy. 'Doyle lost contact with Gina when she left home,' he said. 'He tried to find her, using his own resources, but with his aversion to the law he didn't report it, of course.'

'So I heard,' said Berlin.

It occurred to Thompson that he was sitting here discussing the case with a witness. The whisky was talking.

'When we checked the records her mother had registered her birth but entered "Father unknown" on the form,' he said. 'There's no doubt she was his daughter: we've run the DNA.'

'Doyle doesn't like a paper trail,' said Berlin.

'That's an understatement,' responded Thompson. 'It doesn't look like she used her mother's surname, Baker; at any rate we haven't found any trace of it. Nothing from her clothes. And as you know, her phone, wallet, bag – whatever she was carrying had gone. The divers didn't find anything in the lock.'

'Have you seen the old file on the Doyles?' asked Berlin.

'Not yet,' said Thompson, giving her a meaningful look. She had the decency to look embarrassed and quickly took their glasses and went to the bar. He had to make a decision about all this, and fast.

'I want you to try this,' she said, returning with two single malts.

In for a penny, in for a pound, he decided. 'Look, Berlin, you probably know more about her than anyone at the moment. There must be something you picked up on that would help us.'

He was making it clear that information sharing would be a two-way street. He would probably live to regret it.

'I've given you everything,' she said. 'She was in her mid-thirties. Smart suits and shirts. London accent. Worked as something in the City. Her mum loved the Juliet Bravo television show. Very good-looking. I once saw a sleazy tourist hit on her. I would say she was disdainful of men.'

'That's the first time you've mentioned that,' said Thompson.

'Is it? I don't see how it would have helped identify her though. She's hardly alone there.'

'So what did you talk about when you met with her?'

'The meaning of life.'

He could see she was serious.

'There is something else,' she said, and sipped her whisky.

Thompson had been a copper a long time. He knew patience was always rewarded in the end. He sat back and waited, watching as she weighed up the pros and cons of this new sharing relationship.

'Nestor's voicemail. Someone else was there. But I don't know who it is and I haven't got the tools to enhance it.'

She fished some headphones out of her pocket, plugged them into the computer and offered him an earpiece. He took it, leaning forward, concentrating intensely on the disembodied voices in his ear.

'Play it again,' he said.

Berlin clicked replay. 'Who is it? Do you recognise the voice?'

He drained his glass and stood up.

To his dismay, Berlin did likewise.

51

Fernley-Price hobbled out of the Abbey – a very discreet private hospital – and onto Great Portland Street. Thank God he had managed to avoid the NHS. He didn't know much about these things, but he felt sure that in the public sector they would have dragged the police into it.

A taxi drew up alongside him, but he waved it away and looked around for a bus stop. Actually, he didn't know which number bus would take him home. Christ, he was like a helpless infant. His jaw was wired up, so he could only suck protein shakes through a straw. The dope they had him on was pretty good, but they had dried him out and as the alcohol had left his body an awful clarity hit home. He had sunk about as low as a man could go.

He should go to the police and shop Doyle, good and proper, but it was a high-risk strategy with a huge downside, particularly without a bloody good lawyer. He could make a clean breast of the whole sordid business, but who was going to represent an insolvent hedge-fund manager on the strength of an IOU? The word of a gentleman banker was worthless these days. They would probably hang him high.

Bugger the buses; he would take the Tube. He was heading up Great Portland Street towards the station when a sign caught his eye. The Green Man. Just keep going, old man, he told himself. The door opened as he passed and that unmistakable aroma, *eau de pub*, drifted out. Fernley-Price took a deep breath.

A patron who was leaving the establishment kindly held the door open. Fernley-Price limped across the threshold and fronted up to the bar. The barmaid stood, impassive, as he hung his cane on a stool and fished in his pockets. He found a crumpled tenner.

'Otch. Arge,' he said, without moving his teeth or lips. Just as well I don't have to ask for a gottle of geer, he thought.

The barmaid dispensed a double Scotch from the optic, plonked it on the bar, then plucked a straw from a dispenser and dropped it into the glass.

'That's the short straw,' she said. 'Eers.'

Soon after he'd stumbled into The Green Man, Fernley-Price stumbled out again.

He had a better drinks cabinet at home.

52

Thompson pressed the intercom button. He still wasn't sure how Berlin had persuaded him to bring her along. He'd had a distinct feeling that if he refused she would have followed him, and he hadn't wanted to spend his time looking for a tail. He also had to admit she had some smarts and, unlike Flint, she didn't seem to be motivated purely by self-interest and ego.

He pressed the button again. The luxury warehouse conversion was right on the river. The seagulls and pigeons jostled for roosting space with CCTV cameras, which actually swivelled when you approached. This time there was a muffled response from the intercom.

'Detective Chief Inspector Thompson here, sir. May we have a word?' he shouted into the tiny grille, holding his warrant card up to the camera. Berlin stayed out of shot.

The outer door clicked open and they proceeded into the vestibule.

Berlin would have sworn the scent of rum, sugar and spices was still seeping from the massive oak timbers that hung low over their heads. Trade. It was why the Romans used this port in Britannia. A deep tidal river, good for berthing ships, but narrow enough just here to be bridged. Trade still provided a reason for the city's existence, but now it was in something called 'invisibles'. She reflected that the term was prescient. The invisibles had disappeared.

Thompson pressed the lift button and turned to her. 'I don't want to hear a word out of you, okay?' he said. 'Okay?'

She nodded and put her finger to her sealed lips.

They rode up in the lift in silence. He couldn't be less like Dempster, she thought; he was a man of few words, and a placid, methodical, old-style copper through and through.

When they reached the fourth floor the doors opened onto a carpeted hallway with just the one door leading off. A camera swivelled to monitor their progress. Thompson knocked and a few seconds later the door opened.

Jeremy Fernley-Price swayed before them. The smell of alcohol oozed from every pore. His head was encased in a wire frame, which pinned his jaw. He grunted and stepped aside to let them enter, gesturing with his cane. The flat was about the same size as Berlin's local supermarket.

Fernley-Price followed them into a capacious sitting room with floor-to-ceiling windows overlooking the river. Berlin walked across and looked down on what had once been Execution Dock. The pirates they hanged there were kept in a metal cage, a gibbet, until the tide had washed over their bodies three times. Punishment was poetic then, she thought. Now it was humane, but prosaic. Pity.

'This is Catherine Berlin, sir. A colleague,' she heard Thompson say. She turned back into the room and nodded at Fernley-Price, who couldn't nod back. He raised his cane a couple of inches in greeting then gingerly lowered himself into a leather recliner.

'Been in an accident, have we, sir?' inquired Thompson. She could see he was nonplussed. The whole point of the exercise was to hear the man's voice again, but here he was, speechless.

'We just wanted to clarify a couple of points about your relationship with Ludovic Nestor. But I see you are indisposed. You told us last time we spoke that he was a client of yours. Sir?'

Tap the cane once for yes, twice for no, thought Berlin. This was bloody hopeless.

'Perhaps you could write down the date of the last time you saw him, sir?'

Fernley-Price groaned. Berlin gazed about at the empty pizza boxes, dirty glasses and discarded shirts. He should get a new cleaner, she thought. No doubt he would have a woman who came in 'to do'.

Fernley-Price had levered himself out of the recliner and was hunting among the sea of paper on a massive desk for his diary. Berlin thought it was a ploy. Surely he would have an electronic calendar, probably a Blackberry, as well as a cleaner. He might be unable to speak, but that didn't mean he wouldn't try to treat them like plonkers.

'May I use the facilities?' she asked.

Fernley-Price waved a hand in the direction of a door leading off the sitting room. She avoided looking at Thompson, but could feel him beaming a warning her way. She stepped out of the room into a long hallway and gently closed the door behind her.

Thick carpet ran the length of the hall and the heavy timber doors were beautifully hung on silent hinges. Perfect. She decided to start at the far end, so that she would be back near the sitting-room door by the time Thompson or Fernley-Price came looking for her.

Her movements were swift and precise. The first door opened onto what was apparently a guest room. The single bed was made up, and there was nothing in the wardrobe or on the bureau.

The next room was a library. Floor-to-ceiling bookshelves, with mobile ladder attached. Soft lights that came on as you entered. Deep chairs.

This wasn't how the other half lived in London; this was how the top ten per cent lived. They owned two hundred and seventy-three times more than the poorest, according to *Newsnight*. Berlin doubted that Fernley-Price had needed a one hundred and ten per cent low-doc mortgage. Unlike hers, which she'd only finally managed to get through a broker who advertised: 'No deposit? No credit history? No problem!'

She backed out and closed the library door behind her. Two

doors remaining. She hesitated between them. She could hear Thompson in the sitting room. His voice seemed to be getting louder, and she wondered if he was approaching the door to the hallway or if it was some kind of warning. She took the door closest to her and went for it.

Thompson was becoming increasingly frustrated with Fernley-Price and anxious about what Berlin was up to. He raised his voice, addressing Fernley-Price as if he were deaf. He was obviously drunk and possibly drugged, but Thompson thought he could also detect recalcitrance and a reluctance to cooperate.

There was no point taking him to the station in that condition. Plus he would have to call out the doctor, who would probably deem him unfit for questioning. He'd better retrieve Berlin and depart.

'I'll just see what's keeping my colleague, sir,' he said. Fernley-Price looked puzzled, as if he had forgotten that there was anyone else there.

At that moment, Berlin appeared. Thompson was relieved, until she opened her mouth.

'Where's your coat, sir?' she said to Fernley-Price. 'We'd like you to come with us, if you don't mind.'

What the hell was she playing at? She held Thompson's eye and gave him a nod that said she knew what she was doing. Did she? He decided to play along.

Fernley-Price was bemused. He waved his cane at Berlin, a gesture of dismissal. But instead of backing off, she grabbed it, grasped his arm with her other hand and dragged him out of the chair. Fernley-Price squealed with pain.

'Let me help you up, sir,' she said.

With Fernley-Price settled in the back seat and Thompson at the wheel, Berlin punched a Poplar High Street address into the sat nav.

An imperious voice announced it was calculating the route, which it said was 2.5 miles and would take eleven minutes.

'Liar,' said Berlin. 'It will take at least twenty.' She addressed Fernley-Price over her shoulder. 'This is very kind of you, sir. Given your current disability, we appreciate your assistance by other means.'

Fernley-Price didn't respond. She saw Thompson check him in the rear-view mirror, no doubt hoping he wouldn't throw up or die en route. Berlin hoped that her comment would also reassure Thompson.

Thompson drove according to the sat nav's insistent instructions. It took them twenty minutes to reach their destination. No one spoke. Gentle snoring indicated their passenger was out for the count.

When they arrived at their destination, Thompson gave her a look that she took to mean he was beginning to see a method in her madness. He parked illegally, taking a 'Police' sign from the glove box and propping it on the dashboard. Rousing Fernley-Price was not easy.

'Come on, sir, out you come,' said Thompson, helping him out of his seat.

Berlin positioned herself on the other side of Fernley-Price and together they steered him along the pavement and down a side street.

Thompson spoke through the hole in the thick glass that shielded the receptionist from the germs of the public. He flashed his warrant card and explained what he wanted.

She picked up a phone, spoke briefly into it, then hung up. 'They'll be waiting for you,' she said.

Fernley-Price was leaning heavily against the wall, dazed. 'Air are?' he asked.

Berlin knew this was 'Where are we?' but just smiled and patted his arm. 'Not to worry, sir,' she said. 'Won't be long now.'

The trio made their way down a long, dimly lit corridor. There was a faint smell of antiseptic in the air as they pushed through a set of double doors made of heavy-duty plastic, which swished to a close behind them. It was colder in the small room they'd entered, and the sudden chill seemed to bring Fernley-Price to a higher level of consciousness.

'Ang on,' he said, and tried to dig his heels in.

Berlin and Thompson propelled him forward. A man in a white coat was standing in the middle of the room in front of a hospital trolley. They walked right up to him. Thompson nodded and he stepped away.

Berlin knew what was coming but it didn't help. A shudder went through her that shook the teeth in her head. The air went out of her lungs and she held onto Fernley-Price as much for support as to hold him up.

The body was covered by a white sheet that reached the shoulders. The face was frozen in a pale mask, lips blue, eyes closed. The jagged wound at Gina Doyle's throat was no less livid than it had been the first time Berlin had seen it.

A soft, tremulous moan began deep in Fernley-Price's chest and erupted through his rigid mouth as a strangled sob. He dropped his cane and fell forward, his arms outstretched.

'My darling,' he whispered, as clear as day, and passed out.

Thompson and Berlin watched grimly as the paramedic worked on the unconscious Fernley-Price.

'Could be a clot, with those head injuries,' said Thompson as the doors of the ambulance closed. It took off, siren wailing. 'He might never regain consciousness long enough to be questioned.'

'Think he did it?' asked Berlin.

'The grief could actually be remorse,' said Thompson.

'And Nestor?'

'It's doubtful. The P-M found no sign of a struggle. Then again, he was so pissed it would have only taken a nudge. Email me that audio file when you get home,' he said. 'I'll get forensics to clean it up. We should find his conversation with Nestor interesting.'

Berlin noted the 'we'.

53

Flint parked up on a double yellow line and he and Coulthard poured themselves out of the car. Flint went to the window of The Wild Cherry vegetarian café and pressed his nose against the glass, peering inside.

'There he is!' he shouted to Coulthard, who was pissing up against the wall of the London Buddhist Centre next door. Coulthard zipped up and they pushed and shoved each other, fighting to get through the café door first, schoolboys on an excursion.

They burst in and were greeted by a lull in the patrons' conversations, which were already being conducted in muted tones. They staggered to the table of a solitary diner and flopped into the spare chairs. Bonnington scowled as Flint flung an arm around his shoulder.

'Hello, my little mate!' Flint exclaimed, dragging Bonnington's head down into the crook of his arm.

'You're drunk. What the hell do you want?' muttered Bonnington, shoving him off.

'How about a nice lamb kebab?' Coulthard chimed in.

A couple at a nearby table shuddered.

Coulthard extended his hand to Bonnington. 'I don't think we've met. John Coulthard, Financial Services Agency. I believe in working in partnership with the community. That's you, mate. You probably don't know about us and the very important work we do hunting loan sharks.'

'And borrowing money from them!' added Flint, roaring with laughter.

Coulthard gave him a friendly punch in the arm.

Bonnington regarded Coulthard with greater interest.

'Let's go somewhere more private,' said Flint. 'Your gaff will do nicely, Daryl. I imagine it's not too far from here, right?'

Bonnington didn't move.

'Come on, my son. Hospitality!' said Flint.

Coulthard and Flint stumbled to their feet and stood either side of Bonnington.

Bonnington's flat was spartan and he was clearly not one to entertain. He made dandelion coffee, but Flint and Coulthard were only interested in something stronger. Bonnington gestured to a cupboard, but when Flint flung it open it contained only noodles, spices and shaoxing cooking wine. Coulthard grabbed the bottle and waved it about.

'I saw this on *Masterchef*,' he said. 'It's very good in Hainan drunken chicken.'

'Yeah, but not so good for drunken detectives,' said Flint. 'Daryl here is a Life Addictions Coordinator,' he explained to Coulthard. 'Works with junkies.'

'Substance abusers,' corrected Bonnington. 'And their families.'

Coulthard poured two tumblers of shaoxing and handed one to Flint.

'He's a mine of information,' said Flint.

'Only when it's in my clients' interests,' retorted Bonnington.

'What, no cash incentives?' inquired Coulthard. 'Chocks away!'

He downed the wine, pulled a face and spat it out. He was drunk, but not so wasted that he was impervious to Bonnington's all too apparent disdain. 'What about your precious little cone of silence then?' he inquired with a sneer. 'I thought you lot – social workers and the like – took a very high and mighty stand when it came to your clients' privacy.'

'I look at the bigger picture,' responded Bonnington.

Coulthard wandered over to a computer in the corner. The modem lights were flashing and he jiggled the mouse.

'Don't touch that!' hissed Bonnington.

Coulthard was taken aback by this flash of rage as Bonnington strode across the room. The screen was suddenly filled with weapons and images of bloody combat. It looked like some sort of war game to Coulthard, but Bonnington yanked the plug and the display died. He gave Coulthard a cold smile. 'Just a hobby,' he said, then turned to Flint. 'Now, what is it you gentlemen wanted?'

'Know a loan shark called Doyle? I should imagine your clients are often in need of a few bob to tide them over,' said Flint.

'Why are you interested in Doyle?' asked Bonnington.

This bloke was giving Coulthard the shits with his bloody superior attitude. 'Call of nature,' he announced, and wandered off through the flat.

'Do you know him or not?' said Flint.

'I know of him. Everyone does. Oily Doyley. Is this about Sheila Harrington?'

'Who?' asked Flint.

'The woman whose dog was mutilated and killed.'

'No, mate, sad as it sounds. It's about the girl who was mutilated and killed.'

'I see,' said Bonnington in a flat tone. 'The girl who was found in the Limehouse Basin?'

Flint nodded.

'I heard she was Doyle's daughter. Is that true?' asked Bonnington.

'Yes, mate. It's true. I'm in charge of the investigation actually.'

Coulthard, poking about in another room, could hear Flint. You pillock, he thought. The snout was supposed to give you information, not the other way round. He went back to what could only loosely be described as the living room.

'I believe one of your colleagues is on a similar quest,' said Bonnington, addressing Coulthard.

'What?' He thought about it for a moment. 'You mean Berlin?' said Coulthard. His eyes lit up when Bonnington nodded. 'Has she been around here asking questions?'

Bonnington said nothing, his face inscrutable.

Coulthard looked at Flint. Flint shrugged. He'd made it clear that Bonnington was his snout, and his alone. No one knew about him.

'So how do you know her then?' asked Coulthard.

'I'm going to invoke the cone of silence at this point,' said Bonnington, smug.

Coulthard put it together. 'Fuck me, she's one of your clients!'

Flint shot out of his chair and high-fived Coulthard. 'She's a junkie!' he bellowed.

Bonnington gave a tight smile. Ten out of ten. 'If you find that information useful, gentlemen, perhaps you could do me a favour,' he said. 'I've got a problem with her and an officer called Dempster. You can help me out with that.'

Flint could feel sobriety creeping up. It was a shitty feeling. The sky, the colour of wet slate, was about to dump more snow as he stumbled out of Bonnington's. He got in the car and turned on the motor. Coulthard got in beside him and cranked up the heater.

'I'll take up that offer now, mate. We can meet my needs and those of your creepy snout in one fell swoop,' said Coulthard.

'This is serious stuff,' warned Flint.

Coulthard gave him a look which said 'nervous nelly'. 'You said whatever I wanted.' He waggled his finger and smiled, but there was nothing warm or friendly about it.

Flint was afraid that Coulthard could drop him in it in a heartbeat. He was the sort of bloke that would put the bullets in the gun, then watch with a smirk as you fired it so he had something on you to bank.

'Yeah, okay. So what do you want?' muttered Flint.

Coulthard pushed the car heater to max and laid it out.

Bonnington stood at the window and watched Coulthard and Flint drive away. Guardians of law and order who so rarely acted out of principle they couldn't believe anyone else did. Fools. But useful fools. They could be very handy in getting Dempster and that bitch off his back. God knows, there was plenty of precedent when it came to the authorities fitting people up.

Berlin's behaviour this morning had confirmed what he'd suspected for some time: that the arm of the corrupt State was reaching out for him. He sat down at the computer to read the news on sites he trusted. He never watched television. People were blinded by misinformation from the media, weakened by vice and betrayed by governments who baulked at defending traditional values against moral relativism. Purity of purpose conferred moral authority. Why did so few understand that? The rest would have to learn the hard way. He had dedicated himself to providing the lesson.

54

The police station was busy with all the usual things that came out at night.

Dempster had felt uneasy since the argument with Berlin and sneaking out with the Doyle file. He didn't know why he cared, but it had bothered him. So he had photocopied the file for her and put it in an envelope, even though she had a mind like a steel trap and had probably memorised the contents. It would be a sort of peace offering. He would take it around tomorrow, but he might as well drop the original in to Thompson now. It would save him doing it in the morning.

When he got to the Doyle incident room he could see that the office Thompson shared with Flint was deserted. A constable had his feet up on a desk, chatting on his mobile. He didn't move when Dempster walked over and stood in front of him.

'Hang on,' he said, with a weary sigh.

'I've got a file here for DCI Thompson,' said Dempster.

The constable glanced at the office. 'He's not in.'

A real joker, thought Dempster. 'When will he be back?' he asked.

Irritation crossed the constable's face. He shrugged. 'Dunno. In the morning I s'pose.'

Dempster dropped the file on the constable's desk. 'Give that to him as soon as he arrives,' he ordered and left.

The constable didn't wait until he was out of earshot to resume his conversation. 'Sorry about that. A fucking suit.'

Dempster ignored the jibe. The only people who thrived in this environment were corrupt bottom-feeders and slackers.

The PA system crackled and Dempster heard his name. It was a summons to the control room.

*

Control was not the word that sprang to mind when he entered the hub of station activities. It was hot because of the number of people and computers crammed into a small, windowless space. The walls were hung with CCTV monitors displaying crime hot spots in the area. Radio controllers were barking orders, phones were ringing and in one corner an interpreter was on speaker phone with a distraught woman, trying to establish her address.

A harried sergeant approached him. 'Dempster?'

He nodded and she thrust a post-it note into his hand.

'A call for you to attend this address,' she said and went straight back to her workstation.

'What's it about?' asked Dempster.

She shrugged and continued a conversation on her headset while manipulating a grainy image on a monitor. A mugging was in progress. Three hooded youths were giving a bloke on the ground a good kicking. In a quiet voice the sergeant directed an ambulance and a police car to the location. Dempster watched as the youths left the scene. They didn't even run.

But when Dempster glanced at the address on the post-it note, he did.

55

The relationship between the living and their dead keeps changing. The death of Berlin's father had taught her that. The way you feel about someone the day they die doesn't alter the fact that you will still argue with them, abuse them, adore them, loathe them, miss them, or just be glad they're gone. It can change every day.

You might discover new things about the dear, or not so dear, departed, and about your relationship with them, years later. Or days. Or while you're standing beside their death bed. And you can still fear someone who's dead and buried.

She had seen the beginnings of this awful realisation in Fernley-Price as they prised him away from Gina's body. Fear, regret, anger, love. A relationship distilled into moments.

Berlin feared death and the dead. She had felt a soft, cold touch from beyond when she slid open the door of the master suite dressing room at Fernley-Price's apartment.

A soft spotlight had come up on racks of suits, coats and dresses, shrouded in dry cleaner's plastic. Dozens of pairs of shoes were arranged along one wall, most barely worn. Above them was a shelf of striped shirts, each with white collar and cuffs, fresh and crisp from the laundry, nestled in a layer of tissue paper. A perfume she recognised hung in there: the scent of the dead.

Her fingers had barely touched the pink striped shirt but the shock was electric. She heard the voice of the woman she had known as Juliet Bravo, her clipped, classless intonation disguising the accent that Gina Doyle was born and bred with in the East End long before it was fashionable. Mocking.

'So now you think you know who I really am? What are you going to do about it?'

Berlin shivered as the number eight bus dropped her in Bethnal Green Road, but it had nothing to do with the cold. The driver said it would be the last one on this route because the roads were too dangerous and the council had run out of salt.

It was dark and the icy weather was keeping most people at home. Berlin walked with care, watching out for treacherous patches of black ice and keeping a tight grip on her laptop in its soft sleeve. Snow began to fall again.

She almost envied Fernley-Price his nice warm bed under police guard at the Royal London Hospital. Thompson had left orders to be notified the minute he came around and was capable of answering questions, or at least responding to them. Thompson had extended an invitation for her to be there, a recognition that this breakthrough was down to her.

Of course, in the meantime they had no clue as to what exactly they had broken through, or what they would find on the other side. Fernley-Price's last conversation with Nestor might complete the picture. She would email it to Thompson this evening so he could pass it on to forensics.

The tremor in her limbs was urging her to get home and have a hit. Her breathing was shallow and her brain was on fire. She felt the impulse to retreat into chemical serenity sapping her will.

The blank wall was in front of her again, but this time it was riddled with cracks. Lazenby, Nestor and Gina stood on the other side. The cracks were yawning now and through them she could hear a tumult of whispers. She strained to listen, to decipher what they were saying. But then the voices receded, the faces dissolved, the cracks healed.

She turned a corner, walked quickly across the courtyard into her block and ran up the stairs. The landing light was out again, but she didn't hesitate, her usual caution in these circumstances overridden by desperation. She fumbled to get the key in the lock. As she turned it, two bodies behind her converged from out of the gloom and thrust her through the door.

Both men were wearing body armour, gloves, and riot helmets with the black visors pulled down. One shoved her to the floor and put his foot on her back, pinning her as the other stepped over her and began to ransack the place.

The smell of alcohol came off them in waves.

She had wrapped her arms around her laptop as she pitched forward and now it was trapped underneath her.

The pressure of the foot in the small of her back eased for a moment and she rolled to one side, putting the drunken man off balance.

'Hey!' he cried as he staggered and she leapt to her feet, ready to flee. But he was between her and the door. He yanked an Asp off his hip and swung it at her. It struck her shoulder and she gasped.

'Stand fucking still!' he commanded.

She did as she was told. As the agony radiated down her arm, she saw the other man emerge from the kitchen. He held up a small brown paper bag.

'What have we here?' he asked, as if he was talking to an infant. He jiggled the bag and the ampoules chinked together.

'What the fuck are you playing at, Coulthard?' she said in a hoarse whisper as she broke out in a cold sweat.

'Give me the fucking computer,' commanded the man with the Asp, whose voice Berlin recognised as Flint's.

She clutched the computer tight with her good arm and took a step back. Flint smacked the Asp into the palm of his gloved hand in a rhythmic tattoo. He took a step forward.

'Special delivery,' said a breathless voice from the doorway.

It was Dempster, panting, the armpits of his thin charcoal suit stained with sweat and his shoulders flecked with snowflakes. He held a large envelope in his hands.

'Sorry, mate,' said Coulthard. 'We had to start without you.' He flipped up his visor. Flint followed suit.

Berlin stared at Dempster. He held up his hand as if to ward off the intensity of her gaze.

'Perhaps you would like to do the honours, Detective Chief Inspector Dempster?' said Flint with a sneer. 'Caution her and make the arrest for possession of Class A and pervert the course of justice. That way you get the collar.'

The silence was thick with the scent of fear and betrayal.

'Because if you don't arrest her, I'm going to have to arrest you,' said Flint. 'On the same charges.'

No one moved. Berlin could see that Dempster was snookered. If he arrested her she would have to turn on him to save her own skin, concoct a plea in mitigation that would reduce her sentence. Bonnington's evidence would corroborate her story of a blackmailing police officer.

If he didn't arrest her, Flint would arrest them both. The uniformed officers who had nicked her in the first place would no doubt gladly give evidence that Dempster had interfered in the process and released her without charge, after the heroin had been found in her flat.

There was the sound of a siren approaching. The pitch rose, then fell as it moved away. The Doppler effect. She knew it was just a matter of perception.

There was a ripple in the atmosphere and she watched Dempster smile and saunter over to Coulthard.

'Give it to me,' he said, extending his hand.

Coulthard smirked at Berlin and gave up the bag, but his smirk turned to dismay as Dempster dropped it on the floor. The ripple became a tsunami. Before Coulthard could stoop to pick up the bag, Dempster trod on it. The soft crunch of the ampoules disintegrating reverberated through Berlin's body.

She watched, aghast, as a dark, wet tidal mark of pain oozed through the paper bag. The floor seemed to drop away beneath her.

Seized by a monstrous craving she uttered a cry and flailed at Dempster, smashing the computer into his temple. Flint rushed at her, wielding the Asp, but she ducked under it and Coulthard caught the full force across his arm. Dempster staggered and dropped the envelope. Berlin threw her weight against him and he careened into Flint. They both went down.

She ran, slamming the front door behind her.

*

Dempster and Flint rolled on the floor, each trying to use the other as leverage to get up while keeping the other down. Dempster locked his arms around Flint's neck and smashed his head into the wall. Flint crumpled. Dempster dragged himself to his feet. When he looked up, Coulthard was pointing a gun at him.

'What the fuck?' said Dempster.

Coulthard's left arm hung, useless, at his side. The gun in his other hand wobbled with the tremor of fading adrenalin. Dempster looked into his eyes, which were wide with fear and confusion, and then at the gun. There was only four feet between them.

Dempster stepped forward and raised his arm as if to reach for the gun, but as Coulthard's eyes followed the movement, he kicked out. His size fourteen Peacekeeper boot, handmade in Yorkshire, cracked Coulthard's wrist bone. Coulthard dropped the gun with a yelp and Dempster grabbed him, slammed him to the floor and bent his damaged left arm up his back.

'Where did you get the gun?' he whispered in Coulthard's ear.

'Let me go!' moaned Coulthard.

Dempster twisted his arm a few more inches. Coulthard screamed.

'Where did you get the fucking gun?' demanded Dempster.

'I nicked it. From this bloke.'

Dempster wrenched the arm higher. He was careful. He didn't want Coulthard to pass out.

'What bloke?'

'Bonnington! His name's Daryl Bonnington.'

56

Berlin hadn't bought drugs on the street for over twenty years. In fact, even back then she'd rarely bought from the proverbial shady character lurking on a dark corner. Illicit substances were just part of the culture of her friends and acquaintances in the seventies and eighties. A couple of phone calls, a friendly chat in a pub and a friend of a friend would deliver whatever you wanted.

One day you would be partying at a pop star's flash house in Knightsbridge, helping yourself from a supermarket bag full of cocaine, and the next you would be at a lock-down in a room above a seedy pub in Hackney using cheap H. The IRA would march in, banging their drums, buckets at the ready for your donation. The hard stuff would be on sale downstairs, confiscated from Irish dealers by men in balaclavas who had smashed their kneecaps.

Those heady days were long gone. The people she knew then were either dead or running B 'n' Bs in Todmorden. Or QCs, CEOs and academics who wouldn't want to be reminded of their former lives as party animals. Now they stuck to growing a couple of dope plants at the holiday home in Wales, and drank decent reds.

Berlin blamed the war on drugs.

Her transition from recreational user to career junkie had been seamless and unremarkable. It wasn't until her usual connection failed and she was seized with blind panic, that she realised a relationship she had regarded as casual was now serious. It was love.

The cold was numbing the pain and her head cleared a bit. She realised she was crouched in the lee of the plinths that shouldered the burden of the tall iron gates of St John's, at the crossroads near the Underground station. She had no idea how she had got there.

She peered back down Bethnal Green Road, but the snow swirling in the sulphurous yellow of the streetlights kept visibility to a minimum. She didn't think anyone had followed her out of the flat, but even if they had, they wouldn't be able to see her in this.

The weather didn't deter the dealers and buyers. They nipped up and down the steps of the three entrances that led into Bethnal Green Station, wearing puffa jackets, T-shirts and knock-off trainers.

As she watched, a desperate, wasted teenager missed a step going down and careened into a woman carrying a fractious toddler. He shouted abuse at the woman and kept going. She almost fell, but grabbed the handrail at the last minute and steadied herself as the toddler burst into tears.

Berlin thought of her father lying on those steps, crushed by the desperate and the dead. She felt dizzy and leant back against the church gates. Inside St John's were fourteen famous paintings: the Stations of the Cross. She wondered if in her strung-out state she was getting a bit melodramatic.

Taking a deep breath she turned her attention back to the deals that were being done in the blink of an eye in the short tunnels that led to the ticket hall. Beyond the range of the CCTV.

There were three ways in and three ways out of the station. If the law mounted an operation, which they did routinely, they would have to man up each entrance and have people beyond the ticket barriers. That many plod gathering on the plot was obvious to the experienced eye and most dealers would melt away, leaving a couple of new kids on the block to learn the hard way. It was all part of the game.

In fact, most of the officers working out of Bethnal Green police station were on nodding terms with the dealers. They were more concerned with guns and knives on their patch. Heroin followed the same market logic as all other commodities. If dealers were taken off the streets and there was a shortage of supply, demand would force up the price. The curve of violent crime would follow.

Heart pounding, Berlin stood up, took the few short strides to the brink of the steps and took the plunge.

*

The short tunnels were bathed in the dull yellow reflection of cold light on cream tiles. The slight curve to the walls gave the impression of an endless, inescapable passage.

She approached a tall, skinny boy she had seen doing numerous deals. He was no more than fifteen, his face hidden deep inside a black hoodie and baseball cap. He didn't look at her or acknowledge her presence in any way.

'I'm chasing. Can you help me out?' she said.

The boy still didn't look at her. He raised his arms in a slow, expansive gesture that seemed to convey 'What's the world coming to?'

She swallowed the lump in her throat. 'Please.'

The boy ambled away.

She walked through the ticket hall and checked out each tunnel. The signal had gone up and the dealers had evaporated. No one would sell to her. She wasn't a face, and her profile – middle-aged and female – didn't fit. They thought she was undercover law setting them up. How bloody ironic.

She left the Underground and turned towards Hackney Road, where she knew there was a cheap hotel with a bar and wi-fi.

She couldn't go home tonight; maybe not for some time if they issued a warrant for her. But she couldn't think about that now, or about Dempster's part in what had happened. It was a bloody nightmare.

57

Thompson checked his work email from his home computer for the umpteenth time. He couldn't understand why Berlin hadn't sent the voicemail. She wasn't answering her mobile either. He thought they had reached an understanding but perhaps she didn't trust him. He could hardly blame her, after the way that loose cannon Dempster had jerked her around.

He thought about calling the hospital again. He kept calling to check on Fernley-Price's condition and to make sure that the uniformed officer was still in the room. The nurses on the ward were beginning to get fed up with him. Each time it was the same story: Fernley-Price was stable but hadn't regained consciousness, and the constable was there drinking tea.

The doctor had told Thompson there was no way of knowing at this stage if Fernley-Price's swollen brain was permanently damaged. The injury to the jaw was consistent with an uppercut, the injury to the brain with a kick in the head. Apparently it was a miracle Fernley-Price had been able to stand, let alone prop up a bar, and he should never have been discharged from the private hospital.

Inquiries there indicated his medical insurance had run out, and with it their compassion. The bottom line had been drawn just above the Hippocratic oath in the commercial sector.

No one even knew exactly where the assault had occurred. A Good Samaritan, probably the last one in London, had found him crawling along Liverpool Street and called an ambulance.

Thompson had got the City of London uniforms to do a quick canvass of the immediate area as it was their patch, not Met territory. But they drew a blank. He couldn't pursue it until Fernley-Price woke up.

He stared at the computer screen, his thoughts elsewhere, sifting the information he had and trying to identify the relationships that held the key to Gina Doyle's murder. It was times like these he wished he had a grip on that software Berlin used. He scratched notes in the margin of his newspaper, next to an abandoned sudoku.

Jeremy Fernley-Price was Doyle's son-in-law, unbeknown to Doyle. Doyle's daughter was Mrs Fernley-Price. She had informed on her father. Fernley-Price was also Ludovic Nestor's private bank-er. Maybe when he'd gone down in the crisis, Nestor went down with him.

Nestor had killed himself in the same place that Gina Doyle's body was found. Did he do it there to make a last, ghastly point to Fernley-Price? Was it to leave a legacy of guilt, or was it because he was guilty? It was difficult to believe that Nestor would kill Fernley-Price's wife just to get back at him for his financial losses.

What about Fernley-Price himself? You never looked for motive when spouses murdered each other but in this case there was one. What if he'd found out she had informed on Doyle? By informing on Doyle she was effectively informing on Fernley-Price. At the time of her death only Agency personnel knew she was the inform-ant, and she had used the alias Juliet Bravo. They didn't know who she was then. That last conversation between Nestor and Fernley-Price could really help.

He checked his email again. Nothing. Where the hell was she? He had a feeling she knew a lot more than she was letting on, what with all those charts she had stashed away in her computer. She was testing his patience.

58

The hotel room was bland and lifeless. Everything was screwed to the wall or the floor. Berlin put the internet-access token on the ta-ble and emptied her pockets of the Johnnie Walker miniatures she had bought at reception. She unscrewed two of them and poured herself a double in a paper cup.

She opened her computer and pressed the power button. She

would at least try to keep moving forward with the investigation, and the next step was to email Nestor's voicemail to Thompson. If she stayed on good terms with him perhaps he would help her out of this mess.

The LEDs blinked and the screen turned blue, but there was no Windows welcome, only a noise like a dying lawnmower. Berlin pushed various keys, to no effect. Her laptop was as dead as a dodo, no doubt wrecked by forceful contact with Dempster's head. If this was karma, she must have been Bluebeard in another life.

Before the voicemail could be cleaned up, a professional would have to recover the file from her hard drive. If indeed it was recoverable. She would have to courier the whole bloody computer to Thompson now and God knows how long it would all take. She'd lost her notes and charts too. All the intel she had carefully compiled since Gina's body was found. Which seemed an eternity ago.

She'd lost everything.

A wave of utter exhaustion swept over her. It was all she could do to take off her coat, easing her swollen arm out of the sleeve. A deep purple bruise was spreading from her shoulder to her wrist.

She gulped two more Scotches, lay on the bed and wrapped her coat around herself. Before she could do anything she had to make it through the night.

Suddenly her bowels turned to water and she leapt up, only just making it to the bathroom in time. It could be shock or the beginning of withdrawal. But surely it was too soon for that?

It wasn't too soon for fear. Life without heroin. Terror seized her guts and twisted. It was like the worst flu, food poisoning and sea sickness all striking at once. She crawled back to bed, although she knew sleep would never come. Maybe not ever again.

The dead swarmed out of the ether to keep her company. Gina, Lazenby, Nestor. Saying nothing, just looking at her, reproachful.

Just beyond them stood a young black man and a woman who

seemed to be reaching for his hand. Merle Okonedo and her brother. In the distance, her father. Always her father, with his back turned to her.

59

Frank served his time in the prison of the wakeful. At three a.m. he was busy boarding up the past.

He had too many rooms and only lived in one. He slept on the couch so he didn't have to waste money on heat and light. There were only four light bulbs in the house. One in the kitchen, one in the bathroom, one in the living room and one in the hall. Actually, that one was a waste.

He stopped hammering, dragged a chair down the hall, climbed up and unscrewed the fourth bulb from the socket. Three bulbs, that's all he needed. It didn't pay to shed too much light on things.

He'd noticed lately that sometimes the furniture in the rooms he didn't use seemed to have moved. That would account for the noises that kept him awake at night: the sound of something heavy being dragged across the carpet, then dropped with a thud.

He hadn't mentioned it to Doyle because he knew he would give him one of those funny looks. That boy had no backbone. He was just waiting for an excuse to put him in a home so he could get his mitts on everything. Over his dead body.

He went back to hammering. So many windows.

The Seventh Day

60

Doyle rose with the first hint of light and put the kettle on. Another sleepless night and an excruciating headache. His schedule was up the spout and the lads were skiving off without his watchful eye to keep them in line. He couldn't face Frank last night, and anyway the bloody roads were impassable. He'd better give him a call. He'd have to get out there today even if it meant using a bleeding toboggan.

The truth was that he had been feeling a bit off his game, shaken up by recent events: Gina's passing, Coulthard legging it, having to give Fernley-Price a tune-up. He wasn't a young man any more. He had been knackered. Yesterday had passed in a blur of daytime television and vodka.

He dialled Frank's number and waited for ages, listening to it ring off the hook. He imagined Frank standing beside it, scowling. Finally Frank picked up the phone, but didn't speak.

'Pop, it's me.'

'What?'

'The roads are bad.'

'Why are you telling me?'

For God's sake, thought Doyle. 'I'll be out today, Pop, rain, hail or shine.'

'Make sure you are,' barked Frank, and hung up.

Doyle put the phone down and went in search of aspirin.

Doyle parked opposite the Toy Museum on Cambridge Heath Road, where the lads were supposed to be waiting for him. He liked it in there. They always had lots of stuff about the old East End, and the sort of toys he remembered hankering after as a kid.

He got out of the car and crossed the road, which was strangely quiet. There were usually coach-loads of children pouring through the doors of the museum but today there was only the odd intrepid tourist. For a moment Doyle imagined what it would be like to be a kid again, coming here for the first time, excited and innocent.

Beyond the modern foyer, the glass and iron roof soared above him. He looked down at his feet. Last time he'd wandered in here one of the security guards told him the marble floor tiles had been laid in the nineteenth century by women prisoners from Woking Gaol. It made him think of his mum. He knew she'd been in the nick more than once, although Frank wouldn't talk about it, of course.

Tears came to his eyes. The woman behind the counter watched him, frowning. He'd better leave before they decided he was a nonce or a nutter and called the law.

When Doyle got back to the car, the lads were hanging about beside it, looking as if they'd just got out of bed. Doyle threw the car keys at one of them.

'What time do you call this?' he shouted.

The lads got in the front, sheepish, and he got in the back. They took off towards Hackney.

'Right. We've got a couple of calls to make this morning and I want a result. Geddit? Got the collateral?'

The lad in the passenger seat was clutching a plastic bag. He reached into it, brought out a fistful of foreign passports and held them up for Doyle's inspection.

'Okay,' said Doyle. 'Hassan's mum is on her last legs in Pakistan and he's desperate to get over there, so I'm pretty sure he'll cough up today. Five grand or he doesn't get his passport back and he's going nowhere. Remind him the old lady wants to see her son one last time. We'll start with him. We'll do number fifty-one last. She's overdue again.'

The lads sniffed, yawned and scratched. Preparing for battle.

*

The day was going better than Doyle had expected. It turned out the terrible weather was a bonus, with most people stopping indoors, and then paying up without too much of a fuss because they didn't want to run out the back way into the freezing slush. Doyle whistled the old Bing Crosby number, 'Let it snow, let it snow, let it snow'.

Hassan had legged it the first time they had knocked on the door, so they'd had to go back again later, which had given Doyle the irrits. Now Hassan, who had apparently dredged up enough courage to face his creditor, sobbed and moaned.

He begged Doyle for his passport so he could visit his mum on her death bed, but Doyle knew that he wouldn't be doing Hassan any favours by showing mercy.

Concerned that Hassan might get it into his head to apply for a new passport, Doyle was forced to take extra measures – for Hassan's own good, of course. The kneecap was a very sensitive part of the anatomy and now the state of one of Hassan's meant he wouldn't be going anywhere for a while. Funnily enough, he managed to find five thousand pounds hidden in a cushion to prevent damage to the other.

All's well that ends well, thought Doyle, as he knocked at number fifty-one. The youngest boy opened the door a crack, keeping the chain on and growling like a well-trained Rottweiler.

'Mum in?' asked Doyle, all smiles.

Sheila Harrington appeared behind the boy and steered him away. Doyle heard her tell him to play his game and stay in the living room.

There was the sound of a door slamming and Sheila reappeared. She reached into her cardigan pocket, brought out a wad of notes and thrust them into Doyle's hand through the gap in the door.

'That's everything I owe you,' she said.

You could have knocked Doyle over with a feather. 'Best let

me be the judge of that,' he said.

But she was right. He counted it with care, trying to think of a reason to demand another payment. Then he offered her some back, to keep the loan ticking over. But she refused, point blank.

'Well, Sheila, if you don't mind me asking, how did you come up with this fucking lot? You haven't been disloyal, have you? Consolidated your debts with someone offering an interest-free period and frequent flyer points? Taken your custom elsewhere?' If someone was encroaching on his patch he wanted to know about it.

'No, no,' said Sheila. 'Nothing like that, Mr Doyle. I would never. It was a friend. He gave me a sort of present. You know.'

Doyle didn't know. He folded his arms. He wanted an explanation. 'I think my lads would enjoy that game your boy's playing. Come to think of it, they might enjoy just playing with your boy. They loved taking your dog for a walk.'

He glanced over his shoulder at the two lads, leaning on the car and smoking. They grinned at Sheila.

'Appealing is it, love? A play date?'

She took the chain off the door and opened it. 'Cup of tea, Mr Doyle?'

'That would be lovely, Sheila. A cup of tea and a nice chat.'

61

Berlin trudged through the icy slush, her weak footfall barely leaving an imprint. She had tried to call a cab to get home from the hotel, but an automated voice response system had informed her in cold tones that there was a fifty-minute queue just to speak with an operator.

London was a cantankerous beast; her joints ached and her arteries were clogged. Now the weather had stretched her frayed nerves to breaking point.

With each difficult step Berlin's irritation grew. No one was responsible. No one was in charge. If something went wrong these days you could apply for a voucher as compensation. That was British customer service: don't fix it, just add a quid to the price and then give it back to the customer when it doesn't work. Nothing would change, but they would enjoy a good moan.

With Gallic insight into their temperament William the Conqueror had granted the citizens of London special privileges, no doubt already well aware of their status as world-class grumblers. But he also built a tower in which to incarcerate them if they became too restive. The complaints were little changed, but the methods of containment had been modernised.

By the time Berlin got to the flat she was having trouble seeing straight. She stumbled up the stairs. The key was still in the lock.

The only sign of the chaos she had fled was a dent in the wall, which was about the size and shape of a helmet. She hoped someone's head had been inside it at the time.

She washed down three aspirin with what was left of her Scotch, then lay on the floor near the radiator and tried to conjure up the sensation of her last hit. It seemed an eternity ago, after she had snatched Coulthard from the bereaved Doyle's lock-up. She thought about Gina's blue-tinged flesh at the mortuary, cold as marble, which set her teeth chattering.

She kept telling herself the physical symptoms would resolve soon. The experts couldn't agree on how long this phase of withdrawal lasted. It didn't invariably conform to the 'cold turkey' depiction of the desperate, foaming-at-the-mouth junkie in films, but depended on the individual. The experience could vary from very uncomfortable to hellish. She couldn't remember it ever being this bad, but maybe it was the same as childbirth. You forgot the pain and did it again. Berlin jerked awake feeling as if she had fallen a great distance. She must have dozed off. Dragging herself from the floor to make tea, her fingers clutched at her favourite blue china mug. It went flying and smashed on her bare foot. The urge to scream, to lose herself in an unceasing howl, was almost overwhelming.

Another moment was too much to bear.

She could think of only one person who might be able to help her.

62

Doyle's doorbell played an attenuated version of the children's nursery rhyme 'Oranges and Lemons' and she thought of the final line. *Here comes a chopper to chop off your head.*

Doyle opened the door. He seemed surprised, but not put out.

'You'd better come in,' he said. 'It's bleeding arctic out there.'

The flat was spick and span, and everything in it dated from the eighties. Apart from the plasma television. This must have been the way it was the day Nancy walked out, thought Berlin. Melancholic best described the atmosphere.

Framed family snaps of a pretty woman and a young girl, clearly mother and daughter, took pride of place on the mantelpiece. Berlin felt her chest constrict as she stared at the serious face of an eleven-year-old Gina Doyle, whom she had known only as a woman in her mid-thirties.

Even in death, Gina had been the image of her mother. There were no photos of Doyle with them, and she guessed he was always the photographer. Camera-shy, too. He wouldn't have wanted a pictorial record to assist with any future police inquiries.

He emerged from the kitchen with tea and a plate of biscuits. Berlin just knew they would be chocolate bourbons, and they were. This was England. If Jesus Christ came to visit, tea would be taken before he was crucified.

'You don't look at all well, Miss, if you don't mind me saying so,' said Doyle.

You don't look too flash yourself, mate, thought Berlin. 'I've got a nasty cold. Do you mind if I use the bathroom?' she said. It was a polite gambit, a ritual gesture which they both knew meant she wanted to snoop around a bit.

'Be my guest.' He pointed at a door off the sitting room.

In fact she did need the loo, and didn't bother to open the two other doors off the small hall. She suspected that behind them would be two neat bedrooms and she would bet the farm that one was still decorated for a little girl.

What did surprise her was the calendar on the back of the toilet door: 1986. Faded kittens gazed down on her with big, soft eyes. Doyle seemed an unlikely Miss Havisham, but here was the evidence.

When she returned to the sitting room, he looked expectant. The pleasantries were over.

'So what can I do for you, Miss?'

'Mr Doyle, I have some information for you about your daughter.'

Doyle remained very still but she saw his right knee begin a slight nervous jig. 'This isn't official,' he said.

'No.'

He regarded her for a moment, as alert as any predator. 'So what do you want?'

He was no fool.

'My request might surprise you,' she said.

'I doubt that, but go on. Whatever you need, I'll do my best. I know that everything in this life has a price and you'll find me a ready payer.'

Berlin thought it was a measure of her desperation that she was prepared to take him at his word.

'Did you know your daughter was married?' she asked.

'Married? What, you mean, like living with some bloke?'

It was as if he couldn't quite comprehend that his little girl could be someone's wife.

'Married.'

Doyle sat forward. 'Who was he? Why didn't he report her missing? They told me no one had. Did you know that? If they were together or whatever why didn't he —'

He broke off suddenly, as if he had just realised the implications. His demeanour hardened.

'What's his name?'

Berlin hesitated. There was a limit to her trust.

'Before we get to that, I wondered, that is, I thought perhaps you may have some contacts in certain areas,' she ventured.

She could see he was impatient. What the hell was the point of beating around the bush anyway?

'I need heroin,' she said.

He didn't even blink. Just went to a small bureau and scribbled on a pad. He tore the page off and handed it to her. She glanced at it. The address was local.

'Mention me,' he said. 'Now. What's his name?'

'Fernley-Price. He works in the City.'

Doyle looked at her as if she was mad. 'No. That can't be right.'

'He confirmed their relationship when he viewed her remains, Mr Doyle. I was there.'

Doyle stood up, stunned. She could see he was reeling.

'Jesus H. Christ.'

Berlin stood up too, alarmed by the change that had come over him.

'Mr Doyle, are you okay? What's wrong?'

He stared at her, his fists clenched and she saw the monster within rise up.

'Do you know him?' she asked.

Doyle didn't respond and she saw him recover himself. When he spoke, his voice was steady and very cold.

'I think that concludes our business, Miss.'

The door closed behind her. The view of Weaver's Fields from the landing was a picture postcard. A blanket of snow obscured all shape and colour; the swings and slide appeared to have been coated in thick white polystyrene by the clumsy hands of a giant. It wouldn't last long. Even as she watched, a boy ran into the park and plunged into a drift. Watch out for the dog shit, she thought.

What had she done? Her judgement could be off, given her current condition. Why hadn't Doyle asked any questions about his son-in-law once she'd named him? True, Fernley-Price was a distinctive surname and there wouldn't be too many of them. No doubt Doyle felt he would have no trouble finding him. She could feel the lines reaching out for the dots as she made haste to deliverance.

Thompson had told her that Fernley-Price was a hedge-fund manager who had gone bad in the crisis. Nestor and Fernley-Price were part of the old boys' network and Nestor had every penny tied up with Fernley-Price.

When Doyle was torturing Coulthard he had as much as said his partner was in touch with Nestor. Could Fernley-Price be Doyle's partner without Doyle knowing that Gina was his wife?

By bringing her father down, she would also destroy her husband. Was it a BOGOF – buy one, get one free? Fernley-Price hadn't reported her missing. There could be a very good reason for that. He'd killed her.

He was lucky to be comatose in hospital under police guard. She wouldn't like to be in his shoes when Doyle decided it was time for a family reunion.

Should she alert Thompson? She dismissed the thought. She had just swapped a key piece of evidence in the case for a drug connection. Not a good look. Plus, Fernley-Price was safe where he was. She would tell Thompson eventually. First she had to deal with her own shit.

Pure, dazzling white coated everything: roads, cars, hedges, bins, railings, the tops of walls, streetlights. Everything was covered in a foot of snow. Ice encased gables and downpipes. The world was transformed. She turned her face upwards and felt the soft, icy touch of snowflakes falling on her cheeks.

All sound was muted, nothing moved. The tumult and constant, restless movement of London had been cancelled. It was as if her own turmoil had squeezed out the rest of life. This was the longest she had gone without heroin for more than twenty years.

She glanced behind her nervously, half expecting Gina Doyle, privy to her selfish thoughts, to be dogging her: a persistent corpse dragging her feet through the snow, the gaping wound at her throat hung with bloody icicles. Hanging on, making sure that Berlin didn't abandon her.

God, I am really losing it now, thought Berlin. She had to focus on one problem at a time. The one she was about to solve.

63

After the punch-up at Berlin's flat, Dempster had taken the unconscious Flint's car keys and gone after her. He'd driven around in Flint's car for hours, crawling along to avoid skidding on the black ice, but he had no idea which direction she had taken. Eventually he'd gone home to consider his next move.

Bonnington was the lynchpin. The social worker knew of the connection between him and Berlin, and the fact that she was an addict. The little toe rag had told Flint. Flint had got together with Berlin's hostile boss, Coulthard, and together they had cooked up the scene at her flat to ensnare Dempster and destroy her. But they had been pissed and hadn't thought it through. The last thing they had expected was physical resistance from either him or Berlin.

He knew how it had looked to Berlin. She would think that he was in it with them. He'd crushed the vials of heroin to demonstrate that he wasn't going to allow it to be used as evidence against her. But it had enraged rather than reassured her. He rubbed his temple. His head hurt but, wherever she was, she would be feeling worse.

He tried to think about the situation strategically. One incontrovertible truth of the job was that if you caught a killer, all would be forgiven.

In fact, history showed that it didn't even have to be the actual killer, just some unlucky bastard who fit the crime and the circumstances. If you could get a conviction for murder, you would be a hero. No matter how you did it.

Now the gun he had taken from Coulthard lay in front of him.

Bonnington displayed his teeth in what might have been a grimace or a smile. He seemed to be enjoying this. Dempster wanted to hit him, but sensed that he would welcome the pain.

Bonnington had been talking for what seemed like hours without giving up anything useful. His tone was mild and his speech controlled. He talked about the corruption of the police and the government, the sheep-like population numbed by drugs, alcohol and television, the masses crushed by debt foisted on them by predatory usurers who peddled the illusion of wealth creation: conditions that provided the perfect opportunity for oppressive alien creeds with strict moral codes and self-discipline to insinuate themselves and corrode our way of life.

Dempster drank his cold green tea and waited for Bonnington to pause for breath. He had no idea how to interview this sort of nutter. There was no point in threatening him. He was a zealot, convinced of his own rightness and unafraid. There was no point trying to negotiate. The bloke was beyond reason. Although there was some sense in what he said.

'So you eliminated Lazenby?' Dempster asked yet again. He was exhausted, his head throbbed and his eyes were full of grit. The flat didn't seem to be heated. He shivered. It wasn't like him to feel the cold.

'No,' said Bonnington, sighing as if Dempster was an obtuse child.

'Where did you get the starting pistol?'

It was the same type of weapon that had both fallen from Merle Okonedo's hand and killed Lazenby.

'You can get them on the internet,' said Bonnington.

Dempster glanced at the softly whirring computer in the corner. He noticed the webcam clipped to the monitor, its little green light blinking, the modem lights flashing. Mesmerised by the lights, a slow signal travelled from one part of his brain to another, but he couldn't quite grasp it.

Bonnington smiled.

Then the thought exploded in Dempster's brain. He'd been played.

64

Coulthard and Flint sat looking at each other across the table at Pellicci's, trying to work out what had gone wrong.

'I am totally fucked. He took the work car and my warrant card and nearly broke my fucking neck. And when I came around you were nowhere to be seen. Thanks for that,' snarled Flint.

'You didn't plan, mate,' said Coulthard, pouring brown sauce on his eggs. 'There was no briefing, you didn't scope the plot...'

'You? What do you mean "you"? We did it to shut her down so she couldn't make your life a misery and to see off fucking Dempster, which suited me and Bonnington. That's all there was in it for me!' said Flint, his voice going up an octave.

'Bullshit, mate,' Coulthard tut-tutted. 'You're forgetting the voicemail. You reckoned you could show your boss up if you could get hold of her computer.'

'All right,' conceded Flint, miserably. 'But it wasn't supposed to be the bleeding Charge of the Light Brigade either. We just had to get her drugs, which would have given us leverage against her and Dempster. We fucked up on all counts.'

Coulthard looked offended. 'Well, I'm sorry you feel like that, mate,' he said with a sad smile. 'After all, you're the policeman.'

Flint stared at him, not getting his drift.

'I don't have the authority to do any of those things that you did. I didn't know what you had in mind,' continued Coulthard, pointing at Flint with his fork each time he said 'you'.

Flint couldn't believe it. The prick was just going to walk away from it all. Flint's career was already in the toilet, let alone the possible criminal charges he could face if Dempster played hard ball. He stirred three sugars into his tea and wondered what the hell they could have been thinking. Number one, junkies don't behave in any way that's predictable, and number two, Dempster had simply given them a good thrashing.

Dempster might be a fucking lunatic, but he was a smart fucking lunatic who had been unafraid to take on the two of them. He himself, on the other hand, was stupid and scared; that much was becoming clear.

'Now, if you don't mind,' said Coulthard peevishly as he got to his feet. 'You've put me off my scoff with these wild accusations and I've got an appointment with my doctor to see about long-term sick leave. Stress following a work-related assault.' He smirked.

Coulthard's arm hung at his side, a reminder of his first time on the receiving end of an Asp – and Dempster's boot. If it hadn't been for Coulthard's stuffed arm, and his own stiff neck and blinding headache, Flint would have wiped the smile off his face. Instead, he sat there and watched Coulthard saunter out.

'That bloke is fucking Teflon,' he muttered, and dragged Coulthard's plate to his side of the table. The condemned man might as well eat a hearty breakfast.

65

Berlin's journey to the other side of Bethnal Green felt more like an epic voyage to the North Pole. She slid and slithered through the layers of snow on slush and ice, bent into the headwind, a funereal figure propelled by desperation. She made one stop at a cash machine.

When she finally turned into the estate she was disoriented for a moment. Snowdrifts had softened the contours of walls, balconies and roofs, creating a surreal, Gaudi-esque world without edges. She sought the kerb with the toe of her boot and moved forward slowly.

Her physical condition was already poor; a fracture or even a sprain now would be a disaster.

Neat, ordinary, mundane. Such were the lairs of monsters. She rang the bell and waited, the silence within pushing her almost to screaming point. But then the door opened.

'Can I help you?' said a neat, ordinary woman.

'Doyle sent me,' said Berlin.

The woman stood back and Berlin walked in.

The door of number fifty-one closed behind her.

On the way down the hall the woman shut the living-room door on two boys watching TV.

'They couldn't open the schools today, with the weather. They're driving me mad, stuck indoors all the time,' she said, as she led Berlin into the kitchen and closed the door behind them. 'Can I get you a cup of tea? You look half frozen.'

Berlin was a little taken aback by this resort to the usual social niceties, but wondered what she had expected. A black dude with an Uzi?

'No, thank you. I haven't got much time,' she said and realised as soon as the words were out of her mouth how desperate she sounded.

The woman looked at her with sympathy. 'Okay, love, I understand. Are you a friend of Doyle's or a client?'

'Acquaintance,' said Berlin.

'Because I'd hate you to be borrowing from him to do this bit of business, know what I mean?'

Berlin nodded. 'It's my own money. What have you got?'

'Just sit tight, I won't be a minute,' said the woman, and left the kitchen.

Berlin heard her open the living-room door and tell the boys to stay where they were; she would bring them hot chocolate with marshmallows later if they were good. Hysterical laughter rose in

Berlin's throat at this further erosion of the drug dealer's stereotype and she clamped her hand over her mouth. There were footsteps overhead, doors opening and closing and a minute later the woman returned to the kitchen, closed the door behind her and held out her hand.

In her palm lay two gleaming ampoules of pharmaceutical di-amorphine. A jolt of recognition shook Berlin. They were straight from Lazenby's drug safe.

The woman took Berlin's shudder for desperate anticipation. 'I bet you've never seen anything as good as that before, love!' she said.

Berlin realised she was staring, mesmerised. She looked up and saw the woman through different eyes.

'My name's Catherine,' she said.

'Sheila,' said the woman. 'Pleased to meet you.'

'How much have you got?' said Berlin.

'How much do you want?' said Sheila.

66

When his phone rang Dempster answered without checking the ID.

'Dempster,' he said.

There was a pause and then a quiet voice said, 'It's Flint.'

Dempster didn't respond. Sod Flint.

'Are you there?' said Flint.

'What do you want? I'm busy.'

'I want my car and my fucking warrant card. That's out of order, Dempster, taking my warrant. It will finish me, you know that.'

'Mate, I needed the car for official police business, not for swanning around the manor with my dick hanging out. And I haven't got your bloody warrant card.' He hung up and studied Bonnington.

The automatic aperture on the webcam adjusted focus. How many people were watching them? Dozens? Thousands? Bonnington was a vain prick who had created the perfect soapbox. But he hadn't realised that Dempster was onto him.

'So Daryl, tell me. Where did you get the gun?'

'I confiscated it from one of my client's kids.'

'Why didn't you hand it in, report it to the police?'

'Client confidentiality. The cone of silence. It's so important to maintain trust, DCI Dempster. You know all about that, don't you?'

'Professional discretion then?' snapped Dempster, frustrated. The bastard had an answer for everything.

Bonnington sighed and nodded. 'He said his mum had a box full of them on top of her wardrobe.'

67

The computer arrived with a note that just said: 'It's fucked. Sorry.'

Thompson felt uneasy. He inspected it and saw something that looked very much like blood on one corner. The courier said he'd picked it up from reception at a hotel in Hackney and had been paid cash. Thompson spat on his handkerchief and gave it a wipe. He was better off not knowing.

The computer hummed and creaked when he switched it on, but nothing else happened. He cursed. He had no bodies to do legwork for him. Half the bloody forensic workforce was stuck at home because of the weather and the other half were queuing up at the Australian embassy trying to emigrate.

He was supposed to be pursuing a vicious killer who had taken a chunk out of Gina Doyle's throat, and a psycho who had nearly beaten Fernley-Price to death. It looked like the bloke who ran the agency hunting loan sharks was in the mix somehow and had topped himself. Now the woman in the middle of it all, a junkie, was nowhere to be found.

Happy days.

Sod it. He would ignore all the bloody warnings about the roads and drive the computer down to Risk Control – a private firm in the City who would give him a decent coffee while their highly paid analysts worked on extracting that file.

He could send the bill to the bloody Home Secretary and tell him to charge it to his expenses. They couldn't say no. When it came to the MPs' expenses, he knew where the bodies were buried.

68

Doyle was so agitated after Berlin left that he felt he had to get out of the flat despite the weather. He had a focus now, a purpose. Motivation. He couldn't sit still. It gave him an appetite.

He decided to walk down to Pellicci's, have a sausage sandwich and make some phone calls. The damage he'd done to Fernley-Price would probably have landed him in hospital. If the prick was in a bad way and laid up, one thing was for sure: there was no one waiting at home to take care of him.

The rage in his breast was the best kind. Cold. He was able to consider the situation clinically. When the missus was offed, hubby was the prime suspect. Christ, he should know. He'd been through it himself with Nancy.

He remembered the first time he'd met the banker. The geezer had approached him in The Silent Woman and asked if he could sit down. 'Suit yourself,' said Doyle. Fernley-Price bought him a drink, then another, then asked if he was interested in a business proposition. He seemed to know a lot about Doyle's business. When Doyle asked him how, he'd said 'due diligence'.

What a fool he had been. He thought Fernley-Price must have somehow known one of his clients, looked into Doyle's reputation, been impressed and decided to seek him out as a partner. Let's face it, he'd been flattered by the City gent showing him respect, wanting in on his business model. Here was a chance to show Frank what he was made of, a chance to branch out into big money.

It seemed that Fernley-Price had serious cash salted away – his own and that of a few very special clients. It had to work for them after the crash wiped out their other investments. Doyle knew where to place it for maximum returns. No risk.

But now it was as plain as the nose on your face. Gina had told Fernley-Price all about her dad's business. But maybe she had failed to mention he was her dad. Christ, when she was a kid he'd drag her around with him doing collections. He'd leave her in the car, of course, for the trickier ones. She'd run around at Frank's while they did the tally. That was when Frank had all his marbles. He'd doted on her.

It was difficult for him to understand why Gina had turned him in, but then again, she had always had that thing about her mother. She was sharp, Gina. She must have seen a way to get at him. Then dragged her husband into it. Obviously she had had enough of him too, which showed taste.

He would find Fernley-Price and finish the job he'd started. Gina would be pleased.

69

The windows of Sheila's tiny, overheated kitchen were opaque with condensation. The air was thick with the smell of wet wool from Berlin's coat.

Sheila had gone upstairs to get more ampoules. Berlin's first instinct was to cut and run, but Sheila had taken the 'samples' with her. So this was the woman Pink Cheeks had seen in the waiting room. This was the woman who had shot Lazenby. But this was the woman who had the heroin.

Berlin struggled to master the turmoil in her brain and the frenzied dance in her veins. She tried to think. She could score or she could turn in a killer. Either or.

She was standing between her mother and father, looking up at them, squinting. Behind them the sun was dazzling.

'You can go with him or stay with me,' said her mother. 'You can't have it both ways, Catherine.'

Mute, she stared into the sun and was blinded. When she blinked, she saw her father walking away.

Her mobile was in her hand and she was dialling before she even realised what she was doing. She was flicked to voicemail.

The movements upstairs had stopped and the house was suddenly very quiet. Berlin didn't leave a message. She hung up and dialled again. This time, to her relief, Dempster picked up.

'Hello?' he said. Her ID was blocked.

'It's me,' she whispered. Footsteps were approaching down the hall. 'Lazenby's killer. At number fifty-one —'

'On the estate,' he cut in.

'Yes,' said Berlin. 'But how —'

'Listen to me – get out of there, now. Leave and don't take anything with you. Got it? Go, go, go!'

The kitchen door opened. Sheila stood there with two Tesco

223

bags. She frowned at the sight of the phone in Berlin's hand.

'I won't be long, darling,' said Berlin sweetly, and hung up.

Sheila smiled.

Suddenly there was a dull thud, followed by the sound of wood splintering and men shouting. Sheila spun around. Over Sheila's shoulder Berlin saw the front door shudder and crack open, revealing a queue of armour-encased black bodies.

'Police!' one of them shouted as the enforcer smashed into the door again.

Berlin sprang to her feet and shoved Sheila hard in the back. She pitched into the hall. The two boys emerged from the living room, their faces pale and frightened. Sheila reached out to them, dropping the Tesco bags. The ampoules spilt out onto the floor: a shining carpet that could fly Berlin to heaven.

The front door gave way and the first boots thundered into the hall. Berlin slammed the kitchen door and jammed a chair under the handle, then legged it out the back. The snow had been cleared off the tiny tiled patio and swept onto a narrow strip of dirt. In one corner a small mound bore a cross made of two sticks.

She knew that the police would be on the other side of the back fence. She took a short run up to next door's wall, jumped, hoisted herself over it and dropped to the ground. A jolt of pain shot up her bruised arm and she jarred her knee. She lay there for a moment trying to catch her breath. A delighted Jack Russell terrier ran up and started licking her face.

A scream went up at number fifty-one and there was a sound like rolling thunder as a dozen pairs of Armed Response boots ran up Sheila's stairs. She could hear the enforcer battering the kitchen door.

Berlin got to her feet and scrambled across the garden, searching frantically for a way out. The fence on the far side was in bad shape, and she managed to pry two loose boards apart and squeeze through the gap she'd made. The dog followed.

She found herself at the end of the block, standing in a grassy area now covered with slush. She brushed herself off, walked to the pavement and peered back down the street. Three police vehicles, lights flashing, were parked outside Sheila's house.

'Oi,' said a voice behind her.

She turned around to face a stocky policeman in full body armour with a sub-machine gun slung across his chest.

'What are you up to?'

The dog trotted up beside her and squatted. Berlin and the officer watched as a yellow stain appeared on the snow.

'Good girl,' said Berlin to the dog.

The officer grunted and walked on.

70

Dempster was magnanimous when he took the terse congratulatory call from the DCI leading the local Murder Investigation Team. They had followed Armed Response in and found the box of starter pistols, just as he'd said, on top of the wardrobe. Apparently they belonged to Sheila Harrington's husband. Some had been modified to fire and some hadn't.

Sheila had been taken in and would be charged with dealing and Lazenby's murder. She'd said she had to do it to pay off a local loan shark who was giving her grief. She hadn't mentioned Bonnington.

Dempster hung up.

'Do you wish you had been in at the kill?' asked Bonnington.

Jesus Christ, thought Dempster, I must be an open book. Then again, the bloke was a psychologist, social worker, whatever.

It was his job to read people.

'All guts and no glory – that's me, mate,' said Dempster.

'Will you tell them how you cracked the case?' said Bonnington.

He knows he's going to walk, thought Dempster. What could he be charged with? Giving a desperate woman big ideas? He knew how Lazenby worked, and he knew Sheila had the contacts to deal: she'd watched her husband do it for years.

Bonnington had done her a good turn by taking the kids off her hands twice: the first time while she cleaned up the mess after Doyle had mutilated the dog, and then later that day to give her time to do the deed. In the process he'd given himself an alibi.

'We could do you for criminal conspiracy to murder Lazenby,' said Dempster.

'I didn't expect her to kill him. I didn't even mention him, just the set-up in the surgery,' said Bonnington.

'So what was the idea then?' Dempster was genuinely interested; he just didn't get it.

'Simple armed robbery. Then she would sell the pure heroin and junkies would die in droves before the police caught up with her. There would be an outcry and Lazenby would be finished. There would be a crackdown on prescribing heroin for addicts. The whole system would be exposed.'

Dempster realised he had been right about Bonnington, but for the wrong reasons. Bonnington didn't want the drugs out of circulation; he wanted them to kill as many people as possible. He would never be satisfied with a single death. Or even two. Dempster thought of Merle Okonedo.

He had scored a big win, but felt numb. Looking on the bright side, which didn't seem that bright, matters such as belting Flint and nicking his car would attract a reprimand at the most. He was the senior officer, in any event.

Bonnington was an evil bastard, but in the eyes of the law his worst offence to date was possession of a banned starting pistol. The magistrate would weep when he heard why Bonnington had it. Dempster decided to squeeze every last drop of intel out of this psycho before he left. He wouldn't get another shot.

'So Daryl, you met Merle Okonedo through her brother, who was inside?' He framed it as a casual inquiry, using Bonnington's first name. Establishing a more intimate connection between them.

'He was one of my clients. Unfortunately he OD'd. In one of our drug-free correction facilities.'

'Her death wasn't an accident then? You killed her,' said Dempster.

Was Bonnington mad or vain enough to admit it in front of thousands?

'Why do you do it, Dempster? You work for a morally bankrupt state, rounding up a few degenerates. It's just window-dressing to disguise true corruption.'

'Maybe it's like Churchill said: it's a lousy system but it's the best we've got, or better than the alternative. Something like that, anyway,' he replied. But he knew he lacked conviction.

'She was willing,' said Bonnington. 'But yes, I killed her.'

Something broke inside Dempster. He held his breath.

'The hand is quicker than the eye,' said Bonnington as he tore open his shirt.

Dempster caught a glimpse of the rage that drove him. Bonnington wanted an audience of millions, not thousands. The video would go viral.

He thought of Berlin.

'Everything's connected,' said Bonnington, and pressed the detonator.

71

Flint was on his third cup of tea when Doyle walked in. Doyle seemed preoccupied and didn't notice Flint, even though the place was quiet. The weather was deterring even the usual hardened punters. There was a dull clap of thunder in the distance. Rain would turn the snow to slush. Flint hated slush. It ruined your shoes. At this moment, he hated everything.

He was fuming. His conversation with Dempster had left him in no doubt that Coulthard had done the dirty on him. If Dempster didn't have his warrant card, the only other possibility was that Coulthard had taken it while Flint was lying on the floor, out cold. The prick could get away with murder flashing that bloody card.

Flint was younger than Coulthard, but they looked enough alike that anyone taking a quick glance probably wouldn't notice. Anyway, who looks long and hard at a copper's ID? Coulthard had all the bullshit to go with the badge too, from his time on the job. Bullshit was about all he did have; even when he'd been a copper he was impersonating a police officer, thought Flint bitterly.

He waited until Doyle's order arrived and watched him tucking into his sausage sandwich. He thought about what he was about to do. But not for very long.

Doyle had his sandwich in one hand and his phone in the other. His fingers were a bit fat for the tiny keys, and his rings didn't help. He misdialled, tried again, then became aware of someone standing over him.

He looked up into the beady eyes of one of the coppers who had interviewed him about Gina's murder. A bloke he'd often seen about the manor before that, and who he knew had often seen him. He was the live-and-let-live type, unless there was something in it for him. Flint, that was his name. It suited him.

'What can I do for you?' said Doyle, slipping his phone into his pocket.

'Bloody awful weather we're having,' said Flint.

Doyle waited.

'It gets some people down,' said Flint.

'Does it?' said Doyle.

'Yeah. Like my mate. He's a bit down. More than a bit, actually. He's got stress. From work. He's got a very demanding job.'

Doyle was aware his sausage was waiting.

'He's gone to see his doctor about it today actually. The stress. Not to mention a broken nose, a few busted teeth, very sore ribs and a buggered arm.' Flint's tone was confiding.

Doyle paid more attention. His own ribs were still sore from where he'd been kicked after that bastard had whacked him and scarpered from the lock-up. He made the connection.

'Coulthard,' he said.

Flint's nod was almost imperceptible.

Doyle knew Coulthard wasn't at home, but his girlfriend was still there. The lads had checked. 'Got a good doctor, has he?' said Doyle.

'Very sympathetic. At the Mare Street Clinic,' said Flint, glancing at his watch. 'He's just gone down there. You never know what a man will do when he's in that state of mind. He might do himself a mischief. Nobody would be surprised.'

'Why don't you sit down?' offered Doyle.

Flint pulled up a chair and gestured to Nino for another cup of tea.

72

The café door closed behind Flint. Doyle picked his teeth, contemplative. He had barely said a word. Flint hadn't stopped talking. Some people, he thought. Some people.

He took out his phone and turbo-dialled the lads.

'Yeah?'

He sighed. They were dragged up these days. Didn't they know that was no way to answer the fucking phone?

'Get plotted up at the Mare Street Clinic,' he said.

'What? The doctors?'

'Yes, the fucking doctors! Get down there and wait until our friend from the other night shows up, then ring me. Gottit?' He hung up.

His sausage was stone cold. It was turning out to be one of those days.

'Got a telephone book handy, Nino?' he asked. 'And do us a favour and sling this sausage back in the pan for a minute.'

Doyle tried the Hoxton Hospital, Barts and the Middlesex with no luck. But when he rang the Royal London inquiring after Fernley-Price's health they put him through to the ward. Bingo, he thought. The nurse who answered snapped at him when he mentioned Fernley-Price.

'Is this someone from DCI Thompson's office? Again?'

Doyle responded in the affirmative.

'How many times do I have to tell you? He's still in a coma! Please don't ring again. While we're dealing with your calls, people are dying! Why don't you ring the officer if you need an update?' She hung up.

Well, well, thought Doyle. They've got a man there. Must be expecting trouble. His phone rang. The caller ID informed him it was one of the lads.

230

'Any sign?'

'He's just come out of the Mare Street Clinic.'

'Let's make him an offer he can't refuse,' said Doyle.

73

Berlin was putting as much distance as she could between herself and the estate. Sheila would assume she was a grass the police had sent in to set her up. The minute Sheila mentioned it, no doubt in the same sentence as some choice expletives, the police would be on the lookout for Berlin, hoping to bag a recent buyer as well as their prize trophy, the dealer and murderer.

The sirens seemed even worse than usual and she kept dodging into shop doorways as emergency vehicles and police cars raced past.

Dempster must have ordered the raid on Sheila's place. He had given her a heads up when she called, instead of leaving her to get caught in the raid with no chance of talking her way out of it. So he had her interests at heart after all. Maybe she had misjudged him. She tried calling him again but kept getting flicked to voicemail.

She remembered she also had to check with Thompson about the progress he was making with her computer. She hadn't responded to any of his messages, which, like those she had left for Dempster, were becoming increasingly urgent. He was probably wondering where the hell she was, while she was wondering the same about Dempster.

They were all bound by a chain of unanswered messages: small, untethered pleas drifting in an abstract space. Call me. Please ring. Help me. Banal and tragic in equal measure. She thought of

Nestor's last call, a final, plaintive cry.

She was teetering at the edge of incoherence, not even sure where she was: the streets seemed unfamiliar with their mantle of white. It struck her that the first thing we say when someone answers their mobile is 'Where are you?' Location is critical. Everyone in their place.

Berlin tried to focus on what needed to be done and not on the despair she felt at having seen her last chance at peace of mind scattered across Sheila's floor. She struggled to forget the bright promise that the ampoules held, and the darkness that was now pouring in to fill her chasm of need. Nature abhors a vacuum.

A shadow passed over her and she looked up. A dark pall of smoke drifted to the east.

74

Thompson had never heard a sadder conversation than the one between Nestor and Fernley-Price. He sat in a warm, bright office in a glass tower that overlooked the river, and listened again as a man was driven to a despairing death.

Fernley-Price was clearly drunk, but apparently was soon shocked into sobriety. Nestor had a high blood-alcohol reading according to the post-mortem report, but he only sounded drunk during his opening attack on Berlin.

'Berlin, you think you know everything, you arrogant bitch, but you never knew Juliet Bravo. When I said no further action I meant no fucking further action! Now look what you've done!'

The next sound was an entry phone buzzer, according to the technician. He'd even been able to identify the make. Nestor broke off from berating Berlin, presumably to admit Fernley-Price. The lift doors droned.

'So glad you could make it,' said Nestor to his visitor. His tone had changed completely.

'I haven't got any money,' mumbled Fernley-Price. There was a thud. It suggested the phone had been put down hard onto something timber. Probably the desk, although they had found it on the floor.

Thompson wondered if Nestor had deliberately not hung up so that the conversation would be recorded on Berlin's voicemail.

'This isn't about money, old boy,' said Nestor. 'I'd just like you to take a look at this.'

There was a pause.

'Jesus fucking Christ! What is this?' Fernley-Price's voice was a whisper.

'It was taken by the pathologist. Did you do this, Jeremy?' Nestor asked. His voice had taken on an eerie quality.

'I . . .I thought she had left me,' said Fernley-Price.

'Did you kill her?' thundered Nestor.

'What? Are you fucking mad? Why would I kill her?' shouted Fernley-Price.

'Because she informed on your business partner. Doyle was her father.'

Something crashed to the floor. The computer? Fernley-Price must have swept it off the desk. He was a big bloke and his fingerprints were found on it. The post-mortem photo wasn't pretty.

'You *are* fucking mad!' screamed Fernley-Price. 'You're making all this up. Like at school!'

There was the sound of a struggle, grunting, flesh on flesh, bodies colliding with furniture. Then it was over. Neither man had the heart for it.

'You stupid, vain, greedy fool. It's all your fault,' said Nestor. His voice dripped misery.

'But it was her idea! She said she'd heard about Doyle from a reliable source in the City.'

'I shut down the investigation Gina started,' said Nestor.

'To protect your money,' moaned Fernley-Price. 'She kept on at me to get documents from Doyle. A paper trail.' He was talking to himself. 'But he wouldn't cooperate. We had a terrible row about it the night she walked out. It must have been the same night she...'

Thompson could hear ragged breathing, scuffing on the carpet. Fernley-Price was pacing. 'I don't understand,' he said. 'She was setting me up. Why?'

Thompson knew why. To bring Doyle down she needed evidence. She had used Fernley-Price to try to get it. He was collateral damage.

Nestor wailed, pitiful. 'It wasn't the damn money! I thought I was protecting her. A prosecution would have ruined you. I thought it would devastate her. She... she liked nice things.'

'Oh my God,' hissed Fernley-Price. 'You fell for her. All those foursomes, boring fucking bridge evenings, awful dinners with your bloody wine collection. You fancied her!'

There was a terrible silence.

'What would a woman like my wife see in a pathetic little bureaucrat like you?' Fernley-Price's vicious laughter almost smothered the sound of Nestor sobbing. 'If anyone's to blame for all this it's you!'

Thompson closed the file and shut down the computer. He gazed through the window at the cold, merciless river. He felt that Nestor hadn't intended to kill himself until that moment.

75

Berlin barely heard her phone over the din of sirens. A police heli-copter flew over as she answered the call.

'Where are you?' asked Thompson. 'It sounds like a bloody war zone.'

'What?' she shouted.

'They recovered your hard drive. When the voicemail was cleaned up it was...'

She caught the inflection of emotion in his voice. He seemed to be searching for the right word, but cleared his throat and finished his sentence in a perfunctory, businesslike manner.

'Fernley-Price didn't murder Gina.'

Berlin heard the door slam on another suspect.

'Nestor killed himself because he'd lost everything, but she was his biggest loss,' he said.

'What?' said Berlin.

'It was unrequited, of course, but just being in love can sustain a man.'

Berlin had no idea how to respond to Thompson's sudden bout of sentimentality.

'Doyle told Fernley-Price about your investigation,' continued Thompson. 'Fernley-Price told Nestor his money was tied up with Doyle. When his old school chum had given him the opportunity to recoup his losses, Nestor didn't ask how. He was an honourable man who turned a blind eye. But love prevailed.'

'Love?'

'If Fernley-Price went down, so would Gina. Nestor wanted to protect her,' said Thompson.

Berlin thought of Dempster.

'According to Fernley-Price it was all Gina's idea. She pointed him in her father's direction,' he continued.

If it came to it, Gina was prepared to sacrifice her husband to en-
sure her father's destruction. Berlin had a sudden vision of Doyle's
face when she'd told him Gina was married to his business partner.
'Thompson,' she said.

'Yes?'

'Doyle knows.'

'Knows what?'

'That Fernley-Price was married to Gina.'

She could practically hear his train of thought heading in the
same direction as hers. Doyle would think that Fernley-Price was
Gina's killer.

'Jesus Christ. How the hell? Nobody knows that except you and
me.'

She gritted her teeth, knowing that her silence would speak volumes. She had traded Fernley-Price for the promise of dope.

'We'll discuss this later,' said Thompson. 'I have to sort this out.
Doyle might try to get at him.'

A plaintive beep told her he'd hung up.

Shit, shit, shit. She scrolled frantically through the contacts on
her phone, found Doyle and hit 'call'. It rang. And rang.

'Come on, come on,' she muttered as she turned south. 'Come
on, answer your damn phone.' But Doyle's phone just kept ringing.

She ran.

76

Thompson hurriedly shook hands with the relaxed geek who had
done the computer work for him and pressed the lift button ur-
gently.

'See you soon,' said the geek.

'I doubt it, mate,' Thompson said. 'This was a one-off. Extraordinary circumstances. We just didn't have the resources in-house.'

The geek smiled. 'Haven't you heard? They're scrapping the forensic service altogether. Everything's going to be contracted out.' He rubbed his hands together, anticipating the windfall. The lift arrived and Thompson stepped into it. 'Nice doing business with you,' called the geek as the doors closed.

Christ Almighty, thought Thompson. What next?

Striding out of the lift and across the smart glass and granite lobby, Thompson called the Limehouse Control Room and asked to be put through to the supervisor. There was a delay, during which Thompson felt his nerves fray.

'Send two cars to the Royal London now, and get me the mobile number of the constable who's on duty there,' he demanded as soon as the supervisor came on the line.

'Sir,' the supervisor began to reply, then paused.

Thompson instantly regretted his tone, but it was too late. No doubt the supervisor was sick of detectives snapping their fingers and ordering up resources that didn't exist.

'Sir,' the supervisor spoke slowly and deliberately. 'All teams are attending a major incident. The constable on duty at the hospital is a special and I don't have a mobile number for her. I'm running three shifts with the same number of bodies that previously worked two and I'm not allowed to authorise any overtime. Is there anything else I can do for you, sir?'

Thompson hung up as he reached the revolving doors, which refused to budge. A security guard approached and pointed to Thompson's visitor's badge.

'Sign out before you leave,' he explained.

Thompson snatched the badge off and thrust it at the guard. The guard gave a resigned sigh.

'No good. You have to sign out at the desk. They swipe the card or the doors won't open.'

'For Christ's sake!' muttered Thompson, pulling out his wallet and shoving his warrant card under the guard's nose. 'Let me out, now!'

The guard shrugged, unimpressed.

'Makes no odds,' he said. 'The system doesn't care who you are.'

Thompson sprinted back across the lobby.

77

The Royal London Hospital had hosted the Elephant Man and the surgeon who had assisted with the Jack the Ripper investigation. Now it was home to Fernley-Price, although he didn't know it. Still comatose, he had been moved from intensive care to a surgical ward, at which time the Special Constable had arrived to replace the sworn officer.

The officer told her she'd been given the job because the Control Room Supervisor had asked the DCI how long he thought he could get away with keeping a warm body assigned to one that was almost cold. He thought it was funny, but she was confused.

She was a volunteer, and not entirely sure what she was supposed to do. All she knew was that to get a proper job with the Met, it was now pretty much expected that you would work part-time for nothing for at least a year, despite insistence from the powers that be that this was not the case.

So she would sit there and make sure no one came near the bloke except doctors and nurses. And police officers, of course.

*

'Oranges and Lemons' was Doyle's favourite nursery rhyme. He used to sing it to Gina when she was a little girl, swinging his arms in an axe-like motion when they got to 'here comes a chopper to chop off your head'. She would scream and giggle and run.

His phone kept ringing, but he wanted to hear the tune, so he just let it ring.

When a plainclothes bloke approached the special, gave her a warm smile, flashed his warrant card and told her she could go and get a cup of tea, it didn't occur to her that a detective would never be sent to give a lowly volunteer a tea break. She legged it to the canteen. But she was smart enough to record his name in her notebook.

Berlin felt empty, as if she had no substance. She flew along White-chapel Road, amazed that her legs could still carry her. It was a market day. The Bangladeshi stallholders stamped their feet to stay warm and watched with only mild interest as she weaved through their customers, glancing back to see who was chasing her.

Thompson's cab was stuck behind a number twenty-five bus, which was proceeding tentatively on the icy road.

'Okay, this will do!' he said, thrusting twenty quid at the driver. He jumped out. They'll never cough up for that on expenses, he thought.

Just ahead he could see the brick arches of the hospital's portico, and the clock just above them. The sound of the traffic was drowned out by the rapid approach of the air ambulance. Everybody stopped to watch as it hovered over the hospital. Thompson ploughed on through the gawkers.

The pungent scent of coriander and cinnamon, melded with diesel fumes, caught in Berlin's throat. She gasped for air as she reached the pedestrian crossing opposite the hospital and found herself trapped amid a sea of Bengali housewives toting bright plastic bags of produce, all waiting patiently to cross. Berlin tried to push through them, but they stood shoulder to shoulder, all gazing up at the helicopter, solidly repelling all comers.

Fernley-Price slumbered on, untroubled by the thrum of helicopter blades, or the trembling hand that closed over his mouth and nose. It was merely an instrument of the man who sat outside in the black Merc listening to his phone play 'Oranges and Lemons'.

Coulthard stumbled down the worn stone steps, making a beeline for the car. The passenger door swung open and he got inside.

'There. That wasn't too hard, was it?' said Doyle.

Coulthard couldn't speak. He jammed his hands between his knees and squeezed, as if he could never again trust them to act in accordance with his own wishes.

'Good thing you've had plenty of practice at impersonating a police officer. It came in handy, didn't it?' said Doyle, as he pulled away from the kerb and dialled a number on his mobile.

Berlin saw Coulthard slumped beside Doyle as the black Merc sailed through the traffic lights. He looked as if he'd seen a ghost. The lights changed and the housewives surged forward but Berlin didn't move. She saw Thompson bounding up the hospital steps. She knew he was too late.

In Coulthard's living room his girlfriend sat on the couch between the lads, her elbows pulled in tight. When the mobile rang, one of them answered.

'Yeah?'

Doyle's irate voice carried into the silent room.

'How often have I told you that's no way to answer the fucking phone?'

'How may I help you?' mumbled the lad.

'That's more like it,' said Doyle. 'You can help me by letting her go with a warning. Tell her the weather's cracking in Australia this time of year. Then get your lazy fucking arses down to the lock-up.'

The lad hung up. He gave the girl a slap and Doyle's message, then indicated to his mate they were off.

'That's it?' said his mate, disappointed. 'Pity. I was looking forward to that.'

78

The moment that Thompson stepped out of the lift and saw the special in the corridor crying, he knew he was too late. Nurses were running in and out of the ward and a couple of the hospital's security guards were standing around, slack-jawed, already denying any responsibility. As Thompson approached, four policemen came running up the stairs, led by a wheezing, fat sergeant who looked as if he might have a heart attack on the spot.

'Someone died,' gasped the sergeant.

'Well it's a hospital, isn't it?' joked one of the policemen.

Like the bloody Keystone Kops, thought Thompson. 'Get this lot out of here!' he yelled at the sergeant, pointing at the crowd in the corridor. The special looked up, startled, and burst into a fresh flood of tears.

'Seal it off. It's a crime scene. Call the SOCOs!' ordered Thompson.

'They're all at a bombing,' said one of the uniforms.

Thompson thought things couldn't get much worse. Doyle had

murdered Fernley-Price right under his nose, despite a so-called police guard, and in full view of the CCTV on every floor. Doyle had done it, or had it done, without any bother at all, and had made a complete fool of Thompson in the process.

He beckoned to the special. Eyes wide, she scurried over like a scared animal, cowering in front of him.

'I'm ever so sorry, sir,' she said. 'He said I should go and have a cup of tea.'

'Jesus Christ, you just walked away?'

'He was a detective. He showed me his warrant card!'

Thompson stared at her. 'Are you telling me this is down to a police officer?'

She thrust her notebook at him. At the top of the page neat writing recorded the time of her tea break and the name of the relieving officer. Flint.

Thompson took a breath. 'Get me the CCTV footage,' he said to one of the hospital security guards, who glanced at his mate, who looked at the floor.

'Er... it's on the blink,' said the guard.

When Flint's phone rang and he saw Thompson's name displayed, he was disinclined to answer. In fact, he was thinking he might not ever be going in to work again. He'd disclosed information and compromised an investigation, lost his warrant card and assaulted a senior officer. Dempster would be well within his rights to lay charges.

Now he'd given Coulthard up to a violent loan shark. He'd had misgivings about that, thinking it might come back to bite him. But by the time he'd called Coulthard to warn him, it was too late. Doyle answered the phone. Flint had hung up, fast, praying that Coulthard had Flint's number stored under a name that wouldn't give him away.

All in all, it wasn't a good look for an Acting Detective Sergeant on the rise. Plus, he was sick of being treated like a numpty by Thompson. He'd be better off in the private sector. More money, more respect, less hassle. Once he resigned, the Met couldn't discipline him and they wouldn't want the sort of publicity that would come with a criminal trial. They would let him go quietly.

The only problem was that in the current economic climate it might take him a while to find a suitable gig. He was mortgaged up to his eyeballs and a bit short of the readies. But he had a fair idea where he might be able to lay his hands on some.

He touched his inside pocket, where he had put the envelope Dempster had dropped at Berlin's. The contents had made interesting reading.

Thompson listened to Flint's voicemail greeting but hung up without leaving a message. It was all his own fault. He'd dropped the ball on this one, big time, and ignored all the warning signs of an investigation unravelling.

He felt something inside him snap. He had cut corners, compromised himself and still he was no closer to Gina Doyle's killer. Now he had another body on his hands and his Acting Detective Sergeant was the prime suspect. Someone would pay.

79

The mean winter sun was fading fast. Berlin felt that she would disappear with it – dissolve, absorbed in darkness, a cipher emptied of humanity. Her phone rang and when she saw it was Thompson she switched it off. There seemed no point in listening to his recriminations; she was more than capable of self-loathing.

The market stalls were closing, the crowd was sparse and the pavement was thick with crushed cardboard and rotting vegetables. A few homeless people picked them over, competing with the pigeons for edible refuse, and with one another for the driest pieces of cardboard to sleep under.

Speculators and the poor: the driven and the desperate. She glanced up at the Gherkin, the City's icon, cheek by jowl with the East End. The dying light was trapped in the myriad panes of its diamond carapace. Reflecting history. The South Sea Bubble. The Great Depression. A royal bank bailed out by a levy on the citizens, its barons richly rewarded for failure.

Berlin's mind wandered in lockstep with her restless feet, turning away from the City. Money never sleeps. I never sleep. She would just walk into the night, as she had done so many times before, and at the end it would be just like the beginning. The need that drove her on would find a way.

She tried to look forward to a time when Gina Doyle's death didn't hang around her neck like an albatross and she had a steady supply of good-quality dope. She would talk to Dempster and sort things out with him. He would understand; he would say it was okay. But her natural inclination was retrospective.

It had all started with Coulthard's bastardry and Nestor's weakness. And her stubborn demand for evidence. It had started then. Her compulsion to go back, to find the very heart of things, to seek the source of rage, despair and murder, came from the same place as her addiction. It gave her faltering legs the will to keep moving.

A beggar touched her arm and, startled, she raised a fist to ward him off. He cowered, seemingly resigned to the blow – an emaciated ancient, his eyes pearly with opaque cataracts. It had begun generations ago.

She had looked back and seen a glimpse of her own history, a stray thread that linked her with the Doyles. It was a tangled thread. There was only one person who could draw it out.

80

Delroy closed the front door behind the police officers. Linda, his girlfriend, emerged from the kitchen, none too happy.

'What did they want?' she asked.

'They're looking for Berlin.'

'What's she done now?' said Linda.

Delroy frowned. Linda thought Berlin was trouble and was going to drag down his promising career. Delroy hadn't mentioned the team's imminent demise, which was going to cut his career off at the knees anyway.

'Nothing. The inspector on the Gina Doyle inquiry is looking for her, that's all. Apparently she's gone off the radar.'

'She went off years ago, if you ask me,' muttered Linda.

He hadn't told her the half of it. The uniforms had told him the DCI was on the warpath and had issued a BOLO; be on the lookout. He wanted to interview Berlin about a murder down at the hospital. The bodies were piling up around that woman.

81

'Stay there,' Doyle said to Coulthard as he parked the Merc outside the lock-up. 'The lads will drop you home in a minute.'

Coulthard barely nodded. He was in no fit state to argue. All mouth and no trousers, thought Doyle as he got out of the car. The door of the lock-up opened and the lads hovered just outside, clearly reluctant to leave the warmth of the old-fashioned paraffin heater in the corner.

Doyle strode past them and they followed him back inside.

'Leave the door,' he said. He wanted to keep an eye on Coulthard. 'Any trouble with the girl?' he asked.

'Nah. She was packing her bags before we were out of the house.'

'Good. Now I want you to take him down to the Basin and make sure he doesn't come back.'

The lads looked at each other.

'What?' said Doyle.

'Well, it's a bit different, innit?' said one. 'Breaking a few legs, giving a girl one, all right. But this, this is like, well it's...'

'We want more money,' said the other one.

Doyle regarded them in disgust. The little shits. The Ivans were moving into the manor and they were always looking for muscle. He wondered if the lads had been headhunted.

'My daughter, my little girl, lies mouldering in her grave and all you two can think about is money,' he snarled.

The lads looked sheepish. 'Yeah, well, *he* didn't do it, did he?' said one, chancing his arm.

'No, you bleeding pillock!' bellowed Doyle. 'But we just black-mailed him into killing the bastard who did! Did you think of that? So now he's got the drop on us, on *you*, you fucking genius, unless we get rid of him!'

The lad's face fell. It was clear he hadn't thought of that.

'Sort it!' commanded Doyle.

The lads shuffled out to the Merc.

'And take the fucking Mondeo!' he shouted after them. He glanced at his watch. 'I've got to get over to Frank's.'

82

Frank opened the door and smiled. 'I always knew you would come,' he said.

Berlin glanced back at the rusty iron gates. The padlock on the chain hadn't been locked, but the gates were frozen and she hadn't the strength left to force them open. She'd had to squeeze through the small gap.

Even if she did change her mind, the tail lights of the cab were already tiny red eyes in the distance. She wouldn't get far in her condition. Every muscle felt like wire beneath her skin and she was jarred by a dry, racking cough. Despite the freezing temperature her hair was drenched with sweat and she stank. She felt like she'd lost six pounds already.

But why would she run? The old man who stood before her in his fingerless gloves, muffler and ancient herringbone tweed over-coat looked harmless. His feet were encased in decrepit hobnail boots. She could see the newspaper they were stuffed with peeking through the toes. There was no hint of the villain with the fearsome reputation.

Frank stepped aside and she crossed the threshold into the cold, dark hall. When he closed the front door, it was pitch black for a few moments, then he switched on a torch.

The beam glinted off icicles hanging from a pipe that ran along the ceiling. She was seized by the notion that she was entering an underworld where not only water, but time itself was frozen.

Frank led her down the hall, turning into ever narrower passages constructed out of old doors. They passed doorways boarded up with old planks, their missing doors apparently used to construct the passages. The house was utterly silent. At last he turned into a room and switched on a light. It was the kitchen. A heavy blanket hung at the window.

'For the blackout,' Frank explained. 'Make yourself at home.'

Berlin sat down at the table. 'Mr Doyle,' she began, but he raised a hand.

'Frank, please,' he said. He was looking at her with what she could only describe as benign wonderment. He shook his head. 'You're the spitting image of your father.'

'I'm sorry, Mr Doyle – Frank. I came because... there's something...' *Bothering me.*

'I believe you knew my father,' she continued. 'I only became aware of this recently because of my involvement with Gina.'

Frank filled the kettle from a bucket of water and put it on the gas. Of course, she thought. We're going to have tea.

'Gina,' said Frank with a big sigh. 'A right little madam, but the apple of her granddad's eye, eh?'

The sensation of having fallen down a rabbit hole grew stronger.

'What took you so long?' he asked.

'Well, I – you know how it is,' she said. 'There's always something.'

Frank nodded sagely. 'Hang on,' he said. 'I've got something to show you.'

He left the kitchen, taking the torch, and Berlin heard his footsteps fading into the nether regions.

She was on her feet straightaway, checking the cupboards, drawers, and under the sink. She had no idea what she was looking for, but if this was the only room Frank lived in, anything to be found would be here. It was another habit: the need to know.

But everything was empty. Even the cutlery drawer. A single knife, fork and spoon lay on the draining board. And two cups. She lifted the corner of the blackout blanket. The sash window was nailed down; beyond it a bleak, white wasteland.

She sat down again, overcome with fatigue and disappointment, and decided she was a fool. Maybe she was kidding herself about the real reason for coming all the way out here. She was as deluded as Frank. He was a sad old man, and Doyle, for all his faults, was a dutiful son who kept a close eye on him.

The clump of Frank's boots heralded his return. He came in carrying an old brown photo album, coated in thick dust.

'Kettle's boiling! Don't waste the gas!' he said, plonking the album on the table. He scuttled about making the tea with industrial-strength tea bags, a concession to modernity.

He passed her a cup then sat down at the table, dragging his chair around so he could sit next to her. He flipped through the pages of the album and she saw his eyes grow misty with memories. Each page bore a small black and white photo. Holiday snaps mostly. Post-war. Street parties for the Coronation. Southend Pier. He kept turning until finally he found what he wanted.

'See!' he exclaimed, pointing at a snapshot. 'What did I tell you? I'd have known you anywhere.'

Berlin leant forward and turned the album to catch more of the light from the bare bulb that hung over the table.

Her heart lurched. Two young men stood side by side. They wore wide trousers with turn-ups. Their hair was Brylcreemed into quiffs. One was taller, stocky, his arms crossed to show off his muscles. The other one was her father. Between them stood a little girl, blonde, frowning. Berlin remembered the dress.

Doyle had told her Frank knew her father and here was the proof.

But what was the real nature of the connection between her father and a family of East End villains? She had a feeling she should let it lie. But couldn't.

Bethnal Green was a smaller, tighter community then. Her father had his shop on the high road. It wasn't so surprising that they knew each other. Frank was probably a customer. Perhaps Archie Doyle's rings had once rested on black velvet in the shop window.

The photo implied a closer relationship. Her father must have taken her to visit Frank. They were smiling, standing shoulder to shoulder. She had no memory of the visit, or of Frank, but by the time she would have been old enough to take notice she was living with her mother.

She closed the album and took a deep breath. 'Frank,' she said. 'What about Gina?' And there it was, almost rhetorical, more a plea than a question, out of her mouth before she realised. The thing that was bothering her.

This time, at the mention of the name, Frank frowned. 'Her mother was here a few days ago. Or was it last week?' he said.

Jesus Christ. Nancy's alive, thought Berlin. Maybe she had heard about Gina.

'You mean Nancy, your son's wife?' she asked, very quietly.

Frank looked at her as if he didn't recognise her. 'Shouldn't you be in a shelter?' he asked. 'You should get down the Underground. The Nazis are at it every night, bombing the docks.'

Berlin waited a moment and saw the thought leave him.

'What did Nancy want?' she asked.

Frank's fist came crashing down on the table. 'She wanted the fucking ledger!' he roared, and flung open his overcoat to reveal a thick black notebook tucked into his belt. Confusion clouded his face again. 'But how could she know about it? She was dead before I started the business.'

He seemed to have forgotten Berlin was there.

A gust of wind rattled in the eaves and she shivered.

Retired Senior Constable Marks and his chocolate bourbons came back to her. He had said that Nancy had a nest egg and that Frank Doyle wasn't in the sharking business in those days. He started after Nancy had gone. The juxtaposition of the two facts came into sharp focus.

Her confusion evaporated at the same time as Frank's. He regarded Berlin with narrowed eyes, suddenly completely compos mentis. Coldly rational.

A chill crawled up her spine.

'Who are you and what the fuck do you want?' he said in a quiet, menacing voice.

'My name's Catherine Berlin. I'd like to ask you some questions about Nancy and Gina Doyle.'

In an instant the old man became an enraged, scarlet gargoyle, eyes popping, hands clenched in lethal fists.

Berlin pushed back her chair very slowly and rose with care, afraid of provoking this ferocious creature who glowered at her, ready to pounce.

That's why I'm here, she thought. They're all dead. My father, Nancy and Gina. Her heart was pounding as she saw there were only two possibilities. Either Frank knew Doyle had killed Nancy or he had done it himself. She had disappeared the year they began loan sharking. Using her nest egg.

She took a step back from Frank and the horrible symmetry which presented itself. She had insisted Gina come up with hard evidence, so Gina had come for the ledger. At first the demented old man mistook her for her mother.

'Gina came out here after the ledger. She said it was her birthright,' sneered Frank. 'She said her dad had killed her mum for her bit of capital. As if he'd have had the balls to do it!'

Frank had remembered Gina's mother was dead because he had murdered her. She was trapped in an icy labyrinth with a deranged killer. Just as Gina had been.

Frank reached up and with his bare hand crushed the light bulb. There was a bang and they were plunged into darkness.

83

Flint parked up against the wall, climbed on top of his car and dropped over the wall into a foot of snow, which reflected the full moon and bathed the scene in an eerie glow.

He carefully made his way to a garage attached to one side of the sprawling bungalow. A thin strip of light from one window was the only sign of life, but as he watched, it blinked out. All gone to beddy-byes then. Good.

He pushed the roller door tentatively and, to his surprise, it slid up in well-oiled silence. His penlight picked out racks of tools, cans of paint and piles of junk. In the middle of it all was a car covered with a heavy canvas. He lifted the corner, expecting an old rust bucket, but the Jag was in pristine condition, apart from mud under the wheel arches. It had been used recently.

His instincts were right; the bastards kept their buried treasure out here somewhere. All that cash Doyle collected wouldn't be left hanging around his flat in Bethnal Green, waiting for the burglars to turn up. And he couldn't bank it. Flint tried the door which led into the house. It was locked, and the lock was new.

But the timber was old. He reached for a rusty crowbar.

X marks the spot.

*

Doyle was surprised when he got out of the car and found the gates ajar. He might not have secured the padlock, but he always yanked the chain tight. Maybe it was the wind. He put his weight against the gates and shoved. Bloody weather. At least they didn't grate on the concrete any more – the ice had smoothed their path.

He was glad to get back in the car, which was warmer than it would be inside the bloody house. He drove up the driveway and stopped, but didn't get out, reluctant to leave the cosy cocoon.

There was no light on in the kitchen and Frank didn't open the door. Doyle switched off the motor and sat in the sudden ticking silence, enjoying the peace and quiet. What a bloody life he led. He didn't understand the half of it. Then the silence was shattered by an almighty racket coming from somewhere inside the house.

Berlin felt Frank's hands brush her face as he grabbed at her in the dark. She ducked, and his hand closed around her hair. She kept moving, gripped the edge of the table and overturned it. She heard the torch strike the floor and felt Frank totter as the edge of the table struck him. She struggled from his grasp, but his grip didn't falter and she felt a fistful of hair torn from her scalp as she broke away.

He stumbled about, his heavy boots betraying his movements. He went for the door, no doubt expecting her to do the same, but she edged around the kitchen, reaching out until her fingers brushed the blackout blanket. When he realised what she was doing he flung himself across the room, kicking the table out of his way.

'Come here, you cunt!' he growled.

She felt his hot, fetid breath on her neck as she put all her weight on the blanket and brought it down.

For a moment they were both shrouded in the dense, suffocating fabric. She kicked back, using his body to propel her forward. The window shattered and she fell out into starry nothing.

*

253

Frank flung open the front door and nearly collected Doyle, who was trying to get in. Frank shoved him out of the way.

'Stop the bitch! She knows everything! Get her!' he screamed.

'What the fuck?' gasped Doyle as Frank shot down the steps and ran around the side of the house. Christ, he thought, the old man's really lost it this time, and ran after him.

When he turned the corner he was astonished to see someone crawling away from the kitchen window. Frank was gaining on them fast. The figure was in shadow and Doyle couldn't make out who it was as they staggered to their feet and stumbled across the strip of gravel, which was obscured by snow.

Suddenly the whole area lit up, dazzling Doyle. Frank must have rigged a motion detector to the exterior spotlights. He blinked. When his vision cleared he saw that Berlin woman fleeing across an expanse of tall grass, the glistening tips rigid above the snow. Frank was standing at the edge of it, watching her.

Doyle ran up to him. 'What the fuck's going on, Frank?'

'Don't worry, she won't get far,' Frank replied, suddenly placid, as he tracked Berlin's stumbling progress.

Berlin stopped and looked back at them. Doyle watched her weighing her options. The wall was too high for her to scale and although the gates were only about fifty yards to her right, if they moved fast, they could still cut her off.

'He killed them, Doyle.' Her voice carried across the still night. 'Frank murdered Nancy and Gina. Your wife and your daughter.'

The silence was rent by Frank's enraged howl. Doyle felt it as a blow. Frank had told Doyle to stop Berlin because she knew everything. He realised it was all true. He struggled to breathe, paralysed by the horror.

Frank broke the spell. He bore down on Berlin and she fled.

*

Berlin ran towards the wall she couldn't climb: the wall she faced in her nightmares. The cracks in it were closing now, crushing her father, who was desperately trying to reach her, no longer whispering but screaming at her to run.

The next thing she knew she was pitching forward. A ring of fire bit into her ankle and she struck the ground. Jagged teeth tore at her face. Agony obliterated time.

She lay beneath a sea of towering, frigid thistles on a frozen tundra. The black sky bled sharp, silent crystals, which pierced the swollen skin around each embedded tooth of the spring-loaded trap. It clamped one cheek and jaw at an unnatural angle and crushed her nose flat against the ridge of her shattered eye socket.

Her throat filled with blood from an almost severed tongue. She couldn't open her mouth to release it from the grip of her teeth. She tried to swallow and imagined she was encased in a scold's bridle, the iron muzzle studded with spikes.

Above her, she could hear knuckles crack, bone on bone, and the gasping wheeze of lungs fighting for air.

All she could see were legs and torsos twisted together, a knot of serpents locked in a hissing struggle. Frank's hand clawed at his belt buckle and the ledger fell to the ground. With a fierce grunt he pushed himself free of Doyle, his clothes riding up as he dragged off his belt.

The white expanse of his stomach was scored with deep purple scars, the sort of scars that might be left by lances or burning pokers. Or by the spikes of iron railings that had dug deep into your flesh as you hung over them to haul a skinny boy from the midst of a crushing stampede.

Berlin put her hand on her chest as she felt the breath squeezed from her lungs. She tried to turn her head, but the teeth of the trap bit deeper with every movement. No doubt it was designed that way. She inched forward and a shrill pain shot down her twisted spine. She passed out.

When she came around, there was silence. A figure loomed over her, but she couldn't move her head enough to see who it was. The figure crouched and bent to look her in the eye.

Doyle's face was wet with tears. 'I loved him,' he said. He fell to the ground beside her, curled up like a baby and sobbed, his face inches from hers.

'I loved them, too,' he gasped between despairing sobs. 'I loved them and he killed them. He shouldn't ought to have done that. It wasn't right!' he raged.

The pain of his loss covered them both, a suffocating blanket of horror.

'Gina!' he screamed, calling her out of the night.

But there was no reply, only the explosive sound of ice as it slid from the roof of the house and shattered. Icicles snapped in imitation of bullets striking tin, pipes burst and released a torrent.

Berlin heard the cacophony of the thaw and wept.

Doyle's fingers crept around her throat, finding space to insert themselves beneath the rusted steel bands of the trap. 'It's only right, Miss, to put an animal out of its misery.' His hands tightened, crushing her windpipe.

There were no nosy neighbours to call the cops so Flint had time to search the house before venturing outside to inspect the carnage. He'd heard glass breaking and Doyle's cry for Gina, but whatever was happening was outside, so he took the opportunity to get on with the job at hand.

When he emerged from the house the place was lit up like Christmas. He followed the trail of crushed grass and disturbed snow until he came upon the old man. Two others lay close together in the deep shadow just beyond reach of the floodlights.

He picked up the thick black notebook lying on the ground near the body, flicked through it and knew it represented a gold mine. Coulthard's name was in there, along with dozens of others. He put it in his pocket. There was a collection of cash books like this one in an old tin trunk he'd found inside the house, one for every year since 1986. All the entries were in the same fine, meticulous hand.

There was money stashed all over the place, but he was a trained expert and he'd pretty much managed to find most, if not all, of it. Sod everything. Leave the crooks and the politicians to it. He was off.

A small movement caught his eye. A cosy couple was locked together. He walked towards them and stepped out of the light. In the gloom he could make out Doyle and Berlin. She was caught, head and foot, in two evil-looking animal traps.

Gobsmacked, he realised that Doyle's fingers were clenched around her throat. If she was still alive, he was slowly choking the remaining life out of her.

Flint saw a brighter future beckon. He picked up a slab of broken concrete, held it high and dropped it.

A skull shattered.

He flicked open his mobile and dialled. 'Acting Detective Sergeant Flint here,' he announced. 'There's been a murder.'

The Tenth Day

84

Berlin gasped and tried to claw at her throat. Someone restrained her. She opened her eyes. It was a woman she didn't know.

'Take it easy,' said the woman. 'It's to help you breathe.'

The light was dim and there was a faint purr and click of machinery. A battery of soft blue lights blinked on a monitor. Berlin heard a voice and tried to turn her head, but it was held fast. It took all the energy she had left to raise her hand and touch the cold steel frame that encased one side of her face.

The woman, a nurse, fussed around her then disappeared from her field of vision. A man appeared. She recognised Thompson.

'You're going to be all right, Berlin,' he said. 'Thanks to Detective Sergeant Flint.'

She was aware of someone on the other side of the bed taking her hand. She was able to move just enough to see that it was Delroy.

'Jesus, mate,' he said. He had tears in his eyes.

She must look a sight. She squeezed his hand and saw the surprise on his face. It was probably the first affectionate gesture he'd ever known her to make.

Thompson cleared his throat and she looked back at him.

'We found Gina's DNA in the boot of Frank's Jag. The ground was frozen solid, so he couldn't bury her at Chigwell. Unlike her mum. Nancy's remains were out there. Dug up and moved more than once, from the look of it. We think she was killed for her savings: the capital he needed to start loan sharking. And Frank's wife's bones were encased in the concrete floor of the lock-up.'

How long had it taken them to uncover Frank's secrets? How long had she been unconscious? She hadn't told anyone where she was going. Lack of trust had nearly cost her her life.

She focused hard and mouthed 'Dempster?'

Thompson frowned.

She tried again. The croak she heard was her own voice. 'Dempster. Ask him to come,' she rasped.

Thompson exchanged a glance with Delroy, then made a pantomime of looking at his watch. 'I have to go. We'll talk when you're better,' he said and disappeared from view.

The effort of speaking had exhausted Berlin. She closed her eyes. Delroy whispered in her ear.

'The police found Coulthard's shoes at the Basin. They think he went to top himself but it was frozen over, so he went into the river instead. I reckon he's legged it to Spain.'

Berlin wanted to smile, but couldn't. She had stared into the abyss and it blinked first. The dragon had been put to the sword; hereafter night would mean sleep.

The nurse came back and started to rig up a device. 'You'll have to go now,' she said to Delroy, hooking a tube into the cannula in Berlin's arm. She adjusted a valve.

'What's that?' asked Delroy.

'PCA,' replied the nurse. 'Patient-controlled analgesia. She's going to be in excruciating pain.'

Berlin opened her eyes wide, alarmed. The nurse gave her a brisk, reassuring nod. 'This will fix it,' she said.

Delroy watched as she curled Berlin's fingers around the device and showed her how to control the flow.

'What is it?' said Delroy.

The nurse smiled. 'Morphine,' she said.

Acknowledgements

Sincere thanks to Ben Ball of Penguin Australia and Jason Arthur of Random House UK.

Particular thanks to my very classy agent, Sarah Ballard.

Special thanks to Arwen Summers, my editor at Penguin Australia.

No thanks to those who told me a picture was worth a thousand words.

Heartfelt thanks to Peta Masters for the title, and just about everything else.